She's feeling the heat. Or it might be a hot flash. Sometimes it's really hard to tell.

Psychic Dreams

It's been four years since Monica lost the love of her life to a sudden and devastating heart attack. She's held her family together and picked herself up with the love and help of her two best friends. Now Monica has a new business, a new wardrobe, and a new vision for the future.

As in *actual* psychic visions. Dreams that manifest in reality? Monica's still not sure why or how it happened, but she's been seeing everything from unexpected visitors to visions of fire and destruction.

Separating premonitions from morbid imagination is proving harder than Monica expected, and no one can tell her if these new, violent visions will become a reality.

Added to that, there's a new fire investigator in town, and he's more than a little suspicious about the anonymous and frighteningly accurate tips someone is calling in. Monica is feeling the heat... or is that a hot flash?

Is their town about to feel the burn of a serial arsonist, or can Monica, Robin, and Val figure out the dange smoldering at the heart of Glimmer Lake?

Psychic Dreams is a standalone paranorma fiction novel in the Glimmer Lake series by *USA* seller Elizabeth Hunter, author of the Elemental and the Irin Chronicles.

PRAISE FOR ELIZABETH HUNTER

I love the realness of the characters in this series....
Troubled marriages, dead-beat dads, small town
gossip, death and hormonal teenagers. You know, life.
It's not always pretty, but sometimes it's downright
beautiful.

— MAC'S MEANDERINGS

I loved this book! I always expect amazing stuff from
Elizabeth Hunter, but this was just above my
expectations.

— THE BLUE-HAIRED READER

Monica's story was sweet, heartfelt, down to earth.
And try as I did, I could not guess the ending. The
twists and turns had me guessing all the way till
the end.

— SASSAFRACK'S BOOKS

PSYCHIC DREAMS

GLIMMER LAKE BOOK THREE

ELIZABETH HUNTER

Psychic Dreams
Copyright © 2020
Elizabeth Hunter
ISBN: 978-1-941674-57-4

Cover: Damonza
Content Editor: Amy Cissell, Cissell Ink
Line Editor: Anne Victory
Proofreader: Linda, Victory Editing

Recurve Press LLC
PO Box 4034
Visalia, California 93278
USA

This book is dedicated to the wives, husbands, and partners of our brave firefighters. Thank you for your courage, resilience, and tenacity.

CHAPTER 1

Monica woke from a dream of fire and darkness. She sat up straight in bed, gasping for breath, and reached for the glass of water sitting on her bedside table. She gulped it down as sweat bloomed across her heated skin.

Looking at the clock on her bedside table, Monica realized the vision had come to her just past midnight in the small hot hours of the Glimmer Lake summer. Some women in their late forties woke in the middle of the night sweating from a hot flash. Monica woke up sweating from the visions that had tormented her dreams since a near-death experience three years before.

The doctors told her she'd died for a few minutes, but what did that mean? There had been no bright lights or visions of peaceful tunnels. She hadn't seen Gilbert, her husband of twenty-five years, who had died the year before the wreck.

Monica didn't remember much of anything from the car

accident and near drowning. What she did remember was the first time a vision had come true.

At first it felt like déjà vu. She thought she'd imagined it. Just a little thing, a phone call that came exactly when she knew it would.

Then another thing happened.

And another.

Soon visions of places she'd never seen invaded her thoughts. Violent acts and secret pain became as clear to her as a movie. Instead of having the normal worrisome dreams of a widow and mother of four, Monica was haunted by everything from premonitions of everyday mundane encounters to visions of murder, death, and destruction.

She swung her legs over the edge of the bed and sat up straight, holding the sweating water glass against her cheek. Drops of condensation ran down her neck, over her collarbone, and between her breasts, trailing the drops of sweat brought on by the oppressive summer heat. She reached for the journal she kept by her bed.

Though her heart was still racing, she mentally reconstructed the dream she knew was far more than a dream. Her ceiling fan beat a steady rhythm overhead, wafting air onto the sweat-soaked sheets as she closed her eyes to examine the memory before it faded.

Fire and destruction.

She'd been walking down Main Street, walking past shops and storefronts she knew well, walking calmly despite the ash and sparks that rained around her. She was alone in the dream. The only sounds had been the crack of burning branches and the wind as the town of Glimmer Lake burned around her.

Monica scribbled down everything. She'd been wearing a sundress, the same dress she'd worn the day before, a light cotton outfit that kept her cool but still professional-looking while she was working at Russell House.

She wrote down what she'd heard—the crackle of the fire, breaking branches, the wind. She wrote down everything she had seen—which shops were burning, which cars were on the road, which cars she saw in the lots, and how far she could see in the distance before the smoke swallowed her sight.

She knew the town of Glimmer Lake intimately. She knew who drove each car she'd seen. She knew who owned the shops she'd seen burning. She also knew which fire-fighters would respond to the scene, risking their lives to save the small town in the heart of the Sierra Nevada mountains.

She knew because her late husband Gilbert Velasquez had been one of those firefighters. But though she was a widow, Monica hadn't lost Gil to the ravages of a fire. She'd lost him to the mundane, everyday tragedy of heart disease.

Gilbert had been gone for nearly four years, struck down by a heart condition that had crouched silently until the morning it took his life.

She slept alone and she woke alone. Her four children, the children she and Gil had raised, were all out in the world, living their lives. Only Jake, her oldest, remained in Glimmer Lake, working as a handyman, boat captain, and sometime ski bum during the winter.

Until the year before, Jake been living at home. But once he gained a measure of independence by working at Russell House—along with a much more generous salary than he'd been earning at Max's Pontoon Rentals—he'd moved out of Monica's house and into an apartment with a friend.

Monica glanced at the clock again, noted the time, and realized she wouldn't be able to return to sleep. She finished writing as many details of the vision as possible; then she put her journal down, finished the last of her water, and stood up to go to the kitchen.

She couldn't deny that she missed having Jake around. Sylvia, her second oldest and her only daughter, was working on her master's degree in psychology at the University of California at Berkeley. Her two youngest boys, Caleb and Sam, were working in their own business, a construction company they'd started just after their father passed. They were only in Bridger City, and Monica got to see them every few weeks when they came home for Sunday dinner.

But day to day, night to night, Monica remained alone. Her two best friends both had men in their lives. Robin had repaired her relationship with her husband Mark, and Val had started a new relationship with the local sheriff, Sully.

She wandered through the three-bedroom, two-bath house she and Gil had bought so many years before. It was a good house, the first and only one she'd owned as a married woman. She'd been a teenage bride and mother, and she and Gil hadn't been able to afford their own house for years.

But once Gil was hired on full time at the local fire department, they bought it and then remained there for the next twenty years. It wasn't fancy, but it had been enough. They were happy.

They were *so* happy.

Monica walked into the kitchen and put on water for tea. She reached into the cupboard and took down a bag of chamomile along with a jar of honey.

She'd spent years listening to friends complain about

4

inattentive husbands or neglectful boyfriends. But though she and Gilbert had hardly been more than children when they married, she couldn't have asked for a better man. He was funny and romantic. He put her needs above everyone else, even above his own family. They'd had rough times, but those rough times had never even come close to a fraction of the good.

They had struggled, but just when life seemed to be smoothing out—when they'd raised their kids and sent them out into the world as successful adults—the rug hadn't just been pulled out from under Monica...

The rug up and disappeared.

Gil died, and Monica had been left alone. All the dreams of a joyful retirement—of the adventures they'd been waiting to take together—were gone.

Poof.

It was as if Life had said to her: "Oh, did you think you had a plan? How cute. That's gone now. Figure it out."

As the water came to a boil, she measured out the tea and her mind returned to the vision of fire and destruction from which she'd woken.

It wasn't the first time she'd dreamed of fire. Monica didn't know a firefighter's partner who didn't have nightmares about what their loved one might walk into.

But there were nightmares, and then there was this.

She poured hot water over the chamomile leaves, stirred in a bit of honey, and took her tea to the living room. She sat in Gil's big old recliner that she'd hated from the moment he bought it. She hated the fake leather upholstery and the massive size. It took up too much space, she'd said, and it didn't match anything else in the room.

Nevertheless, Gilbert had loved that chair, and now that he was gone, Monica couldn't bear to part with it. She sat in it and looked over the wooded yard. Monica knew that she didn't need a big house anymore, but parting with it felt like losing another part of Gilbert, and she wasn't ready for that.

But as she looked into the dark, shadowed forest, she felt a sense of foreboding like she hadn't felt in years.

Maybe she'd never felt darkness like this.

Monica had seen ghosts and helped capture murderers, but she'd never experienced a feeling of dread like she felt after waking up from that dream.

A violent and destructive force was coming to Glimmer Lake. She didn't know when, she didn't know why, but she knew in her gut it was coming.

CHAPTER 2

*M*onica pulled into Russell House a little after eight a.m. She had just under three hours to meet with Jake and Kara about the week, have a financial meeting with Grace and Philip, then oversee checkout and turnover before their largest party of the summer came in. It was an end-of-summer bachelor party with some very wealthy businessmen from the Bay Area, and they had a schedule of activities that would keep the guests very busy.

She parked her creaking minivan in front of the kitchen, next to a shiny new luxury minivan that served as the shuttle for the hotel. Then she jumped out of the car and hustled into the grand old house.

"I'm here! Sorry I'm late."

Russell House had been the familial home of Monica's best friend, Robin Brannon. She hadn't been raised in Russell House, but her mother had. In fact, just after the car accident, Russell House had been the site of their very first adventure banishing a ghost.

It had been Robin's grandfather, and it hadn't been fun.

But that was over, and since Grandma Helen had passed, Russell House had undergone a massive transformation into a boutique hotel. The family bedrooms had been converted into ten luxury rooms and suites. They hosted conferences, parties and fancy dinners, and weddings on the massive front lawn. Since Russell House sat directly on the edge of Glimmer Lake, the views couldn't be beat, and they had perfect waterfront access.

Their first season had been a test run, but this season they'd gone all in, and Monica had been thrilled with the results.

"Jake?" She set down her purse. "Kara?"

"Coming!"

She heard Kara approaching from the dining room, which had been converted into a small café where a branch of her friend Val's Misfit Mountain Coffee had taken residence.

Monica heard Val's manager Eve and Kara exchanging a few quiet words before the swinging door pushed into the kitchen and Kara came through.

She was a tiny young woman with a giant smile; Monica had hired her last winter when she realized she needed someone with more hotel experience than she had. She knew how to run a busy household and a business, but the high-end hospitality aspect was still new.

"Good morning!" Kara's dazzling smile spread across her pale, heart-shaped face. She had dark brown hair clipped into a pixie cut and beautiful green eyes.

Monica sometimes got the urge to pinch Kara's cheek, but she resisted. The girl—the young lady—was a year older than her daughter Sylvia, and she bubbled. She had impressed

Monica with her energy, organization, and references. Kara loved hospitality and she loved the outdoors. It was the perfect combination.

"How are you this morning, Mrs. Velasquez?"

"Please." Monica squeezed Kara's shoulder. "How many times have I asked you to call me Monica? You make me feel old."

"Sorry." Kara's cheeks went a little pink. "I was just speaking with a guest who was asking for your card, so I was calling you Mrs. Velasquez to her."

"Event interest?"

Kara smiled. "Her daughter just got engaged."

"Nice!" Monica did a little fist pump. "Gimme that sweet, sweet special-event cash."

Kara laughed. "It's not until next summer, but I told her we were already filling up, so don't wait too long to call."

Monica mentally paged through her calendar. "June is filling up. July is still good. May's got space too." Spring could come late in the mountains, so a May wedding would be beautiful. The dogwood trees that surrounded Russell House would be in bloom, along with all the tulips and daffodils that Helen had planted.

Thinking about weddings still made Monica think of Gilbert and their rushed wedding at the county courthouse. She'd been embarrassed then—eighteen and pregnant—but she could smile about it now. She and Gil had gone all out for their twentieth wedding anniversary, but Monica still had the cream-colored dress with puffy lace sleeves she'd gotten from the prom sale rack at Macy's department store in Fresno.

Her baby was twenty-nine now, and as he walked

through the door from the garden, her breath caught just for a second.

Jake was the picture of Gilbert at that age. A little taller, but with the same barrel chest and thick dark hair. He'd start growing his fall beard soon; he liked having a beard during ski season.

"Hey, Mom!" The broad smile was Gil's too. Dimples were the only thing Jake had inherited from his mother. "You need a new car."

"I like my car—stop trying to get me trade it in."

"Trade it in?" Jake glanced out the window. "I'm not sure anyone would take the old van at this point."

"It's not that old." Monica looked at her old minivan. "It still runs great."

"Tell me that this winter when the heater is giving you problems again." Jake poured himself a cup of coffee. "Kara, you want one?"

"I'm good."

Kara watched Jake's back as he stood at the counter. Her eyes slipped down to Jake's backside before she quickly looked away and shuffled through her binder. Her cheeks went a little pink again.

Oh.

Oh!

Monica's baby had an admirer. It was hardly surprising. At twenty-nine, Jake had had more than his share of seasonal romances, usually with girls from down the hill who were just at the lake for the summer or ski season.

But Kara?

Oh, Monica was telling Robin and Val about this one. She could definitely see Kara and her son hitting it off. They had a great working relationship and a lot of common interests.

"So." Jake sat down. "The Donner party is coming in this afternoon." He grinned. "Should we have appetizers out early so we don't have to worry about any guests getting eaten?"

"Will you stop calling them that?" Monica whacked his arm a little harder than she meant to. "The best man is Jonathan Bacon. It is the Bacon party."

"Which makes them sound extra edible, but the groom is Alex Donner," Jake said. "I'm sticking with the name."

Russell House had never hosted a bachelor party before, and Monica couldn't lie that she'd been skeptical when the best man called and asked for a quote. He'd convinced her they were far more the cigars, whiskey, and outdoors kind of bachelor party than the debauchery kind.

Jake had immediately come up with an activities calendar that included waterskiing, rock climbing lessons, and whiskey and wine tasting. The best man had been thrilled, and Monica was hoping it would all go well. Their reputation as a wedding venue was growing, but with a lack of luxury spas and shopping in Glimmer Lake, they were limited in hitting the bridal party market. Maybe becoming a luxury outdoor escape for grooms was the way to go.

Kara said, "As long as the Bacon *or* the Donner party are laughing about it and not resorting to cannibalism, I don't care. You all set for this afternoon?"

"I've got the pontoon boat at the dock already, and Dylan's coming in at four to set up."

Jake's friend Dylan owned a bar in Bridger City that had a specialty liquor store attached. The store and the bar specialized in whiskeys and bourbons, and it had been Jake's idea to make whiskey tastings an option for guests. Dylan came with samples of each and bottles to buy. It had proven to be a very popular event on Fridays.

The pontoon boat was a rental from Jake's old employer. Russell House had their own ski boat and waterskiing equipment, but they had to rent the pontoon.

"Do you have everything set up for Saturday?"

Jake looked at his battered yellow legal pad, which was as organized as Monica and Kara could make him. "I gotta call the lodge to confirm their dinner reservation since they added another guy to the party."

Monica's eyes went wide. "They added another guy? We're already maxed!"

Kara held up her hand. "Don't panic. We got it sorted. I called Philip and he said Grace has another rollaway in storage. He's bringing it this morning when they come."

Philip and Grace Lewis were the owners of Russell House, and Monica was in partnership with them for the hotel. They were also her best friend's parents and like surrogate parents for Monica, who hardly spoke to her own mother even though she only lived twenty minutes away.

"Philip has another rollaway?" Monica jotted down a note in her calendar. "Do we know what shape it's in?"

"I kept some of that black spray paint from the last one we cleaned up," Jake said. "He says it's just banged up a little, but the mattress is nearly new."

Grace had been an antique dealer for most of her life, and she loved shopping at auctions. She'd managed to pick up a surprising amount of hotel equipment on her buying trips. Most of it stayed in the Lewis garage until they had an emergency; then Grace and Philip popped in with supplies like fairy godparents.

"Okay, so that's *sixteen* people, not fifteen." Monica's eyes nearly popped out. "This is quite the party. We're definitely going to need another ski boat for tomorrow."

"Already arranged," Jake said.

Kara said, "And they've already worked out who the extra person is staying with, and they agreed to pay full price for him even though it's just a rollaway. To make up for the inconvenience."

Monica closed her calendar. "Then welcome Mister...?"

Kara closed her eyes and Jake started laughing again.

"What?" She looked between them.

Kara cleared her throat. "The new member of the party is named Josh. Josh Trout."

Monica shook her head. "So Mr. Bacon and Mr. Trout are throwing a Donner party." She gave in to the laughter. "Why not?"

Kara said, "It's going to be great, Monica. I promise. Don't worry at all. These guys are paying big bucks, and we're going to make it an amazing weekend. Don't worry for a minute."

"Exactly, Mom." Jake turned his grin on Kara. "You think there's any guest Kara can't handle? Please."

Oh yeah. There were stars in Kara's eyes. And Monica was starting to think that there might just be some stars from Jake too.

But she was an observer only! She'd learned long ago that indicating she thought any person was a good match for one of her kids was a sure way to make them lose interest.

"Okay." She stood. "I have a meeting with Grace at nine. How many guests have already left?"

"Four rooms are out, and Pam and Joelle are on it. The other four look like they're taking lazy mornings, so we'll just have to be fast on turnaround when they're gone." Kara looked down at her binder. "Also, the fire chief is coming Tuesday. I forgot to tell you about that."

"The fire chief?" She frowned. "We already had our inspection."

"It's about the perimeter." Kara motioned to the trees outside. "Defensible space prior to fire season, all that stuff."

"Oh sheesh." It had been a constant balancing act with Gil in their own home. He would have cut down every tree in the vicinity to protect their house, and Monica wanted at least a little shade. "Okay, just remind me Tuesday morning."

She might have a battle on her hands with this one. She'd grown up in the mountains and had more than a healthy respect for forest fires, but she also knew that the lush gardens and woods around Russell House were part of what sold the hotel.

For a second, her dream from the night before flashed in her memory.

Fire and ash and sparks raining down...

Okay, maybe they were going to have to alter the gardens after all. That was another thing she'd have to bring up with Grace when they met. "Kara, I'm going to meet with Grace now. Just text me if you need anything. Jake, be careful on the lake today."

"I will!"

"You got it, Mom." He was already looking at something on his phone.

Monica gathered her purse and papers and headed toward the dining room. "And let me know if you need anything. I can pitch in if we're in a rush."

Monica might have been the manager, but the one thing she'd learned about running a hotel—even a small one—was that if something needed to be done, all hands were on deck. She'd changed sheets and washed laundry. She'd scrubbed showers and unclogged toilets when no one else was available. She regularly delivered the morning pastry boxes and coffee trays if the hotel was full.

Russell House was her baby and the first real job she'd ever had. She viewed each guest like they were staying in her own home, and she busted her butt to make sure they felt welcome.

It was hers, and it would be a success.

CHAPTER 3

Monica stopped at the coffee bar to check in with Eve. "Hey! How's it going?"

She could see guests milling around the front of the house, drinking their coffee at tables on the lush, wide lawn.

"Good." Eve was cleaning the espresso machine. "Just sold the second round for the late crew." Eve had been Val's second-in-command at her coffee shop until she'd taken over the stand at Russell House.

She'd turned the simple coffee stand into something a lot more than Monica had originally envisioned. She'd expanded their pastry selections and introduced a special-event formal tea held once a month that sold out every time. It was a hipster take on a British high tea and had proven really popular for birthdays and special occasions.

Monica watched the lawn and the café, gauging the mood of her guests. She wanted happy repeat customers and good online reviews. They'd already booked around a dozen parties for a repeat stay the next summer, and she was hoping Russell House became a yearly tradition for wealthy families who wanted a taste of the outdoors without too much grime.

"You ready for this weekend?"

Eve smiled. "You mean the Donner party?"

Monica rolled her eyes. "Not you too."

"Jake has been having way too much fun with that name."

"I'm surprised he didn't latch on to Bacon."

Eve tamped down a shot of espresso and slid it into the machine. "Nah. Bacon's great, but cannibal jokes are too good to pass up. Your son keeps people laughing around here, I'll give him that."

"He certainly seems to have found his niche."

Jake was the only man working in a group of women, most of whom were pretty young, and he got to walk around fixing things, playing with boats and skis, and doing much of his job shirtless. Working at Russell House was Jake's dream job; Monica was just fortunate that he was really, really good at it.

Eve asked, "You want your usual?"

"Please." A "usual" for Monica was a plain old latte with a shot of hazelnut. Not too much sweetness, just a little. "I haven't seen Grace yet."

Just as she said it, Philip's truck appeared from beneath the trees that sheltered the road to Russell House. The shiny charcoal-grey vehicle drove around the decomposed granite drive and headed toward the kitchen where Monica parked her own car.

"That's my cue." Monica grabbed her latte as soon as Eve finished it. "I'll see you later."

"Tell Grace I'm making her coffee for her."

"Will do."

Monica sat near the end of the dining room at a long square table that was usually reserved for business meetings. She spread out her monthly report and sipped her coffee while she listened for Grace.

A few minutes after nine, Grace Lewis, elegant matriarch of Russell House, entered the foyer. As always, though it was nine in the morning and she'd probably been lugging around dusty antiques all morning, Grace was immaculately put together.

Her shoulder-length hair was a blend of blond and silver grey, and her makeup was applied expertly to highlight her cheekbones and beautiful eyes.

"Good morning." Monica stood. "I think Eve has a coffee ready for you."

"Oh." Grace put a hand over her heart. "That young lady always knows just how to make a perfect coffee, doesn't she?"

"She's a professional."

Grace sighed. "I just wish the tattoos... Ah well. The world is a different place now."

Monica smothered a smile. "Yep."

Grace couldn't exactly be labeled fashion forward. She was wearing a yellow summer blouse tucked into a cream-colored pair of linen pants with a bright blue belt and a pair of matching sandals.

Stuffy? A little. But her heart was in the right place, she was generous, and she made a hell of a gin martini.

Grace was also unfailingly polite to everyone on staff, even if she didn't approve of "outlandish hair" and tattoos.

Monica had raised four children through too many personal-expression trends to count. She didn't make any dress code at Russell House other than "work appropriate." So far her biggest problem was reminding Jake to put a shirt on around guests.

"So we had a wonderful summer," Grace said as she returned with her coffee. "The ladies at the library lunch were raving about the tea that Eve is doing now. They loved it."

"Great." Monica made a note to tell Eve. "That's wonderful to hear. I've been talking over the idea of doing it every other week instead of once a month. What do you think?"

They chatted about marketing ideas for about half an hour, brainstorming for promotions that could keep the hotel busy through the fall and late winter.

Between the lake in the summer and the ski resort in the winter, Glimmer Lake was a year-round getaway for people across California, but Russell House was still new and it was small. So far that had worked in their favor, but Monica liked planning ahead.

"You remind me of me."

Monica looked up from scribbling in her notebook. "What?"

Grace smiled. "You remind me of me when I was younger. I was very certain I could plan for everything. I had plans, backup plans, and backup-backup plans."

Monica laughed a little. "Well, four kids in six years will do that to you."

Grace looked at her for a long time. "How are you doing?"

"Fine. Good!" She waved a hand around the dining room. "Busy, but good."

"I know you're doing well professionally. You were born to be in hospitality, and you're thriving in it." Grace leaned forward. "But how are you doing personally?"

Monica's stomach dropped. "I'm fine, Grace. Really."

"I remember being where you are," she said. "I remember that point where my kids were out of the house and really independent—they're not when they're still in school, you know? But where you are right now, with Sam and Caleb busy with their business, Jake doing so well here, and Sylvia just thriving—"

"Her advisor is encouraging her to apply for PhD programs. Did I tell you that?"

"No, but I'm not surprised. She's a brilliant young lady." Grace took a deep breath. "I remember this time, and it's a special time. It's almost like going out into the world again. Like being on your own for the very first time. The world seems so wide open."

Monica laughed. "Yeah... I mean, I didn't have that. I didn't go to college or anything because Jake—"

"I remember." Grace's eyes danced. "I was there."

Yes, she had been. Robin might have had her issues with her mother, and Monica knew Grace was far from perfect, but she would never, ever forget that when her own parents had disowned her for getting pregnant at eighteen with her high school boyfriend, Grace and Philip had immediately welcomed her into their home. She'd stayed with the Lewises for three months before Gilbert arranged for them to move into his Uncle Eddie's house.

"My point is," Grace continued, "during this time in my life, I remember being excited. I was older, I knew what I wanted and what kind of person I was. And I felt free."

Monica nodded. "I get that. I do feel free."

"But you're facing that without Gilbert." Grace's eyes teared up. "And I can't imagine that. That was the time when Philip and I reconnected. We took trips we'd always planned on but hadn't had the time for when the kids were young. We danced in the kitchen and slept in and got to be spontaneous. If I wanted to drive to Reno for an antique expo, we just packed the car and went."

Monica's heart hurt. "Yeah."

"You have that same freedom, but you lost your partner in crime." Grace blinked rapidly. "So" —she took a deep breath— "I want to know: How are you doing?"

Monica didn't give her a flippant response. She didn't say *fine.*

"I'm... lonely." She cleared the roughness from her throat. "I miss Gilbert every day. I miss waking up next to him. I miss going home at night and telling him all the stories about guests here or what the kids are up to." She shrugged. "But I can't do anything about that."

The wound Gilbert's loss had left wasn't bleeding anymore. It just sat in Monica's chest, hollow and aching.

"Did you like being married?"

Monica smiled. "I loved it. We had our moments, but I loved Gil so much."

"But did you like being *married*? Did you like having a partner, a friend, a second in your life's duel?"

Monica had never thought about it that way. "Yeah. I did. I liked always having someone at my back, you know? Other than Robin and Val."

Grace nodded. "Monica."

"Mm-hmm?" She was jotting down an idea she'd just had for a fall promotion.

"I think it's time you started dating again."

She dropped her pen. "Excuse me?"

"I'm not talking about those odd people who are convinced that the way to grieve a dead spouse is to date the first available person they see. That's ridiculous."

Oh. Oh no. Not this. "Grace—"

"You are a young woman and you were a wonderful wife. You don't like being alone—I can see it every day—and you're holding yourself back from seeing new men. Why?"

Monica was still trying to process what Grace was saying. "I... um..."

"Have you considered online dating?" Grace asked. "For professional women it seems like a very sensible choice, though I have no idea what kind of men those sites attract. Still, I imagine some of them might be... *entertaining* even if they're not good long-term prospects."

"I'm sorry." Were her eyebrows permanently frozen in a shocked expression? Possibly. "I'm still trying to process what you're saying." Was her best friend's mom—traditional, kind-of-stuffy Grace Lewis—telling Monica she needed to get laid?

"If you're interested in my suggestions, let me know." Grace closed her financial folder. "But if you're holding back because you think you need more time to grieve or because your children would disapprove—"

"It's not that."

"Good." Grace nodded decisively. "Like I told you, I recognize myself in you. You're a planner. You like having a road map, and you're excellent at following a plan. But you have to leave room for the unexpected. I know you'd be happier with a partner at your side. Like me. I would miss Philip horribly if something happened to him, but I would hate to be alone."

"Right." Monica was still blinking. "Is Philip—?"

"In excellent health." Grace waved a hand. "He'll likely outlive all of us with his relaxed approach to life. The man does not even entertain stress."

"So you think—"

"A dating site." Grace nodded. "Or a matchmaker. Does anyone use those anymore?"

Monica muttered, "I honestly have no idea."

"Make sure you play the field for a while. You've only ever been with Gilbert if I remember correctly."

"I... Hmm." That was it. She was out of words.

Grace winked. "There are a lot of possibilities out there for a beautiful woman in the prime of her life. You should enjoy yourself before you think about settling down."

What universe had she passed into? Was there a hidden camera somewhere? Would Grace even participate in a prank show? Of course she wouldn't. She'd consider it gauche. But prior to this conversation, Monica wouldn't have expected Grace to suggest she "play the field" either.

Grace stood and picked up her folders. "Well, you and the girls will figure it out. Sully seems to make Val very happy. Maybe he has a friend or two."

Two? She didn't need two! "I really don't think—"

"I'll call Robin. I'm sure she'll have ideas. First Friday of next month still good?"

"For?"

Grace looked at her like she'd lost it. "Our monthly finance meeting."

Oh, were they talking about the hotel again? *Thank God.* "Yes!" Monica stood. "First Friday of the month is good."

"Excellent." Grace walked around the table and gave her a hug. "Have a wonderful weekend." Her eyes lit up. "Maybe you'll have a romance with one of the guests. Wouldn't that be exciting?"

No. That sounded like a disaster. "Have a great day!" Monica reached for her phone. "I think someone is texting me. I better check it."

"I'll see you later, sweetheart. Enjoy the weekend."

Monica walked away before her head exploded. She looked at her phone, only to see a series of messages from Robin that she'd missed.

RED ALERT. You're meeting with my mom this morning, right? CALL ME.

The following message was fifteen minutes later.

Oh God, you're meeting with her already. Please know I TOLD HER not to bring this up.

At least Robin had tried to warn her. Not that it would have made the meeting any less awkward.

Another message had come a few minutes after the first two.

She means well.

And another message five minutes later.

Wine at your house tonight? I'm buying. Just tell me how many bottles.

Monica walked to her office and shut the door before she texted Robin back.

Yes. Wine. Lots.

CHAPTER 4

*M*onica leaned her elbows on the counter at Robin's house and massaged her temples. "I'm trying to pretend it didn't happen."

Robin filled her glass of wine to the brim. "I am so sorry. There is no explanation for her. She should never have pressured—"

"She didn't pressure me. Exactly. It was more like..." She sat up straight. "Do people actually walk around town thinking, 'Oh, poor Monica!' when they see me? Do they?"

Val shrugged from her perch near the sink. "Not me."

"You don't count—you know me."

Val pointed at Monica. "It's Glimmer Lake. Everyone knows you except tourists."

"You know what I mean. I mean do the people I see every day at the coffee shop, at church... are they all thinking, 'Poor Monica'?"

Even the thought horrified her. She'd experienced a lifetime's worth of pity when she missed going to college because she got pregnant. The last thing she wanted was her entire community thinking she was a pity case at a time when she was finally getting back on her feet.

"I'm not 'poor Monica,'" she said. "I started a successful business. My kids are all independent, functioning adults who still speak to me. No drugs. All employed. All— You know who's poor? All those women I see bitching about their marriages! The ones who don't do a damn thing about fixing them or starting over." She had moved past horrified and was leaning into pissed off. "Poor Monica, my foot."

"No one is saying poor Monica." Robin reassured her. "Everyone knew how amazing Gil was, so I mean, we all feel for you. But no one is acting like you just gave up or anything."

"Because I haven't!"

"Fuck no, you haven't." Val popped an almond in her mouth. "Is the pizza ready?"

"I'm awesome!" Monica said. "I don't need a man to be happy." Not that it wouldn't be nice to...

Not the point.

"I honestly don't think my mom was thinking that you needed a man to be happy," Robin said. "She just knows... I mean, you did like being married."

"Yeah. To Gilbert." She had no confidence that anyone would even be close to a match for Gil. "So why does she think I want to get out there and sow my wild oats at forty-eight?"

Robin and Val exchanged a look.

"What?" Monica looked between them. "What was that?"

"I mean..." Val shrugged. "It's been a while. You don't have any urge to get laid at all?"

"Oh my God." She clapped her hands over her cheeks, already feeling the heat. "Valerie Costa, I am not some horny teenage—"

"I'm not saying you are," Val said. "But it's been almost four years. I'm just saying if you want to get laid? You could totally get some. So that's an option."

"Why would I want to have sex with some random man?"

Robin stifled a laugh. "I don't think either of us is suggesting you go out trolling at the lodge or anything."

Val piped up. "We're not *not* suggesting that either. A woman has needs."

Monica leaned back on the counter and covered her eyes with both hands. "I'm going to pretend this isn't happening. I don't have the time, energy—"

"I think my mom just meant to say that if you want to look around, maybe date a little, there's not some magic alarm that suddenly goes off and tells you it's allowed. You've had time to grieve. You were an awesome wife and you had a wonderful marriage. If you met a man you wanted to spend time with, that would be great."

"Okay." Please let them move on to something—anything!—else.

Val said, "So do you want to start one of those dating profiles?"

Robin's eyes lit up. "We could help you fill it out!"

Monica was going to kill them both.

THEY WERE MUNCHING on pizza by the time Monica was able to steer them toward something resembling a normal conversation. "So I had a strange and disturbing vision last night."

Okay yeah, not normal for most people, but normal for them.

"Murder?" Val asked. "Theft? Giant asteroid hurling toward the earth?" She looked at Robin. "I read that at any given time, there's one in fairly close proximity."

"Thanks," Robin said. "I definitely needed to know that useful piece of information so I could worry about it."

"Why worry? If a giant asteroid hits the earth, we're fossils."

"Hello?" Monica waved. "Disturbing vision here?"

"Right." Val turned toward her and mimed zipping her lips. "Tell."

"I was walking down Main Street and everything was on fire." She put down her pizza. "I was alone and I was wearing my white dress with the little red flowers on it. I think I was barefoot."

"Summer," Robin said. "Sounds like summer."

"Sundress and barefoot," Monica said. "Okay, yeah. That makes sense. So this is something that's going to happen this summer."

"What do you mean, everything was on fire?" Val asked.

"I mean it looked like a forest fire, but not like we'd evacuated. There were all the normal cars around; I could see people in shops and at restaurants. But all the buildings were in flames. The trees were dropping sparks everywhere."

Robin asked, "And you're sure this was a vision? Not a bad dream?"

"I can't lie—I've had nightmares about fire for years. It's impossible not to have nightmares about fire when you're married to a firefighter. But this didn't feel like a dream. It was definitely a vision."

Val's mouth was set in a grim line. "So Glimmer Lake is going to have a forest fire?"

"Not necessarily," Robin said. "Maybe this was a metaphor. Maybe this isn't an actual fire. That's happened before, right?"

Monica nodded. "Sometimes things don't happen exactly the way I see them. Sometimes it's just a symbol or a mood. Unfortunately, this doesn't feel that way. Not this time."

Val and Robin both watched her with frightened eyes. No one lived in the mountains or foothills of California without understanding how devastating fire could be. Homes, neighborhoods, and even entire towns could be consumed.

"So what do we do?" Val asked. "Should I tell Sully?"

Robin asked, "Tell him what?"

"We can at least warn him about the vision."

Monica thought about the fire in her dream. She tried to remember the feeling of creeping dread and the unnatural darkness that had hovered over her when she woke. "Robin, have you noticed anything unusual around town lately with the... less alive community?"

Ever since the accident, Robin had been able to speak to ghosts, hear them, and even summon a few if she'd met them before. "If I think about it, it's been pretty quiet. But it's also been high tourist season the past couple of months, so I guess I assumed they'd retreated because of that."

Val asked, "Did they do that last summer?"

"Yes, but if I think about it, not as much."

Monica nodded slowly. "Okay. Val, there's not really

anything you can touch and read right now." Val was a psychometric able to read energy and sometimes memories off of objects. "But it might be a good idea to give Sully a heads-up anyway." Val was dating the sheriff in Glimmer Lake, and he knew about the three of them and their powers.

"For now," Monica continued, "all we can do is wait. Something about this dream feels different. I've only had it once, so it's possible that it might change, that it's trying to tell me something else, a metaphor like Robin said."

"Did you get any sense of time?"

Monica shook her head. "Just the sundress and bare feet. And I agree with Robin—I think that means this summer."

"It's August," Val said. "Summer's coming to an end.

"Which means that whatever is going to happen" — Monica took a deep breath— "might happen pretty soon."

SHE DREAMED AGAIN THAT NIGHT, the ceiling fan wafting cool air down on her sweating body as she tossed and turned.

She was hot. The proximity of the flames felt blistering on her skin. Though she walked on sparks and ashes, she couldn't feel the burn on her bare feet, only the piercing grit of gravel, stones, and bark that had blown into the road.

The stores around her were open, people walked in and out carrying packages, looking at mobile phones, and checking purses and wallets. Two girls walked out of Sandy's Scoops with ice cream melting down their hands.

The fire raged above her, dancing from treetop to treetop. The canopy of pine and cedar crackled as it was consumed by the heated wind whipping up from Glimmer Lake.

She could see the water in the distance, obscured by dark brown smoke. The whitecaps that usually danced in the wind were gone, and the water was completely still.

Monica walked through the dream, and this time she felt calmer. This was sent to her. There was something she needed to see, something she needed to discover.

"Hello?" she called out, and that was different too. She didn't talk in her dreams; she saw things. "Hello?"

A figure in shadows appeared at the edge of the forest, and Monica walked toward it. The brush rustled and crackled as the forest detritus simmered with red-gold coals. There was someone in the shadows; high, panicked breathing came to Monica's ears.

Whomever she'd seen was running away, crashing through the burning trees and bushes.

"Don't go there!" Monica tried to follow the shadow, but the fire burned hotter. The flames were right in her face.

She rolled over, and he took her mouth in a long, lingering kiss. His lips moved slowly on hers as he inched his body closer.

"Come here," he murmured. His hand stroked down her back and his other hand cupped her cheek, angling her mouth to his.

They were naked, skin to skin, and the light sheen of sweat on his shoulders glowed in the low light of her bedroom. She pulled away, looking at him.

High cheekbones and an angular face. Dark, arching eyebrows over deep brown eyes. His eyes were so dark she fell into them. Silver threaded through his jet-black hair. It was a little bit long. He needed a haircut. She twisted a curl around her finger, and he let out a rough sigh.

Who are you?

His kisses made her drunk; her body answered his. She threw her knee over his thigh and pressed her body into his.

"Yes," he murmured. "Yes."

She was so hungry for him. *It had been years.*

Monica threw her arms around his shoulders and thrilled in the heavy, corded muscle across his shoulders and chest. The sun had turned his brown skin darker—she could see where the edge of his undershirt ended and his tan began.

Their bodies moved together in perfect time. This wasn't the first time they'd made love. Was it? The planes of his body were as familiar as her own soft curves and dips.

He grabbed a handful of her backside and she lost all focus.

"Say my name."

MONICA WOKE from her dream and sat up, gasping for entirely different reasons than the night before. She was flushed and sweating. Her thighs were damp, and her hair stuck to her neck. Her breasts felt heavy, and her lips were swollen.

What the hell?

She'd never had a sex dream like that. Ever. She'd never had a sex dream about anyone but her husband. It was kind of hard to imagine sex with anyone else when you'd only ever had one partner.

But that hadn't been Gilbert.

Who are you?

She could see his face as clearly as if she'd seen a picture.

He was Latino and around her age. Short curly hair dusted with silver, and an angular jaw. He wore a short beard and he had beautiful eyes.

He was familiar. Wasn't he? Was she having random sex dreams about strangers now?

Oh hell, maybe Robin and Val had a point.

Groaning, Monica fell back into bed and reached for her journal. She tried to focus on the vision of the fire again and not the vision of the man in her bed.

That wasn't helpful at all.

She jotted down everything she could remember. There was something new about this vision. She'd interacted with someone in it. To a point. She'd spoken, and that had never happened before. Before, she had always been a bystander. Most often it was as if she were watching a movie with familiar actors. But this time she was in the dream. She was participating.

Hell yeah, I'd call that participation.

She choked when she remembered the sex dream again.

Sex dream or sex vision?

For heaven's sake, she could practically feel the man's hands on her. This was ridiculous. She blamed Robin and Val. And Grace. This was definitely their fault for getting her imagination going about seeing new men.

Forget the mystery man. Monica had seen something else in her dream. She'd seen *someone* else, and she had a feeling that person knew something about her visions of fire.

Monica had a suspicion that whatever was coming to Glimmer Lake, there was someone—or some*thing*—behind it.

CHAPTER 5

*S*ylvia laughed. "Mom, maybe they have a point."

Monica nearly tossed the phone across the room. "Not you too."

It was Saturday morning, and her daughter had called for their weekly chat. They usually grabbed a cup of coffee, and Monica sat on the front porch, looking at the mountains, while Sylvia sat on her tiny balcony in the East Bay. They caught up on the week, shared gossip, and talked about "the boys," aka Sylvia's brothers.

"I'm just saying" —her daughter was laughing at her— "I don't think Dad would have wanted you to stay single for the rest of your life. You're young. I don't think any of us expect it."

"Caleb would be upset."

"No... Okay, maybe, but that's only because he's the most sentimental and he's young and probably still believes in eternal love and all that."

"He's only two years younger than you, Syl."

"You know what I mean though."

Sylvia, having grown up as the only daughter with three brothers, often sounded more like the oldest than Jake did. She knew all her brothers really well, and she knew Monica was right about Caleb. Her youngest by ten minutes, Caleb had always been her softest child, which was completely belied by his massive frame and heavy beard.

"Caleb would be a little sad, but if you met someone who made you happy, you know he'd be the first to be all in. He's a romantic."

"Do you think him and this girl—"

"Yesssssss." Sylvia started a stream of gossip about Caleb's new girlfriend, who was a teacher in Bridger City and a couple of years older than him. They'd been dating for just over a month, and Jake and Sylvia were already bugging Caleb to bring her home. So far, Caleb's twin brother Sam was the only one who'd met her.

Monica adored her kids. She'd loved raising them, and she loved being a mom of adults too. Watching her kids take flight and soar in their own lives was a thrill. She'd worried initially when Sylvia was the only one who wanted to go to college, but she shouldn't have.

Her boys were too much like their father. They all loved the outdoors. They loved working with their hands. Caleb and Sam had started Velasquez Brothers Construction after they graduated from trade school, and they already had a great reputation in Bridger. Jake had wandered from one thing to another for a while but seemed to have found his niche doing handyman work and planning outdoor adventures for the hotel.

Monica's children were thriving. Her own business was taking off.

And her daughter had circled back around to her love life.

"You know," she said, "you should get one of those online profiles. Just to see."

"My daughter, the future *psychologist*, is recommending online dating to me?"

"Why not? It's a perfect way for busy career women to meet men. If nothing else, you can get an idea of what men are out there and what you might be interested in. Maybe you just want someone to go out to dinner with every now and then. Or go dancing. Don't you miss dancing?"

She did miss dancing. She and Gilbert had regularly driven down to Bridger City to dance at the single salsa bar or go to a salsa night at a local club. They had friends they only saw dancing. One of the women they knew had called after Gil passed and encouraged Sylvia to still join them and maybe find a new partner, but Monica just hadn't felt the urge to dance with anyone at that point.

But now...? She could admit she missed it.

"Maybe I should just go to a salsa night or two," Monica said. "I could dance with some of our friends—"

"I mean, you should definitely do that if you want, but dancing with some of Dad's old friends might just feel kind of weird, you know? I don't know. Don't listen to me. Do what you want." The words rushed out. "But I'm glad you're thinking about doing something, and I still think an online profile is a cool idea. But have Val and Robin help you fill it out, because you'll be too modest about your accomplishments."

Monica snorted. "My accomplishments? My business isn't even two years old. I think I'll hold off on bragging."

"Uh, you were also married for twenty-five years and raised four nondysfunctional kids who all have jobs and all speak to each other. You're practically a unicorn, Mami."

Monica smiled and sipped her lukewarm coffee. "I love you."

"I love you too." Sylvia made long kissing noises on the phone. "I have a three-day weekend soon, and I'm coming for a visit."

"Please."

"And Jake and I will make Caleb bring his girl to dinner. Six weeks is past time to introduce her to the Velasquez crazy."

Monica laughed. "Don't scare her off."

"Pfft. If she can't handle us, she's not the right girl for Tiny."

"Yes, make sure you call him that in front of her. She'll be nice and confused."

Tiny had been a joke since Caleb was seven years old and had shot past his brothers and sister in height. He'd eventually slowed down and topped out at just under six feet, but he had Gilbert's chest and muscular frame, so the nickname was still hilarious.

"Hey, Mom, I'm thinking about using Glimmer Lake as part of my research project."

Monica frowned. "Glimmer Lake? I thought your new project was about generational trauma or something like that."

"It is, but I'm thinking about giving it an environmental focus. How does losing an environment or experiencing gentrification and removal affect a community and the individuals in it? Something along those lines."

Monica looked at her nearest neighbor, whom she could barely see through the thick sugar pine and cedar trees that surrounded the house. "I don't know how much gentrification Glimmer Lake has experienced, Syl."

"I'm not really talking about Glimmer Lake. I'm talking about Grimmer."

Grimmer was the old ranching town that had been flooded to make way for the dam and modern development at the beginning of the twentieth century. The new town of Glimmer Lake had grown on the edge of the lake that had formed.

According to Robin, more than one ghost in town was from Grimmer, still haunting the lake that had taken their home.

Even the thought of the town at the bottom of the lake gave Monica chills. "You want to research Grimmer?"

"Yeah, like... why Grimmer? I know it was flooded because of the dam, but why did they pick Grimmer? Was it because of the river? Or was it something else? How did they get permission? And what happened to all the families who lost their homes?"

"You know, I think Robin's done some research on that" —*when she was solving an eighty-year-old murder*— "and I know the library in town has a lot about town history. Not sure about the families though."

"I just thought it would be an interesting historical example since most of my research is more contemporary."

Did this have anything to do with her dreams of Glimmer Lake burning?

The loss of Grimmer. Generational trauma?

Why Grimmer?

38

"Yeah, it's an interesting avenue. What weekend are you coming to visit?"

"Labor Day. I know it's the end of the summer season and you're probably busy, but—"

"Never too busy for you or your brothers, baby." Monica sat up straight. "Why don't I stop by the library today and talk to Gail? She's probably closed Labor Day weekend, but if she knows it's for a research project, she might make an exception."

"Give her my email! I'd love to talk with her."

"Sure thing."

Monica sat across from a library table while she chatted with Gail, the town's librarian and the closest thing they had to a historian.

"Why Grimmer?" Gail smiled. "Such a good question. I love that Sylvia's doing this project. And I'm very relieved she has a bigger library to access now."

Monica laughed. "I think she may have met her match at the university library." Sylvia was a notorious bookworm and had read her way through pretty much every novel and biography in the Glimmer Lake library when she was a child.

Gail was sorting through a stack of children's picture books, erasing marks and taping pages as they talked. It was something Monica remembered doing when she'd volunteered at the library when the kids were young.

"Why Grimmer? It's a complicated question, and it wasn't an easy decision. Believe it or not, there was something of a competition to be the valley that got the lake."

"You mean some towns *wanted* to be flooded?"

"Oh yeah." Gail finished one book and opened another. "Because the power company that built the dam was offering money to all the property owners, quite a few towns wanted to be the one. I'm sure not everyone in the towns was on board, but we're talking about small communities that were mostly run by the richest man in town, whoever that might have been."

"In Grimmer?"

"The Russells obviously. Very wealthy. But the Grimmers had money too, and they definitely had the most property. But Grimmer was split on whether to submit."

"Do you know what the deciding factor was?"

"It was pretty well covered in the Sacramento papers. The dam was big news." Gail frowned. "I think everything from that era has been digitized, so you can look on the computer. But the main reason it ended up being Grimmer was the fire."

Monica felt a chill go down her back. "There was a fire?"

"It happened years before they started building. This was all in the early thirties." Gail set a picture book down and opened the laptop on the table next to her. "Let me see if I can find the article."

"A forest fire?"

"Oh yeah. Big one. Nearly destroyed the entire town." Gail frowned at the screen. "No way of knowing how it started."

"It wasn't natural?" The dry air of the late summer and fall in the Sierras combined with electrical storms meant some fires were inevitable. Lightning strikes happened, and fires were part of the ecological cycle. Flames burned though underbrush, clearing the way for new trees to sprout. Meadows were opened. The natural cycles were older than any manmade structures and had zero respect for humans making homes in the middle of the forest.

"Here it is." Gail flipped her computer around. "It started in a house, but we have no way of knowing what happened really. A cooking fire is the most likely explanation."

Monica skimmed the article about the Sanger family and their home that burned, causing the tragic 1932 fire that destroyed most of Grimmer.

"Families along the river were able to save their homes, and they were the most prosperous anyway, like the Russells, the Grimmers, and the Roberts clan. But many of the smaller ranchers lost their houses and barns. There was no insurance back then, so most of them just left. By the time the subject of the dam came up, at least a third of the town had already been abandoned."

"Interesting. So if the power company that built the dam had to compensate the residents of whatever town they flooded, and Grimmer was already two-thirds of its original population..."

"Exactly. The Russells made the argument that the town would cost more to rebuild than it was worth, that they should take the deal from the power company and start over."

"And the power company got a good deal because the town was already partly abandoned."

"Gordon Russell had a point. The town really had been devastated. The fire that killed the Sangers—"

"They died?" Monica's head shot up. "The family whose house burned down?"

"Oh yes. A father and two daughters. They burned in the

house, according to reports. Those were the only deaths though. They were fortunate; a storm rolled in the day after the fire started. The rest of the town was able to shelter by the river."

"Huh." Monica turned the computer back to Gail. "Thanks, Gail. Let me give you Sylvia's email. I think she'd really love to talk to you."

"I'd love to catch up with her!"

While Monica jotted down her daughter's information for the librarian, her mind was whirling. Grimmer hadn't been random. A fire had destroyed the town and sealed its fate.

Now another fire threatened Glimmer Lake, and something in Monica's gut told her that somehow there was a connection. She needed more information. She needed to know more about what had happened to Grimmer.

She needed to talk to Robin.

CHAPTER 6

"So you think the old fire is related to your vision?" Robin looked up from her turkey-and-avocado sandwich. It was Tuesday, and Monica, Robin, and Mark were eating lunch at Misfit Mountain Coffee, and Val was joining them for five-minute bursts while she juggled the lunch rush.

"I think it's a weird coincidence that I'm dreaming about a fire when the old town at the bottom of the lake was destroyed by one too."

Mark looked skeptical. "But forest fires happen. I mean, it's kind of predictable even. Forest gets too dense, fire happens, forest thins out. The town is kind of incidental." Robin's husband was a computer programmer, knew all about their psychic "gifts," and believed them. He was a good sounding board when things got weird.

"Not here." Monica was sure of it. "Not now. What I'm dreaming about isn't an ordinary fire."

Robin asked, "Do you think it's arson?"

"Oh yeah. There's something behind it. I'm positive on that. It's not random or natural."

"How are you so sure?" Mark asked.

"Because in my last dream there was a... presence. I'm not sure if it was male or female. I'm not sure what it was, but there was something there and it felt terrified. Excited too, but kind of with this desperate, panicky edge."

"Sounds like it could definitely be an arsonist," Mark said. "What do we know about arsonists? Is there like a... profile or something on them?"

Val sat down at the table with half a sandwich in her hand. "Okay, I'm taking a real break. What are we talking about?"

"The fire in Monica's dream," Robin said. "She's pretty positive it's arson."

"Okay, so we have a future arsonist in Glimmer Lake." Val took a bite. "Not great. Any clues on identity?"

Mark waved at someone behind Monica's back. She turned to see Sully enter the coffee shop. He was walking toward them, carrying a travel mug.

Sully dragged a chair over and wedged it next to Val. "Hey."

He wasn't a man of many words.

Val glanced at him. "Hi. I'm not sharing my sandwich, but I'll tell Jojo to make you one if you're hungry."

"Nice." He reached out and snagged one of the chips on her plate. "I'll go up to the counter and order."

She slapped a hand over her chips. "Careful."

The corner of his mouth turned up. "She doesn't share her food."

"Not in the middle of the day I don't."

Sully turned to the rest of the table. "Val mentioned something about a fire?" Sully knew about their psychic gifts too, and he wasn't a skeptic. His face was already grim. "I'm not gonna lie, this is looking like a bad fire season already. We had a lot of snow, so there's a lot of brush and it's all dry now."

"It's not a fire *yet*," Monica said, keeping her voice down. "But I'm having a recurring vision of Glimmer Lake on fire."

Sully frowned. "And with that stuff, how certain is it? I mean, can you change things you see in a vision? Or if you see it, that means it's gonna happen for sure?"

"Not for sure. Things change all the time. It changed slightly from the first vision to the second. Seeing the future is..."

"Tricky," Robin said.

"Fuzzy." Val took another bite of her sandwich. "You're really only seeing one possible future."

Sully swiped another chip. "You really shouldn't talk with your mouth full."

"Bite me."

"I do. You like it."

Val must have kicked him under the table, because Sully's half smile turned into a full grin.

"Okay, you two, stop flirting," Robin said.

"Don't," Monica said. "It's adorable."

"See?" Val pointed at her. "You're a romantic. You need to start dating again."

Sully frowned. "I actually just ran into an old friend—"

"I'm not looking for a date." Monica cut him off. "These two think I should be dating. I am not looking."

Robin said, "So the friend you're going to set Monica up with, what is he—?"

"Stop." She slapped a hand over Robin's mouth. She hissed, "Can we talk about the possible disaster that is going to descend on our home please?"

"Right." Sully stole another one of Val's chips. "We need to figure out how to change the future."

"Some things seem to be set in stone," Monica said. "And some don't. How do we know that if we try to change this, that won't bring on the fire?"

"We need a physicist," Val said. "Aren't they the time experts?"

Mark perked up. "We actually know a physicist."

"Do you?" Monica was curious. "But would she believe in a psychic vision?"

"I don't know, but Kat's pretty flexible mentally. She might not rule it out."

"Oh, is that..." Robin was snapping her fingers. "That really nice girl who didn't marry Dan?" She turned to them. "Dan was one of Mark's roommates in college."

"He was my best man." Mark took a drink. "He and Katherine were engaged for almost a year, but they ended up breaking it off. I think it was mutual."

Robin said, "They stayed friendly. I remember that."

Mark continued, "She's superbrilliant. We ended up being in the same running club, and she still emails me sometimes when there's a trail run at the coast."

"Where is she?"

Mark said, "She's a professor now, Central Coast State. She married another professor—I don't know him though—and they live in Swann Cove."

"That's such a pretty town," Monica said. "Gil and I went there for our anniversary one year."

"Yeah, she likes it." Mark frowned a little. "If you wanted to talk to Katherine about your vision, I bet she'd be open to it."

Monica cringed at the idea of exposing herself to an actual scientist. "I don't know. She'd probably think I was just... out there. Silly housewife imagining things."

"I doubt it," Mark said. "If I remember correctly, she was really interested in theoretical stuff. She took a lot of philosophy and psychology classes too. She's a really interesting woman."

"Also," Robin said, "you're not a silly housewife. You were a badass domestic goddess for twenty-five years, and now you're a successful hotelier."

Val reached over and gave Monica a fist bump. "Badass domestic goddess."

Sully stole another chip while Val was distracted. "Might be a good idea to talk to her. You're seeing a fire that sounds pretty devastating. Might be worth knowing if this is a foregone conclusion and we need to figure out a way to convince people to evacuate or whether something we do might change it."

Mark looked at her. "I really don't think she'd be dismissive. If you want, I'll give you her number."

———

MONICA SPENT the rest of her afternoon at Russell House. After paperwork was done, she found herself walking around the perimeter of the house, examining the tree canopy and trying to imagine a way to expand the safe zone without sacrificing the lush, forested look of the hotel.

They could expand the garden, maybe even create another event space in the back of the house where now there was only forest. The ropes course Jake had built was closer to the lake, and the back of the house only had a broad porch with a view of the trees.

If they pushed the tree line back and created a forest gazebo...

"Hey, Mom!"

She was standing on the north lawn, which led to the boathouse, when she heard Jake running up.

"Mom!"

She turned and saw her oldest jogging up the path. Goodness. How had he gotten to be a man? He was twenty-nine, and it still surprised her sometimes. She could picture him at every moment of his life. The chubby baby so eager to walk he crashed into everything. The little boy with red cheeks and a soft heart for worms in the garden. The boy obsessed with Spider-Man and the teenager who lived for anything that took him outdoors. Skiing, snowboarding, rock climbing, dirt bikes.

"Hey!" He wasn't even panting when he reached her. "Whatcha doing?"

She nodded toward the back of Russell House. "Remember all Dad's lectures about defensible space?"

Jake cringed. "Oh yeah. He would not approve of that." He swiped his hand along the tree line. "He'd want it all gone."

"I know. I'm trying to think of a happy medium. What if we do cut back some of the trees—"

"Most of the trees?"

"Okay, most of the trees that are really close to the house. We push that back and then maybe do some new plantings? Lower trees like dogwood and redbud that would offer some spring and summer color. Build a gazebo and make some paths with flowering bushes and seasonal color." She turned to Jake. "What do you think?"

Jake was his father's son. "I think that definitely reduces the fire hazard close to the house, and also, wedding parties would go crazy for a forest gazebo. Kara would call it Instagram-worthy."

Monica smiled. "If Kara would like it, then you know it's probably a winning idea. I still have to run all this by Grace and Philip of course, then find room in the budget—"

Jake sighed deeply. "This means I'm going to be stuck with that minivan for years, doesn't it?"

"Do not hate on the minivan!" Monica punched his arm. "That is a luxury minivan, Jake Velasquez."

"It's still a minivan," he muttered. "An SUV would be cooler."

"And cost more to maintain." She patted his shoulder. "If anyone can make a minivan cool, it's you, Jakey. I know you'll survive."

He stayed silent, staring at the back of the house.

"What's up? You have your deep-thinker face on." Which wasn't typical for Jake. Caleb and Sam were her deep thinkers. Sylvia, her sharp-witted strategist. Jake was far more in the throw-yourself-in-with-enthusiasm-and-figure-out-the-details later camp.

"So... does Russell House have a policy about... um..."

Monica frowned. "A policy about what? Russell House is

pretty much me and Grace, so whatever it is you're worried about—"

"I'm not worried." His cheeks were a little red. "I was just wondering about maybe possibly asking someone out. Someone here that I work with. And I was wondering if, you know, that was okay."

Oh yes! Monica tried not to do a happy dance. "Is this person someone you supervise in any way?"

"Absolutely not. We have very separate jobs. If anything, she's my sup— Mom, you know I'm talking about Kara."

"I figured, but I didn't want to assume."

"I think all the other women who work here have husbands or boyfriends anyway."

"And if you wanted to ask any of them out, I'd have a much bigger problem than you working together."

"Mom, can you just tell me—"

"I have no problem with you and Kara going out." She really thought about it. "In theory."

"But...?"

She turned to her son. Her very gorgeous son who had left a trail of brokenhearted girls through Glimmer Lake High School. "If things don't work out—"

"I think we can stay friends," he said. "I'm friendly with most of my exes. Not that it wouldn't be awkward, but—"

"Maybe just... go slow?" She winced. "I hate giving you dating advice. I just know that she is interested in you, and—"

"You think so?" His eyes lit up. "I can't tell with her. She's always friendly, but then she's friendly with everyone, you know? So it's hard to tell... I mean, that's cool." He turned away and nodded. "I think I can go slow."

Really? 'Cause you're so not good at doing that in any other area of your life.

Monica didn't say that. "Good. I think slow is good when it's someone you work with. And that is all I'll say about that."

"Okay. And that's all I needed to know." His cheeks were still a little red, but he crossed his arms over his chest and nodded back at the house. "The gazebo and garden is a good idea."

"Thanks. I think Grace will like it too."

Monica's phone started buzzing in her pocket. She grabbed it and looked at the screen. "Okay, meeting's over. That's Kara. The fire inspector is here."

"It's probably someone you know."

She shook her head. "New chief for the region. Case Jorgensen retired last year."

"I hadn't heard that."

"Yeah. Pretty sure it was a surprise to everyone." Monica started walking around the house. "But he'd been at the department for over thirty-five years I think? I'm sure he and Sheila were ready to be done."

"Okay, have fun with that. I'm going to get the oil changed on the boat. It's overdue." He bent down and kissed her cheek. "Thanks, Mami."

"Be safe." Monica watched him jog away from the house and toward the lake.

She turned the corner of the house and saw the familiar red-and-white pickup truck of the state fire service pulled up in the gravel drive in front of Russell House. A man stood beside the truck, marking something down on a metal clipboard. He was nodding at whatever Kara was saying and appeared to be taking notes.

"Oh! There's Monica." Kara pointed at her. "She'll definitely be the one who can answer your questions."

The man turned, spotted her, and Monica froze.

She didn't know this man—didn't know the first thing about him—but she'd seen him before.

Who are you?

The man of her dreams was literally standing in front of her. Fortunately—*or unfortunately?*—this time he was wearing a uniform.

CHAPTER 7

*H*e stepped forward and held out his hand to shake hers. "Ma'am. Gabriel Peralta. I'm the new unit chief for the area. Nice to meet you."

Monica blinked twice and cleared her throat. "I'm... Monica. Monica Velasquez. I run... I mean, this is my hotel. It's a partnership actually. I'm a partner in the hotel, but I run it. With Kara, I mean. Whom you've met. Obviously."

Dear God. What was she doing?

Monica reached out and grabbed the man's hand, shook it, and dropped it like it was on fire.

Chief Peralta cocked his head. "Have we met?"

"*No.* Nope." She'd maybe said that too forcefully. Monica cleared her throat. "I don't believe so. I knew your... I mean, I knew Case. The chief before you. My husband worked with him."

Peralta's eyes lit up. "Oh, is your husband in the fire service?"

"He was, but he died."

The man's eyes went wide.

Sexy dark eyes...

Stop. It.

"I'm so sorry," he said. "Was it—"

"It wasn't in a fire. He had... I'm sorry, can we start over? You caught me at a weird moment." She was acting like a lunatic. In her defense, Monica had never met someone in real life she'd only ever seen in a sex dream. "I'm Monica. I'm the manager and part owner of Russell House." She put on her customer smile. "You're Chief Peralta, and I believe Kara said you were here to talk to me about defensible space around our structure prior to the fire season."

"Sure." Chief Peralta started on the safety spiel. "So, as I'm sure you know, Russell House backs up to national forest land, which makes it a little different than county."

"Mm-hmm."

He was as handsome as he'd been in her dream. More, in fact, now that she had a clear picture of him. Gabriel Peralta had high cheekbones and wide arched brows that gave his face dramatic planes. Full, expressive lips that drew the eye when he talked. His jaw was clean-shaven and sharp, with a slight cleft in his chin. She could see a hint of silver stubble on his cheek which—judging by how early it was—told Monica he could probably grow a full beard in a matter of days if he wanted.

His shoulders were broad and his hips narrow. He had to work out religiously, because the normal middle-aged spread had not seemed to touch him. His dark blue uniform was crisp and familiar. It wasn't exactly like Gilbert's since Chief Peralta worked for the state fire service and not the county, but they were pretty similar.

"...so with your permission, I'd like to do a full walk

around of the entire complex so I can give some recommendations." He clasped his metal clipboard with both hands and stood at casual attention.

Monica did not look at his arms. Much. For long. "I think that sounds fine. Having been married to a firefighter, I'm pretty familiar with the ideals for defensible space, and I have some ideas about the backside of the house that I'm going to broach with my partners. They actually own the house, so I can't make any changes without their approval."

He nodded. "A written report with suggestions might go a long way to convincing them the changes are necessary. Would you like to walk with me and tell me what you have in mind?"

"I..." Kara couldn't do it? Shit. Of course she couldn't. Monica hadn't talked to her about any of her ideas. "Of course." She glanced at her assistant in a panic. "Do we have any...?"

Kara looked at the giant watch she wore on her tiny wrist. "You're free for the next forty minutes, then you have a phone appointment on your calendar."

A phone appointment with a physicist to talk about precognition.

"Right." Monica looked back at Peralta and had to clear her throat again. "Let's say thirty minutes so I have time to get my notes together for the call. Does that work, Chief Peralta?"

"More than enough time. And call me Gabe please."

He smiled, and it was absolutely devastating. Butterflies took off in her belly. Monica was pretty sure Kara squeaked... something before she retreated from the blistering male charm of Gabe Peralta.

"Gabe." She nodded. "Of course." She pointed down the path she'd walked around when she was examining the back of the house. "Let's start this way."

He tucked his clipboard under his arm and reached for his phone.

No wedding ring...

"Do you mind if I take some pictures? This place is incredible."

Monica smiled. "Thank you, and of course not. Take all the pictures you want."

"When was the house built?"

"In the early 1940s. It was built by Gordon Russell, who was the founder of Russell Timber Company, and it was a family home for many years. He wanted it to be very grand, so it was based on older designs like—"

"National Park Service rustic, right? Kind of arts and crafts, like the old lodges."

She turned, surprised. "Yes. It borrows a lot from those styles."

Gabe nodded, still staring at the facade of the house in admiration. "They did an incredible job. It looks like it's been here for centuries. I can see they used local stone. Whoever designed it was really thinking. Was it Underwood?" Gabe muttered, "Maybe a student of his."

"You're an architecture fan?"

"My ex-wife is an architect. I wasn't really into it before I met her—I just liked what I liked, you know?" He continued taking pictures, walking closer to Monica. "But she was always talking about it, and I got interested. After we split, I was kind of hooked. And thinking about how the natural world and human buildings work together is part of my job."

Gabe looked down at her. "I can already tell you're going to have some issues with the perimeter though."

Monica was trying hard not to think about the slight scent of cedar on his skin. "Let me tell you what I have in mind."

Because I have so very much on my mind.

SHE PLOPPED down at her desk after half an hour with Gabriel and leaned her face fully into both her hands.

Dear Lord. What was she going to do about this?

She was attracted to this man. Wildly, ridiculously attracted to this man whom she'd already had a sex dream—sex vision?—about. But she didn't know him! She didn't know if she wanted to know him. And she was acting like a bumbling idiot.

She'd handed him off to Jake, knowing that her son would understand everything the man was talking about. After all, he'd been raised by Gilbert and knew way more about fires and fire safety than the average ski bum.

Monica took a bottle of water from the fridge in her office and held the cold glass to her neck.

So do you want to start one of those dating profiles?

Val's question hit her like a slap.

Yes. That's what she needed. She was having his ridiculous reaction to Gabe because she hadn't even been near a man in four years. She just needed to get out there. Flirt a little. Wear a pretty dress and be around men who might find her attractive. Sure, she was a little round in more than a few places, but there were lots of men who liked that. She had a good smile. She had great hair. And she was interesting. Right?

Maybe to someone who liked hotels?

Oh hell. Monica was going to go for it before she second-guessed herself. She opened her laptop and put in the address of a dating site that was all over TV ads. Within a few clicks, she was enrolled and had put up a picture. She didn't waste time answering too many questions—she had a phone call to make—but she put up some basic information, two pictures, and a list of her favorite movies.

There. That was a start.

Shutting down her computer, she reached for a yellow legal pad where she'd written some questions and grabbed her phone.

Okay, don't chicken out now. Sure, the woman has a PhD and is probably ten times smarter than you, but she's friends with Mark and she offered to answer some questions.

She entered the number for Dr. Katherine Bassi and touched the Call button.

"Hello?" Monica said over a crash in the background. "Hello?"

"Hi! Hey. Yes, can I help you?"

"Is this Dr. Bassi? My name is Monica Velasquez, and Mark Brannon—" There was another tumbling sound. "I'm sorry, but are you okay?"

"Uh, yeah. Sorry. Yeah, this is Katherine. Mark's friend? Oh right! Right."

"Are you okay? Do I need to call the paramedics?"

The woman on the phone laughed. "I have the day free of classes, and I decided to organize my pantry. It's way more of

58

a disaster than I thought it was. I'm not injured, but how do I have so many nearly empty boxes of spaghetti?"

Monica smiled. "Pringles cans."

It sounded like a door shut. "What?"

"Pringles cans. Use an empty Pringles can to keep the extra spaghetti in when you don't use the whole box. They're the perfect height and they're easier to store."

"Oh, that is a really good idea. They are the right size, aren't they?"

"Pringles cans come in useful for all sorts of stuff."

Katherine said, "And to get them, you have to eat potato chips. There's really no downside to that."

"Not really, no." Monica was already set at ease. Dr. Katherine Bassi might have a PhD, but she sounded like someone Monica would like. "So this is Mark's friend, Monica."

"Monica, it's nice to meet you. Mark said you had questions about parapsychological phenomena?"

"Wow, that sounds so much more official than psychic stuff."

"Ha! Well, scientists like their fancy labels. Just so you know, I'm definitely a scientist. I think most of the stuff you see on TV and in movies is nonsense."

Monica felt her optimism shrinking.

"But," Katherine continued, "I'm also a biophysicist, so I know how much about human biology and the brain we don't know at all."

"So do you believe in parapsychology, or...?"

"I think most of what human beings have referred to as psychic phenomena or supernatural abilities will eventually be explained by science we don't have yet. I have witnessed personally and retrieved secondhand information from sources I trust about things that cannot be explained by current science. But much of what we know now was unexplained at one time. Does that make sense?"

Monica nodded. "I think so. So you don't think there's anything unnatural about psychic powers. You just think they're misunderstood."

"I think they are probably evolutionary relics—senses that we had or found useful at different times—that we gradually grew out of. Or spontaneous mutations that still occur. There's no way of saying for certain right now. But that doesn't mean we'll never know. Neuroscience and biophysics progresses every day."

"Right." Monica blinked. "And you're a..."

"Biophysicist."

"Right." Monica was questioning everything but decided to plunge in anyway. "What do you think about time?"

"That's... a very general question."

"Yes, but... Okay, what do you think about visions?"

"Visions? As in precognition?"

"Yes."

"Oh, I don't think that's possible."

Monica blinked. "But you just said—"

"I was talking about humans perceiving energy fields left by the dead or communicating on unknown neural levels that most people can't understand, things like that. But there's no scientific basis for believing in precognition. The future is too random to be predicted."

Monica felt her heart pounding. "But... if I have a friend, one I believe without question, like you mentioned having sources you trust, because she's a levelheaded, honest—"

"I don't see any scientific bases for precognition. As I said, the future is far too variable to be predicted. That said... I understand trusting a friend, and nothing I say is going to make you *not* trust that person. Who am I? I'm just a physicist from a little college in the middle of California. You know your friend, and you trust them."

Monica's heart was still pounding. "I do. I know this person, and she's... she's had visions that have been verified by multiple people. Including Mark. It's not just her imagination. And she's having a recurring dream that might indicate a horrible tragedy is coming, and she's basically wondering if it's set in stone or if it can be changed."

"Okay. I am putting myself in the position of someone who does believe in precognition. I think... I would warn her that the future is very malleable. And predicting it... If it was possible, there would be no way of knowing if her actions to prevent this tragedy might inadvertently bring it about. So perhaps try using the dream as a tool to find the cause of this event. Or intercept the perpetrator if it seems to be caused by a person."

"Okay. I think I see what you mean. See the bad future like a sickness or a disease and use the vision to diagnose the problem before it gets really bad."

"Not a bad way of saying it." Somewhere in the background a door opened and closed. "Time is fluid and changeable. Nothing is set in stone. I believe that. So if there's something she can do to prevent a tragedy, I truly wish her the best of luck."

CHAPTER 8

"So she just flat out said that precognition wasn't possible?" Val said. "What did you even say to that?"

Monica paused pouring the oil-and-vinegar dressing over the salad. They were having dinner at her house, and she'd been telling Val and Robin about her chat with Dr. Katherine Bassi. "I just told her that I had a friend I trusted implicitly who had verified visions. And she said working from that premise—"

"Which obviously she doesn't believe," Val muttered.

Monica shrugged. "I mean, she doesn't, but I didn't feel like she was brushing me off either. She respected that I believed my 'friend.'"

Robin raised her hand. "I have a friend who sees ghosts. I know she sounds nuts, but it's true."

Monica smiled. "She said that if precognition was possible, that the future was still very changeable. Malleable, she said. And that there was no way of knowing if, by trying to prevent events, we wouldn't end up causing them."

"So what are we supposed to do?" Val asked. "We can't do nothing. An arsonist in Glimmer Lake could kill a lot of people."

"She recommended trying to look for an underlying cause. Like using the dream as a symptom to figure out the disease."

Robin nodded. "Okay. I think I get that. We can't know what actions might trigger the fire, but if we think someone is behind it, we can use the dream to find that person, which would be the best way to stop any bad stuff from happening."

"Exactly." Monica finished preparing the salad and put it on the counter. "Which is why I want Robin to start asking the ghosts about the previous fire."

"I'm still not sure the two are related." Robin put the salad on the table next to the grilled chicken Monica had cooked. "Like Mark said, fires happen. It's part of the natural system in the forest."

When Gil had been alive, she never touched the barbecue, but with Jake gone, she'd had to figure it out. Come to find out, she was pretty good at grilling! Especially chicken. Jake had always burned it because he was impatient, but Monica had figured out how to cook it perfectly.

"Cheers." Val clinked her beer bottle against Robin's wineglass. "Here's to figuring out who wants to burn down Glimmer Lake."

Robin hadn't let go of the ghost question. "Why do you think the ghosts would know something?" She sat down across from Monica. "Do you think some of them died in the fire?"

"I don't know. It was just an idea. You're right—the old fire might have nothing to do with the new one, but it might be worth just asking around if anyone on the other side has seen anything strange."

"Well, like I said, they've been quieter than usual, but I'll see if I can talk to Bethany."

Bethany was the ghost of a girl Robin had seen almost as soon as she developed powers. They didn't know much about her, but she seemed to like Robin and often hung around even when nothing was going on. She was a pleasant spirit and more aware than the average ghost.

"Hey, Monica." Val reached for the chicken. "Sully said you met his friend yesterday. He tried to tell us about him the other day. The new guy with the state fire service? Cabe? Gabe? Something like that?"

Monica dropped her fork. "Um... who?"

Val frowned. "He said his friend met you? He did some inspection out at Russell House?"

Robin asked, "Is there a problem at Russell House? I thought you and Mom already updated all the fire-code stuff."

"Right." Monica picked up her fork. "Um, it's not the inside. He came by—Gabe, Gabriel, I think his name is—to talk about the perimeter." She motioned to the windows. "You know, keeping a defensible perimeter around the structure, cutting some of the trees back, stuff like that."

"Oh right." Robin frowned. "Oh, that could be difficult at Russell House."

"I think I have a plan that will really add to the building and create some space too." *Please don't ask about Gabe. Please don't ask about Gabe. I do not know what to think about hot-sex-vision Gabe, so please do not ask about him.*

"And it might even give us extra event space too. For weddings, parties, stuff like that."

"Oh cool."

Val smiled. "But what did you think about Gabe though? Sully showed me some old pictures from when they worked together down south. He's hot. Or he was."

"Oh, I just..." Monica shrugged. "He was very professional. I really didn't notice... You know, Kara and Jake talked to him more than I did."

Robin and Val exchanged a look.

"She noticed," Val said.

"She definitely noticed." Robin nodded firmly. "That was stuttering. He must still be hot."

"You know, firefighters have to maintain very strict physical regimens," Val said. "You think he lifts? I bet he has great arms."

Robin said, "I've never met a firefighter who doesn't have great arms."

"Mmmm." Val smiled. "Especially forearms. Really thick forearms—"

"I didn't..." Monica huffed out a breath. "I mean, yeah. He was handsome. Are we twelve? Do we really need to spend dinner talking about cute boys?"

Val blinked. "Uh, yeah."

Robin said, "The need to talk about cute boys is timeless, Monica. When we are old and grey, we will talk about cute boys. Or handsome silver foxes, whatever."

"We're both old and coupled up now," Val said. "We have to live vicariously through you."

"Thanks." She dumped salad on her plate. "He was very professional, very friendly, and yes, very handsome. Happy?"

"No. I need to know about the arms," Val said. "Sully gave me nothing."

Robin turned to Val. "You mean you actually asked your boyfriend about his friend's arms?"

"Yes, but like I said, he gave me nothing." She huffed. "I told him I was doing research for Monica."

"Val!" Monica dropped her fork again. "Can you not?" How on earth was she going to get them off this topic? "You know what I was thinking? I think that... trying to date again might be a great idea."

Robin and Val lit up.

"And if I'm going to do that, I should go out with someone we know. Like the friend of a friend." *Who do we know? Who should I—*

"You mean the friend of a friend, like *Gabe*?" asked Val. "I think that's an awesome idea."

Not Gabe! "I was thinking someone like... West."

Robin frowned. "Who?"

Val's eyebrows threatened to collide with her hairline. "West? My friend West? *Biker* West?"

"Yeah." *Oh shit.* What had she done? "Didn't you say he thought I was cute?"

"Cute is not what he thought of you, but that's the PG version. Okay." Val shrugged. "I mean, if you want to go out with West, I can set you up. But if... I mean, I'm pretty sure he's a very good time, but I don't know if there's anything more—"

"That's all I want," Monica said. "Just someone fun. To try dating again." She had a feeling she'd made a terrible mistake, but she'd be damned if she backed out now. "I haven't gone on a first date in literally thirty years. Over thirty years if I'm being honest. And I bet West dates a lot."

Val nodded slowly. "Dating might not be the right term, but he has a lot of experience with women."

Oh God. "See?" Monica was committed now. "That sounds perfect. It'll be like going out with a professional."

Robin choked on her salad, and Val burst out laughing.

"I mean, not a *professional* professional." The hole was just getting deeper. "Not like that! You know what I mean."

Val put both her hands on the table. "Okay, tell you what. I'm going to call West tomorrow and give him your number and tell him he should call you. That sound good?"

"Yes." Monica took a deep breath. "Sounds perfect."

Robin looked skeptical. Val looked amused.

And Monica was terrified.

SHE WAS WALKING through the woods, barefoot again. The pine needles and cones cut into her feet. She walked over rough granite and raised tree roots.

Through the trees she could see a dilapidated old cabin leaning to one side. It was a hunting cabin, one of those countless summer and fall shelters built by old residents of Grimmer, places they would retreat to when the valley became too warm.

The stone chimney was leaning but still intact. The wood cladding was falling down in places, but the rest of the cabin was sound.

In the distance, an outbuilding like a small barn stood with its doors hanging open.

She could smell woodsmoke in the air.

From the top of the stone chimney, she saw a thin line of smoke coming from inside the cabin. Was it a cooking fire? It was too warm for anything else. The outdoor kitchen lay empty, the rocks from the oven falling from the concrete where they'd been set. Birds had created a nest in an alcove.

Monica walked toward the cabin, drawn to the sound of a child singing inside.

Who are you?

Just as she reached the steps of the cabin, something made her pause. She backed away, a sense of dread making a knot in her stomach.

"Hello?" Her voice was damp and muffled. "Hello? Is anyone here?"

A peal of wild laughter was the last thing she heard before the cabin in the woods burst into flames.

MONICA BOLTED UP in bed and reached for her dream journal. Scribbling everything down as fast as she could, she felt her heart start to slow.

What was this? Everything about these dreams felt different. She'd never felt so present in them before. Everything about these visions felt personal.

She knew where the cabin was. She'd spent time there in high school. The old Alison place was a regular haunt for kids looking to hang out, drink beer, and generally feel free of their parents.

Monica reached for the phone as soon as she finished writing. She dialed Val's number.

"Hello?"

"Val."

"Monica?" Val sniffed. "What's wrong?"

"I just had a dream about the old Alison cabin. There was a fire there. What do you think I should do?"

"You had a dream about an actual fire at an actual place?"

"Yes. The old Alison place. Remember that?"

"Oh man. Is that still standing?"

"Pretty sure. Jake and his buddies used to go drinking there. Gil caught them one time and scared the shit out of them, but I'm sure they went back."

"Um.." Val cleared her throat. "You have to call it in."

"How? How am I supposed to explain that I know about a fire, but I'm not the person who set it? If I call 911, they'll know my number. And if there is a fire there, I'd be a suspect."

"Um..." Val sounded so tired. "Sully."

"What?"

"Call Sully. He's used to answering his phone in the middle of the night, and he knows about you. He can say he got an anonymous tip or something."

"Right." Monica nodded. "Okay, let me call him."

She hung up on Val and called Sully's number.

He picked up after two rings. "What's wrong?"

"It's Monica. I just had a very specific vision of a fire starting at the old Alison cabin. Do you know the one I'm talking about?"

"Teenager hangout, right?"

"Yes. It's off old Timberline Road. You take that fire service road past the pump station and—"

"Yep." Sully coughed. "Yep, I know where it is. You see any faces? Anything recognizable?"

"Nothing except..." She tried to remember the exact sound. "Laughter. Like either a kid or a woman. High-pitched laughter."

"Right." Sully's voice had turned grim. "Monica, I'm gonna drive out there, okay? If I see any smoke, I'll call it in. I'll leave you out of it, all right?"

"Thanks, Sully." She hung up and waited in her bed, clutching her hands as she thought about the call the fire-fighters might get.

A blaze in the summer could quickly burn out of control, risking lives, loss, and devastation of the forest and the town. Though fire was part of the natural cycle in the forest, uncontrolled wildfires were every mountain resident's nightmare.

Half an hour later, she got a text from Sully.

There's smoke.

A choking sensation overtook her as she heard the first sirens cut through the night.

CHAPTER 9

Two days after the fire had been extinguished, Val and Monica walked through the remains of what was left of the old Alison cabin.

Val looked up at the scorched chimney. "They got it out pretty quick, thanks to you."

The clearing around the old cabin had been torn up by fire engines and dozens of boots. The trees in immediate proximity were blackened but not burned. The main loss was the cabin, which had already been a wreck. The surrounding forest was fine and had been soaked by the fire hoses. The firefighters had raked the rubble left over into the center of the clearing and doused all of that too, just to make sure no sparks escaped.

If Gil were alive, he'd call it a good day and be done with it.

It was cold comfort to Monica. "What if I don't have a vision next time?" She walked through the frame of the house. The floor was still solid, but the walls were falling around her and the roof of the old cabin was completely gone. "Do they know where it started?"

"I think Sully said Gabe was pretty sure it started right in front of the fireplace." Val pointed to a large black mark on the floor. "Spread from there."

"Do they have any suspects?"

Val kicked an empty beer can across the clearing. "Unfortunately, the fire service thinks it was just kids because this is a hangout, so they're not really looking for much more. And since Sully told them the tip was anonymous..."

"They think kids were goofing around and called the sheriff when the fire got away from them."

Val nodded. "Pretty much, yeah."

Monica sighed. "It's a good theory. If I didn't know better, I'd believe it." She walked away from the house and toward the barn. "This wasn't damaged."

"No." Val followed her. "I don't think they even went inside. Maybe just to check if anyone was there."

Monica swung the barn door open and poked her head inside. The building smelled like smoke, but it didn't appear hurt. Other than the damage that was already there.

Graffiti covered the walls, and cardboard boxes of old paperwork had been kicked over and spread across the barn floor. Someone had clearly used it for storage sometime in the past, but time and a roof leak had led the paper to warp and swell. Blankets and a rotten sleeping bag were in one corner underneath an old ladder leading up to the hayloft.

"Looks like someone was sleeping here." Val squatted down and picked up an empty tin of canned pasta with an ungloved hand. "It's old. A homeless man, I think?" She closed her eyes. "Years ago." She reached for another can.

"He stayed here, but I don't think anything bad happened to him." She reached for one of the blankets. "Nothing bad really." She made a face. "Gross, but not bad."

Monica walked toward the ladder and put both hands on it. "You think it's stable?"

Val looked up. "The ladder looks okay, but I'm not too sure about the loft."

She craned her neck and tried to see into the overhead area. "I feel like there's something up there, and the ladder has been used recently." She pointed to the wood. "See? No dust."

"Right." Val brushed off her hands and stood. "Well, only one way to find out."

Monica gingerly took the first steps up the ladder. It was solid as a rock—the thick-cut pine boards hadn't rotted or cracked. She slowly walked up the ladder, feeling each step and testing her weight. "I should have had the skinny girl go up first."

"No way," Val said. "You're clearly more of a daredevil than I am."

"Three boys and an adrenaline-junkie husband will do that to you."

Val laughed. "Was Gil an adrenaline junkie?"

"He was a firefighter. To one degree or another, they're *all* adrenaline junkies." She reached the top and looked around at the dusty loft. "Besides, don't you remember what he was like when we were young?"

"I mean, he rode bikes and stuff, but everyone does that around here."

"He rode dirt bikes. He mountain climbed. He water-skied. He snow-skied. If he went too long without a call or without a training exercise, I swear the man would climb a tree." She crawled off the ladder and stood, her head nearly reaching the sloped roof. "Careful not to hit your head."

The loft took up half the space of the barn and had clearly been used for storage too. Only this storage was more of the rustic kind. There were a few old tools and three musty bales of straw. The edge of the loft was railed off, with an opening for a pulley system to bring things up.

"Wow." Val looked around. "This is in pretty good shape. I don't remember ever coming up here, do you?"

"There were always gross kids who came up here to have sex while everyone else was drinking," Monica said. "I steered clear."

Val snorted. "I wonder how many Glimmer Lake children have been conceived in this loft."

"I have no idea, and I don't want to know. I got knocked up like a respectable teenager," she said, "in the back of Gil's pickup truck."

That made Val laugh. Monica just shook her head.

"You shame our family. You shame yourself." She still heard her mother's voice like it was yesterday. *"You are not my daughter."*

And from that day forward, she really hadn't been. Gil and Monica had moved in with his Uncle Eddie, and for years Monica didn't even speak to her parents. Not when Jake was born, not when Sylvia came. The parents who'd called her their princess had cut her off when she "embarrassed them" in front of their conservative Catholic friends. Her dad had passed away when Sylvia was a baby, and Monica cried in the back of the church with only Gil holding her hand.

Her mother wrote her a letter once after seeing Gil's picture in the paper at a ceremony. Monica was pregnant with twins, had two active preschoolers, and she didn't have the emotional energy to deal with her mother's guilt.

Twenty-some years later, they were still estranged. Monica sent her mother a card on her birthday and Mother's Day. She saw her at church every week. Her younger sister kept her apprised of major family news, but for the most part, her friends and Gil's relatives were her family now.

"Someone was living here."

Val's voice snapped Monica out of her musing. "What?"

"Look at this. These blankets look new." Val bent down and pointed to a mound of hay that had been covered with blankets to form a simple bed. "They're messed up a little, but they're new. You can still see the fold marks. And there's a pillow."

Monica cocked her head. "I've seen that kind of blanket before. Have you? What is this reminding me of?"

"I don't know." Val flipped a corner up to look at a tag. "Seems like a pretty standard plaid camping blanket to me. They sell them at the sporting goods store, at the market... I don't think we're going to be able to identify who bought it."

Monica crouched next to her. "Want to see what you get off them?"

Val took a breath and touched the blanket with her bare hand. She closed her eyes and concentrated. "It's all messed up. I'm seeing things through their eyes."

"Man or woman?"

"Woman? I think?" Val shook her head. "I can't be sure. The energy feels female."

"What else?"

"I'm just getting feelings. Restlessness. Confusion. She... she doesn't know how she got here." Val pulled her hand away. "It's like she woke up here and didn't know why."

"Okay, that's weird. You couldn't tell who it was?"

"I'm pretty sure it's a woman, but no."

Monica looked around the loft. "Okay, so we have the memories of a woman who wakes up in this place and doesn't know why. Was she drugged? Was she a victim of something?"

"There's no sign of struggle or fighting." Val stood and walked across the loft. "If anything, this place almost looks like it was cleaned up. Did you notice that? The floor..."

Monica spotted an old brush and dustpan in a corner. "Someone swept the floorboards." She walked to the straw bales and looked at the marks near her feet. "These were pushed back along the wall. They used to be over there." She spotted dark marks on the floorboards near the railing.

"So someone came up here, cleaned up the space, and brought a woman here who didn't know what was going on?" Val shook her head. "Nothing about that makes sense."

Monica nodded toward the blankets. "Do you get just one person off the blankets? What about the pillow? Maybe we're talking about two completely different people here. One who cleaned up and the other who woke up confused?"

Val knelt next to the bed and touched the pillow, only to yelp and fall back.

"What?" Monica rushed over to her. "What did you see?"

Val's face was completely white. "Fire. I touched the pillow and all I saw was fire."

THE LAST THING Monica felt like doing that night was going on a date with West, but she'd made a commitment when the man called the day before, and she wasn't going to back out now.

Even though she wanted to. She really, really wanted to.

"I look ridiculous." She straightened her skirt in the mirror. "The man rides motorcycles. He doesn't look like he goes dancing."

"You look sexy as hell," Val said. "You better wear this dress."

"If you reach for that jumpsuit again, I'm gonna slap your hand." Robin snatched the striped jumpsuit from the end of the bed and walked it to the closet. "Wear the sexy dress!"

Val and Robin had convinced her to wear one of the wrap dresses she normally only wore when she and Gil used to go salsa dancing. It wasn't very short—it came to just above her knees—but the cinched waist and plunging neckline made Monica feel incredibly exposed.

She turned to face her two best friends. "Don't you think jeans and a nice shirt would be better?"

Val looked up from Monica's shoes. She was still debating between a heel and an open-toed wedge. "I mean, do you want him to swallow his tongue or not?"

"Ew." She made a face. "I don't want him to do anything that's going to mean an emergency call."

"Metaphorically," Val said. "You have to wear this; you look amazing and sexy and ready for fun. Isn't that the mood you're going for?"

"I guess?" The mood Monica was actually feeling was "dear God, how do I get out of this, it was a horrible mistake."

"You do look amazing," Robin said. "But you should also

feel comfortable. This is your *first* first date in a long time. Why do you feel nervous in this? You wore this stuff all the time when you went out with Gil."

"I know. Because I was out with Gil." How could she explain? "Before, if I wore this, if someone hit on me, there was a giant dude standing next to me with really big muscles. Now I'm meeting a dude with muscles who may or may not hit on me and... I don't know, it's just not the same."

"But you *want* the big dude with muscles to hit on you," Val said. "Which is not going to be a problem."

Robin muttered, "I have a feeling she could wear a trash bag and West would make a pass." She shrugged. "Just saying."

"You're not wrong." Val took Monica by the shoulders and turned her around. "Wear this. You look gorgeous. You have an incredible figure and boobs that many people pay lots of money to have."

"I envy your boobs," Robin said. "Always have."

"We all envy your boobs," Val continued. "And you still have those boobs after nursing *four kids*. Remember when I had boobs? That's right, it's only a faint memory because they disappeared after the second kid. But yours stuck around! And they're not even saggy, Monica. They're not even *saggy*. You're practically disrespecting your girls if you don't show them off a little."

"Your boobs should get a medal or something." Robin stood straight and saluted. "Well done, ladies."

Val nodded. "Well done indeed. Monica should let you out to play."

Monica shook her head and crossed her arms over her

chest. "How are you both so strange? It's getting worse with age. Stop talking to my tits, or I'm going to call your mothers."

"Are you going to wear the sexy dress?" Val asked.

"Fine! Yes. I'll wear the sexy dress." Monica kicked off the heels and grabbed the open-toe wedges. If she had to feel exposed, at least her feet would be comfortable. Plus she wasn't thirty-five anymore and her ankles would be screaming if she wore heels for more than an hour. "But I am *not* letting my boobs out to play. It is a *first date.*"

CHAPTER 10

*M*onica stared across the table at West, who watched her with amusement on his handsome, rugged face.

"You don't do this much, do you?"

They were sitting at a booth at a cozy brewpub in Bridger City that Monica had been to before. Sam and Caleb had taken her there for lunch, but she'd never experienced the evening crowd.

She glanced around, then down at her ringless hands. "I don't do this. Dating, I mean. At all. Or I haven't done this in a while."

West raised an eyebrow. "How long?"

"Since my last first date?"

He nodded. He was wearing a pair of dark jeans and a black button-down shirt open at the neck. The sleeves were rolled up to his elbows, exposing a slew of colorful tattoos.

"Um..." She laughed a little. "My last first date was about thirty-one years ago."

West threw his head back and laughed. "Damn."

"Yeah." His laughter set her at ease. It wasn't anything close to mocking. "So there's that."

"Why now?"

Because I'm avoiding a sex dream about a random man I hardly know and you were an easy distraction. "Gil's been gone for about four years, and everyone tells me that I should at least try dating again."

"And you thought of me?"

She felt her cheeks warm. "I remember you from last year when we were looking for Val's ex, and... you seemed cool. Val said you're a fun guy and that you might be interested, so..."

"I was." His eyes fell to her cleavage before returning to her face. "I am. You're a very beautiful woman, Monica."

"Thank you. And you're very handsome."

"You're sweet." His smile turned wry. "Not too sure I've dated the sweet kind much, but I'm starting to see the appeal."

"Is that patronizing?"

"No. Just honest. I don't usually attract the professional type."

"Hmmm."

The corner of his mouth turned up. "What's that about?"

"I think you *attract* the professional type—because you're very attractive—but they probably wouldn't ask you out. Or ask to be set up with you."

He leaned forward and put both elbows on the table. "Is it the tattoos?"

She waved her hand. "It's the whole package."

The corner of his mouth turned up. "I assure you, there's nothing wrong with the package."

Monica almost snorted her beer. "Good to know." She bit her lip to smother a laugh. "I just meant you have the dangerous-biker vibe. If you weren't a friend of Val's, I would have been intimidated."

"Interesting. But I *am* a friend of Val's..."

"And she says you're a good guy."

"Oh, I am." West smiled again. "I'm very good."

Monica felt her cheeks heat again. "Wow."

"I'm just saying, depending on how hungry you are, we can skip dinner and head back to my place."

She blinked. "I don't even know how to answer that."

"I would encourage you to answer 'Yes, West, let's get out of here.'"

"Do I look—?"

"You look..." He leaned over and let his eyes graze Monica from her shoes to her hips and all the way up. "You look like a smart, sexy, hell of a woman." His voice dropped. "Who probably hasn't been... appreciated in a few years."

"West, I—"

"Now, if you want to hang out, flirt a little, get to know me better so you feel more comfortable, that's just fine." His blue eyes gleamed. "You're cute as hell and I have a feeling you're funny too. But if you're looking for something else, need to stretch your back a little... I'm game for that too. Just say the word."

Monica was speechless. And turned on. And... way out of her depth. "You're very direct."

His crooked smile appeared again. "Too old to play games, sweetheart. And I have a feeling you like the direct approach."

"I don't mind it. But I also don't think I'm quite ready for... that."

He nodded. "Fair enough."

They were both silent for a while as the waiter set down their beers and a bowl of tortilla chips.

"Too direct?" West asked.

"No." Monica sipped her beer. "No, not too direct. You're not wrong. I miss that part of being married; I miss sex. I can't lie."

"But..."

She laughed. "First date in thirty-one years, West. I'm still working with training wheels, okay?"

He chuckled. "I get that."

"Val said you were divorced, but it's been a few years, right? I have a feeling you jumped back on the dating horse a little faster than I did."

"Two days after we split."

Monica's eyes went wide. "Seriously?"

"I was faithful to my woman," West said. "When I was married, she was *it* for me. Not to say that there weren't plenty of temptations, but I didn't even look. That's not me. After I found out she cheated with that pansy-ass ex of Val's?" He scowled. "I wasn't gonna give her the satisfaction of coming back to anything but a well-fucked man."

Monica blinked. "Well, that's definitely one approach."

He shrugged. "We all cope in different ways."

"I just feel..." She sighed. "*Weird.* I never expected to be here again, you know? I'm not saying that Gil and I were perfect, but we were *good.*"

West nodded. "I thought my ex and I were good too. I

know what you mean. Believe it or not, I was happy feeling settled. I roamed for a lot of years."

"And Gil was always it for me, from high school. I figured I might be a widow one day, but I'd be too old to want to have another man, you know?" She laughed. "But I don't feel old."

West smiled. "You're not. You're a grown woman, and you know what you want in life. That's sexy as hell. I'm surprised it's taken you this long to go out with anyone."

"People tried to set me up but..." She shrugged. "I didn't feel ready."

"So what changed?"

"Um..." *I'm avoiding another man.* Wow, that sounded bad. "I just felt like it was time. I had to at least try. And like I said, you seem fun."

"Are you having fun?" West took a drink of beer and watched her over the rim of his glass. "Or did I scare you off?"

Monica smiled. "I'm having fun. It feels good to... have someone pay attention to me again."

"Pay attention?" He glanced at her cleavage again. "Trust me, coming to attention isn't ever going to be a problem with a woman like you."

Her cheeks warmed again. "It just comes automatically, doesn't it?"

"Do you want me to stop?"

"I don't think so?"

He smiled. "Good."

MONICA WAS on a high the next day from flirting with West. She hadn't had a single disturbing dream the night before.

She felt sexy, desirable, *younger* somehow. She didn't feel like a mom of four grown children; she felt... free.

She and West had eaten dinner at the brewpub; then they'd gone to one of the bars West usually frequented. Monica had insisted and they'd had fun. It was a total dive, but the people were friendly, the beer was cold, and they'd played pool until midnight.

By the time Monica was ready to drive home, she felt like a new woman. She'd given West a kiss on the cheek, and he'd squeezed her hip a little.

He also restated his offer for her to call him if she needed to "stretch her back," but Monica wasn't really sure he was her speed.

"You seem happy." Kara brought Monica a cup of coffee and a folder. "I included the housekeeping report from last month. I think the bonus system you have going will be a big success. The rooms are getting really high customer-satisfaction ratings, and the staff seems happier too."

"Sweet." She sipped her caffe latte and looked over the report.

Kara smothered a yawn.

Monica looked up, surprised. "Late night?"

The young woman laughed a little. "I wish it was for a fun reason. I heard you had a night out." She wiggled her eyebrows. "Eve and Jake were talking about your date."

"Seriously?" She shook her head. "Why is my son discussing that?"

"It was really sweet actually! He was happy for you. Excited even."

"That kid." Monica smiled. "He and his sister have been

encouraging me to get out there. The younger two are the harder sell."

"I still can't believe you have four kids in their twenties." Kara shook her head. "You do not look half old enough to have grown kids. It's almost like you're Jake's older sister or something."

"Oh, make no mistake. I changed that boy's diapers."

Kara covered her face and her shoulders shook. "I'm going to try to rid myself of that mental image."

"He runs around without a shirt on often enough that I don't think you'll get stuck on the diapers thing."

Kara's cheeks went pink. "Yeah, he does like his tan."

Monica rolled her eyes. "He likes showing off." She rose and put the report to the side. "Don't let him fool you. His tan..." She took another drink of coffee. "What's on the agenda for today?"

"Two parties checking in around four, and Chief Peralta will be here at eleven with an updated report and recommendations."

Monica nearly choked on her coffee. "Chief Peralta?"

"Yes. You didn't get my note?"

She frowned. "When... Oh shit. It's Tuesday, isn't it?"

"Yeah. It's been a week, so..."

"Right." Great. Not even a day to bask in the boost of self-confidence going out with West gave her before she had to deal with Chief Sexy-Eyes again. "Text me when he gets here, okay?"

"Will do." Kara backed out of the office, her dimples showing. "You know, I think Chief Peralta might be kind of interested too. Just saying. If you're looking to 'get out there'—"

"Out." Monica pointed to the door. "Not you too. I already have enough busybodies interested in my love life."

Kara was laughing when she shut the door, but Monica was already distracted. Going out with West had been fun. She found him attractive, but he was also pretty easy to read. West was all out there. Gabe Peralta, on the other hand, had that stoic, reserved, unflappable thing going on.

Watch out for the quiet ones. Isn't that what they said? Monica shivered. She had a feeling Gabe was a quiet one. Reserved? Yes. Cold?

Not even a little bit.

SHE SAW his truck pull up to the hotel, and she noticed a new addition to the party. By the time it parked in front, she was at the door, opening it and greeting Chief Peralta like the professional, sexy, smart, confident woman who had gone out with a very hot biker the night before.

"Chief Peralta." She held out her hand to shake his. "How are you? Nice to see you again." *I am not thinking about you naked this time. Okay, maybe just a little bit.* "And who is this?"

A lanky teenage boy with long dark hair slid out of the truck. "Hey."

"This is my son Logan. And again, please call me Gabe."

"Gabe." Monica nodded. "Logan. How are you?"

"Logan is staying with me for the summer, and I thought I'd give him an idea of what I do all day."

Logan's arms were crossed over his chest. "Yeah, it's superexciting."

Monica recognized the teenage ennui immediately. She also recognized the gritted jaw Gabe was wearing. "I'm sorry to say that what we have to talk about isn't the most exciting, but why don't I call my son Jake? He can show Logan around, maybe take him out in the boat for a spin around the lake."

Logan's eyes went from bored to lit. "A boat?"

"Yep." Monica grabbed her phone and texted Jake. "That will give your dad and me time to go over the stuff we need to without you having to hang around and listen to the fire code."

Gabe said, "You really don't have to—"

"It's fine." She smiled. "I have three boys, and they were all teenagers once. Way better to get outdoors and stay in the fresh air, right?"

"I've never been on a boat," Logan said. "But I'm a good swimmer. Will I have to wear one of those stupid orange vests I've seen on TV?"

"It's the resort boat, so you'll have to wear a vest, but we have some of the adult ones that the river guides use. Trust me, you won't look like a dork."

"Cool."

Monica saw Jake in the distance and she pointed to Logan as she waved. "Gabe, why don't we let them hang out and you can come in my office to go over the report?"

"Dude! Hey, welcome to Russell House. I'm Jake Velasquez, the activities director here. What's your name, my man?"

"Um, Logan."

"Logan, awesome to meet you. I heard you have to hang out for a while. I could use some help in the boathouse if you have a minute."

"Really?" Logan focused on Jake. "How many boats do you have? Are they like the ones with sails or engines? Are they for fishing?"

"Dude, come with me." Jake nodded at Monica and took the boy by the shoulder. "I'm working on the ski boat engine right now. If you can help me out, we can take it for a spin later."

"Cool."

Gabe looked flabbergasted as Jake led Logan toward the boathouse without a backward glance, waving at Monica over his shoulder.

"Wow." Gabe watched them walk away. "What did you text to Jake?"

"Red alert: bored teenage boy at the main house." Monica shrugged. "He's the oldest of four. He's great with younger kids."

"I'll say. Your son managed to get more conversation from Logan in three minutes than I've been able to eke out all summer."

"He usually lives with his mom?"

Gabe nodded. "In the East Bay. He's been here most of the summer, and he thinks Glimmer Lake is the height of boring. No offense."

"None taken. He's a city kid. It's a totally different life here. I imagine Jake will entertain him though. Everyone loves Jake."

Gabe smiled a little and looked at Monica from the side. "I have a feeling I know where he gets that from."

Wait, was that a compliment? Was Gabe... flirting?

"Why don't we go to my office?" Monica said. "We can talk more there."

CHAPTER 11

*G*abe and Monica settled in her office with coffee and lemon scones from Misfit Mountain. Instead of sitting on opposite sides of her large desk, Monica moved them to the long table that had been part of the Russell family library.

"This is a great office." Gabe looked around at the tall bookcases surrounding her desk. "Kind of... masculine though."

"This was Gordon Russell's home office," Monica said, immediately going into the spiel prepared for guests. "From this office, he ran Russell Timber, which remains one of the most prominent logging operations on the West Coast. Russell Timber is the leader in sustainable tree farming and logging; it's also at the forefront of several green-energy initiatives now."

Gabe raised an eyebrow. "Rehearsed that one, right?"

Monica smiled. "There's a historical tour we offer guests if they're curious about the family."

Gabe ran his hands along one bookcase. "Imagine growing up here."

"You don't have to imagine," Monica said. "Grace Lewis, my partner in Russell House, likes to hang out at Val's coffee shop. She did grow up here." She smiled. "Or you can ask me. I spent most summers here growing up."

"Really?" He peeked out the window that looked over the broad expanse of lawn and the glittering blue water of Glimmer Lake. "Pretty incredible."

"We didn't come in the house much" —because it had been creepy as hell with the ghost of Robin's grandfather haunting the third floor until they banished him— "but we spent hours and hours in the lake. When Grace's mother passed and she was trying to figure out what to do with the property, I was the one who thought of turning it into a small hotel. I just figured why limit that fun to family only, you know? Russell House's beach is one of the best on the lake."

"I can see that." Gabe turned around. "So it's open to the public?"

Monica shrugged. "Within reason. Anyone can boat over and enjoy the lake. Mostly it's just guests or friends and family of the staff. We don't have all the facilities and restaurants the beaches in town do."

Gabe shook his head and turned back to the window. "You know, I thought Logan would have such a good time being up here all summer, but he's barely left the house. We live right off Ponderosa Creek Road. You know the street?"

"Yeah. That's not too far from my place."

"Biking distance to the lake, right?" Gabe stood with his hands on his hips, the sunlight framing his profile as he talked. "He doesn't have his license yet, but he's got a bike. I thought he'd be at the beach every day up here."

Monica shook herself from staring at his ass the moment he turned from the window.

"It's tough." She cleared her throat. "At that age, it's all about their friends. All four of my kids grew up here, so all their friends grew up doing the same stuff they did, camping and boating and fishing and skiing. For a kid like Logan, who's new to the area, that can all be pretty intimidating if they don't have someone like Jake introducing them to the scene."

"I swear, all he wants to do is stare at his computer."

"Oh, that was my daughter Sylvia. She's the bookworm of the family, doing graduate work at Berkeley right now. But all my boys would live outdoors if they could."

Gabe gave her an appreciative glance up and down. "I have to say, you do not look old enough to have four grown kids."

Monica resisted the urge to squirm, but her body felt hot all over. Something about the interest in Gabe's eyes reminded her of the heat in his gaze when she'd dreamed about him. "Well, my late husband and I got started early."

"I guess so." He smiled. "We should probably get to these reports."

"Sure." She sat next to him at the table. "I briefed the Lewises about our conversation, and Grace liked the gazebo and back-garden idea."

"And that should work with the amount of defensible space I would recommend, so I'd suggest starting on that as soon as possible. I did want to talk to you about the area around the boathouse though."

Monica nodded and tried to concentrate on the plans he'd sketched out. She could tell he'd put a lot of thought into the rough design, so she really tried to focus.

He smells good.

She could feel the heat from him and couldn't help but remember the visceral feeling of his large, callused hand on her naked shoulder.

No! Bad Monica. This was why you went out with West, remember? To forget about Hot Gabe!

Forgetting didn't seem to be on the menu. Sex visions were not the same as sex dreams. Monica felt like they'd already been intimate, she could remember everything so well.

"So with this part" —she cleared the roughness from her throat— "you're saying we need to clear even more trees from along this path?"

"I'm saying that you have to think about your evacuation routes. And while your plan is very good—the front lawn is more than enough to keep guests safe—you still have to think about getting there. And if anyone is in the boathouse, keeping some space around the path there will keep guests from possibly walking through a fire storm in order to get to safety."

"I'm not disagreeing," Monica said, "but why would anyone come to the house in a fire if they were already at the boathouse?"

"Your son lives and works there, right?" He raised an eyebrow. "You think in a fire he's not going to rush to the main house to help?"

"Fair point." Jake wouldn't like it, but Gabe had a point. "I'll talk to him about that."

"That one is a suggestion, not a necessity, but again, I'd really think about clearing that significantly, or at least cutting some trees and planting lower, lusher plants like ferns that provide some protection."

"Got it."

Gabe leaned his elbow on the table and angled his body toward hers. "I have to say, you're a lot less argumentative than most homeowners and businesspeople."

Monica smiled. "I supposed being married to a firefighter for twenty-five years probably helps. This is not an unfamiliar conversation. Gilbert was fanatical about keeping the trees around our house cut back."

"And you didn't mind?"

"Of course I did. It was a battle every time he got out that chain saw. I told him he'd build a Walmart parking lot around the perimeter of our house if he could." She laughed. "He'd be horrified by how many little trees have sprung up since he passed." A wave of guilt hit her. "I should probably take care of that. It always seems like it'll never happen to you, you know? It'll be other towns, other forests."

Gabe was silent for a long time. "We always want it to be."

"Yeah."

"If you want me to come around your place and give you a hand, I'd be happy to."

Monica's cheeks heated. "Oh?"

Gabe drew back. "I meant... with the trees. Give you a hand tagging the trees and that kind of thing. It's my job."

"Right." Monica took a deep breath. "Thanks. That's very generous. I have your card, so I might call you."

"That's my personal number I wrote on back." His voice

was a little rough. "It's my mobile, so you can text me too. If you'd rather text." He was staring at her, his eyes on her mouth. He cleared his throat and looked away just as his phone started buzzing in his shirt pocket.

Monica heard the distant sound of sirens on Granville Road, where the fire station was located. "You have to go."

Gabe looked at his phone, not looking away from the screen even as he stood. "Fire south of town, over by the dam."

"Right." Monica felt the familiar rush of dread. She knew what was happening right now, the heavy jackets being thrown on in sweltering summer heat. The heavy-duty masks being counted and the calls being made.

She stood and ran to the window, searching for smoke. The dirty brown-and-grey sign of imminent disaster threaded from the trees and drifted over the south shore of the lake.

"Be careful." She turned to see Gabe running out the door. "Gabe, be careful."

He paused at the door. "Can you get Logan—?"

"Jake and I will take care of him. Don't worry, go."

<hr />

Two hours later, she dropped Logan off at his father's house on Ponderosa Creek Road, making sure he knew where Monica's house was located if he needed anything. Sully had texted Val and Val had texted Monica and Robin. The fire was out, but not before it had completely consumed another old hunting cabin in the woods. They thought it had been started in the early-morning hours; they'd gotten to it later than the one at the Alison cabin and the house was completely consumed, along with part of the forest.

As soon as Logan was safe at home and he'd gotten a text from his father, Monica drove to Misfit Mountain Coffee and walked to the door.

The coffee shop was closed, but Val was wiping down tables and waved. Monica got on the phone with Robin. "I'm at Misfit. You heard about the fire?"

"Yeah. Sully texted Mark that it was contained?"

"Uh-huh."

"He also said it was arson."

Monica froze as Val unlocked the door. "I hadn't heard that."

"Sully told Mark it was definitely arson."

Monica put her phone on speaker so Val could hear. "Robin, you're on speaker. I'm with Val. How do they know it was arson?"

Val's eyes went wide, but she remained silent as Robin answered.

"Accelerant, for one. Gabe Peralta took samples and said he'd have to get them to the lab in Bridger, but he could tell by the scent that kerosene was used inside the cabin."

Val asked, "Robin, do you know if they found any evidence I could read? I asked Sully, but he didn't know when I talked to him."

They heard Mark speaking in the background.

"I don't think so," Robin said. "It sounded like the cabin was completely consumed. Might have been empty before that anyway. It was another one of those old hunting cabins people built before the dam. Probably belonged to someone who lived in Grimmer."

"Weird," Monica said. "That's two hunting cabins burned."

"Are they taking a second look at the Alison cabin?" Val asked.

"I don't know."

"They need to."

Monica turned when she heard the sound of a vehicle pulling into the small parking lot of Misfit. It was Sully's big department truck. "Robin, Sully's here. Why don't we call you back after we talk to him?"

"Okay." Robin took a breath. "I think I need to get pushier with the ghosts around here."

Sully opened the door and stepped out of the truck. He looked utterly exhausted, dirty, and covered in sweat.

Val walked to him and put her arms around him as Monica told Robin goodbye.

A thousand images of Gil coming home from a call filled her mind.

Dirty and sweaty Gil after a successful call.

Ashy and sad Gil after a loss.

Hyped and horny Gil after a training exercise with his company.

"It's contained," Sully said, his arm around Val. "They're watching it right now and laying down more water. They were lucky the cabin backed up to a creek. The ground around it was pretty damp and the fire hadn't reached the canopy yet, so it consumed the cabin but didn't develop much past that."

"That's a relief," Monica said. "Val, can we get a drink?"

She looked at Sully. "You off duty?"

"Not technically, but I don't think anyone's going to give me a hard time if I have a beer."

"Sounds good." Val ushered them both inside and flipped on a single light near the counter. "Gabe was at Russell House with Monica when he got the call."

"Oh yeah?" Sully raised an eyebrow. "He was right in there with the guys."

"Somehow that doesn't surprise me."

"He's never been a desk guy."

"Yeah." Good Lord, did she want that again? She'd imagined Gil dying a hundred times before he passed from a heart attack. Did she want to even think about getting involved with another firefighter? Because even though Gabriel Peralta was a chief and an administrator, Monica knew Sully was right. Gabe wouldn't ever be content to sit behind a desk if his company was answering a call.

Sully was staring at her. "So you didn't see anything about this one?"

Monica shook her head. "Nothing. I was out pretty late last night in Bridger and I was exhausted by the time I got home. I passed out and didn't have a single dream."

Sully grunted and took a drink of the beer Val placed in front of him. "Well, until we get this guy... maybe think about taking more naps."

CHAPTER 12

Two days after the fire, Sully went with Monica, Val, and Robin to the site of the burned-out cabin. The scent of blackened pitch and scorched pine was a pungent stain on the clear morning air. Smoke still lingered, and ashes hung in the air despite the amount of water that had been spread on the site.

There was nothing left of the small hunting cabin that had stood in the clearing for over one hundred years.

Sully walked over and leaned on a scorched pine near the ruined chimney. "I think this belonged the Harrises maybe?"

"Drew Harris?"

"His family anyway." He patted the stones. "Don't think they ever used it. It was falling apart. Roof was mostly caved in."

"This isn't too far from the old Grimmer place," Robin said. "Did you notice that? It's on the same creek."

"Oh yeah." Val walked around the blackened foundation. "Sully, that's one of the places we found clues about Robin's Grandma Helen and Billy Grimmer's murder."

"Right." Sully hadn't been with Val when all that had happened. He'd only known that Robin's car went into the lake and came up with the bones of an old skeleton in the back seat.

It hadn't been an ordinary car accident.

"So all three places that have burned were old and abandoned," Monica said. "Clearly this isn't someone who wants to harm people."

"We can't say that," Sully said. "I've been talking to people about what a serial arsonist is, what to look for, that kind of thing. It's usually about power or acting out internal anger."

Robin looked up from examining a toppled post. "Male or female? I'm guessing male."

"Yes. By a high margin, serial arsonists tend to be male."

Monica said, "But the readings Val got from the last scene were of a woman." She turned her attention to Val, who had her gloves off and was concentrating on the area in front of the stone chimney, which was still standing.

"It was a female," Val said. "But we don't know if the person staying in the Alison barn has anything to do with the fires." She huffed in frustration. "I'm not getting anything from this. It's dead."

Sully walked over and rubbed the back of her neck. "It's too damaged, Val. Don't stress about it. You gave us something to go on with the blankets."

"Robin, what about you?" Monica looked for her friend. "Robin?"

"Over here!"

Monica spotted Robin across the creek, sitting on a fallen log that leaned over the water. "I'm trying to call Bethany."

Sully cleared his throat. "Do I need to be here for that?"

"You've met Bethany before," Val said. "Remember? She's the ghost who found the path for us up at the cabin last year."

"Right." Sully still looked uncomfortable. "I'm just saying, isn't she more comfortable with just you ladies?"

Val smiled. "Sully, are you afraid of the ghost?"

"No." He shrugged. "Maybe not my favorite thing, that's all."

She patted him on the shoulder. "Go ahead and wait at the truck. I can't read anything here, so we're probably almost done."

"Okay." The man departed so fast you'd think something was chasing him.

Monica snorted. "Men."

"So weird about talking to the dead," Val said. "Probably a good thing Robin hasn't told him how many hang around town."

Robin frowned. "Well, not today. I'm not having much luck calling Bethany."

Bethany was usually quick to answer Robin's call when Robin summoned her by drawing her portrait, so Bethany not showing up for Robin was notable.

"When was the last time you saw her?" Monica walked across the creek and over to Robin.

"She came by the shop and hung out for a while last week. She didn't say anything though. It felt off. Her energy seemed... worried maybe? Cautious? She sat in the children's area with Clara."

The ghost of the woman who'd lived in Robin's antique shop still haunted it, but she was a friendly ghost, a young mother who'd died in childbirth. She was peaceful and was happiest when children came to visit the shop.

"Can Clara and Bethany communicate?" Val asked. "Does it work that way?"

"Bethany seems to be aware of her, and Clara sees her. So they know about each other; they don't really chat. But Clara was singing to her and it seemed to calm Bethany down."

Val groaned. "Oh, there is definitely something spooky going on in Glimmer Lake."

"You mean spookier than normal?" Monica asked.

"I mean we have old cabins burning down, ghosts who usually love Robin avoiding her—"

"Maybe she's scared," Robin said. "There was violence here. I mean, it wasn't a gunfight or an assault, but a fire creates a lot of violent energy. Maybe Bethany is just afraid."

"Should we try somewhere else?" Monica asked.

"I have to go," Val said. "Andy and Jack are coming back from their dad's today, so I need to get home."

"Go," Monica said. "I can go with Robin."

"You're sure? You don't have to get back to the hotel?"

They didn't like letting Robin talk to ghosts alone. If Monica or Val wasn't available, Mark was usually the one anchoring his wife. It wasn't that most spirits were angry or violent, but some of them could be, and when Robin was talking to a spirit, she was hardly aware of her surroundings.

"No, you can head home. I'm good. Kara's been distracted lately, but I think that's Jake's fault." Monica smiled. "She's still super on top of work."

"That's great to hear. Eve really likes her."

"Everyone loves her. She's perfect for the position." Monica nudged Robin. "Hey, hon. Let's head back."

"What?" Robin looked up, her eyes slightly unfocused.

"Why don't we try calling Bethany somewhere else? I think this place is too disturbing."

"Right. Good idea."

Monica helped Robin cross the stream and head back to the path that trailed along the creek. "You okay?"

"I'm just worried," Robin murmured. "You're right. Something bad is definitely coming."

———

MONICA AND ROBIN waited by the lakeside, sitting on rounded granite rocks and the exposed roots of giant pines that lined the west side of Glimmer Lake. They had pulled off the road that ran past the dam and headed up to Glimmer Lake Lodge, the same road they'd run off of when Robin had been startled by a ghostly white stag.

Robin was sitting cross-legged on a rock, her eyes closed as she let her fingers move over the page where she was drawing. The afternoon was waning, and gold light shone across the water.

A chill touched the air, causing Monica to shiver. "Anything?"

"She's here." Robin opened her eyes a little and focused on a stand of trees. "She's near, but she's keeping her distance."

Monica kept her voice low. "That's unusual, right?"

"Bethany?" Robin spoke softly. "Bethany, we're looking for help."

Long silence followed the gentle request.

"She's thinking," Robin said. "She's moved a little closer, but she's still not talking."

"She's worried?"

"I think so."

What made a ghost afraid? "Is she avoiding *me*?" Monica asked. "Should I wait by the car?"

"She knows you. She knows all of us. She's not too sure about Sully, but he's not here."

Silence stretched over them, lapping at the edges of the clearing like the water lapped at the pebbled beach.

"I know you're scared," Robin said. "What can we do to make you feel better?" Robin frowned at something in the distance. "Make him go away? Make who go away?"

More silence. "Bethany, can you tell us about the fires? Did you see any— No! Don't leave."

Monica almost started at the urgency in Robin's voice.

"I can tell something is scaring you. Does it have something to do with the fires?" She listened longer. "You don't have to talk about it if you don't want to." Robin's voice fell to a soft whisper. "Is someone hurting you?"

Monica felt the pain in Robin's voice to her toes. All three of them were mothers, and the idea of someone hurting a child, even a ghost child, filled Monica with a fierce kind of rage. "Who?"

"She won't say," Robin murmured. "Bethany's being very elusive, which is unlike her. She's usually very direct."

"Okay. Just... focus on whatever she can give us. Try to pick up anything you can from what she's—"

"She?" Robin asked. "Is the person starting the fires a woman?" She frowned. "Not a woman."

A girl? Monica had been doing her research, and the

number of arsonists under eighteen was truly astonishing. Arson seemed to be a way that young people acted out, especially if they were abused or traumatized.

"Could the arsonist be a ghost?" Monica whispered.

"No." Robin said it firmly. "Sully said Gabe was sure accelerant was being used. Ghosts can't manipulate physical objects without expending an incredible amount of energy, like Billy getting us out of the car. This person has used physical things only a few days apart. A ghost wouldn't be able to do that."

"Is Bethany still here?"

"Yes." Robin's hand was still moving over her sketch. "I've never seen her like this before. She's practically sulking. She's not happy I called her. She wants to leave."

"Should you let her go?" Monica asked. "We don't want to piss off the friendliest spirit we know."

"There's something here. She knows something more."

"Maybe she—"

"What was that?" Robin nearly shouted it. "Bethany, I need to know..." Her eyes went wide. "Who didn't mean for it to happen, Bethany?" Robin leaned forward, her body poised to charge off the tree roots if necessary. "Bethany?" Her body relaxed. "She's gone."

"She gave you something though."

Robin smoothed her hand over Bethany's sketch. This time she'd drawn Bethany in her usual nightgown, but the girl was curled into a protective ball, her knees drawn up and her arms wrapped around them. She was on the edge of the bank, her back leaning against a knotted pine tree. She didn't look at the artist—her eyes were narrowed, concentrating on something just out of the frame.

"Is this how she looked just now?"

"Yeah."

"She looks... angry."

"She is. She's angry and sad. I think she knows what's going on. She might even know who's starting the fires."

"How?"

"First she said: I can't talk about the fire."

"So clearly she knows nothing about what happened." Monica rolled her eyes. "What else?"

"After she said that, she hummed a song. What was it?" Robin frowned. "Lavender's blue, dilly dilly... You know that old song?"

"Only a little. I think it was in a movie?"

"It's an old, old folk song."

Monica felt a shiver trail down her back. "That's not creepy at all."

"And then... right before she disappeared, she turned to me and said, 'It wasn't her fault. She didn't mean for it to happen.'"

"She didn't mean for the fire to happen?" Monica took a deep breath. "So we're looking for a woman again. Sully's profile said a man. Is that out the window?"

"I don't know. Maybe she's talking about something else. *Someone* else. Maybe what she's scared of doesn't have anything to do with the fires happening now. Like I said, a ghost can't do these things. Lighting a fire is too physical."

Monica walked over to Robin and held out her hand. "Let's head back. You can tell me more in the car, but the sun's going down and it's getting cold."

Monica could already feel the nip of fall in the air. But while people in the low country thought about pretty fall colors and pumpkins getting ripe, in the mountains the cold dry nights of autumn meant fire. Risk of fire was there in the summer, but the risk of fire was at its highest just as nights were getting colder and people craved a nice cozy fire to warm up.

Campfires could quickly turn into accidental fires. Was that what had happened at the Alison cabin? Had it all started as an accident? Did seeing that fire unlock something in their arsonist? Had they gotten a taste of release? A taste of chaos?

Who was lighting fires in Glimmer Lake? Where was this anger coming from? And what did the ghosts know?

CHAPTER 13

Three days passed in Glimmer Lake, but Monica could feel the tension. While the out-of-towners seemed unaware of the increased stress in town, everyone Monica ran into mentioned the three fires. More of her neighbors were cutting back their trees and bushes, cleaning off the roof they'd meant to clean after the snow melted.

She saw more than one plastic tub go into a garage. They were go bags for wildfires. Emergency supplies, nonperishable food, medicine, documents, and other things that couldn't be replaced. The baby pictures would go in there. Grandmother's quilt. Memories.

Monica had lived in the mountains her whole life, and living in the mountains meant living with the threat of fire. But she'd never felt anything as close as the fear she felt in Glimmer Lake now. She had her own go bag packed in her trunk, and she took it back and forth to Russell House every day.

She pulled up to the kitchen parking area a few minutes before eight on Sunday morning. They had five rooms checking out today and seven parties checking in, families sneaking in one last week of vacation before school started.

Visitors didn't seem to be worried. Because the fires had been taken care of quickly by the local company and their branch of state services, the incidents hadn't hit the national or statewide news.

She parked and grabbed her purse before heading in. She had a lot on her plate that morning, getting ready for the coming week, and she also needed to call Sam and Caleb to see if they were available for building the gazebo after the trees behind Russell House were cleared.

Nevertheless, she wasn't too busy to notice the quiet conversation between Kara and Jake when she walked in. They were both leaning against the counter, coffee in hand, looking very cozy.

"Good morning." Monica put her purse down and pretended she didn't notice how Jake and Kara darted apart.

"Hey, Mom." Jake walked over and gave her a one-armed hug. "How's your morning been?"

How's yours been? Monica didn't say it. She didn't really want to know. He might be twenty-nine, but he was still her first baby. "Good. You?"

"Good. Great weather today. The, uh, the campfire cocktail thing Kara organized went really well last night."

"Great."

"Yeah." Kara cleared her throat and stepped forward. "I think that's something we can start implementing every night, or at least weekend nights. Complimentary cocktails were snapped up, but we got really good reorders too. And Eve sold a ton of hot chocolate for the kids."

"Nice." Monica smiled at Kara. "Great idea."

"Thanks, Monica." She smothered a yawn. "Sorry."

Monica glanced between Jake and the young woman. "Late night?"

Kara's cheeks went pink. "Just busy with cocktail night. Lots on my mind."

Monica took out her calendar as they joined her at the table. "What's on the agenda for today? We've got five out and seven in. Will our rooms be ready? Is Jacqueline working this weekend?"

"She's coming over after noon. She has church in the morning."

Monica hadn't been to Mass in weeks. Eek. She should go to evening mass for sure. "Make sure Jacqueline and all the ladies know we're continuing the bonus program going forward. It's not just a summer thing anymore."

"Will do."

Monica looked at her son. "How about you? All our equipment ready to go?"

"I'll probably be working my butt off today and tonight. One of the families wanted a fishing trip this afternoon, but other than that, I'm clear until tomorrow. But I've got to get all the waterskiing equipment organized and do some patches on our tubes."

"The kids' equipment?"

Jake nodded. "Just end-of-season stuff. Need to restring some badminton rackets, patch a couple of nets, replace some blankets from the boathouse, things like that."

"Roughly the same as last year?"

"A little more upkeep, but this season was busier than last, so I'm not surprised."

"You should have time during the fall lull." Monica was

looking forward. How would they keep guests coming in once school started again? What did Glimmer Lake have to offer in the fall between summer lake season and winter snow?

Was it irresponsible to tempt people to Glimmer Lake when a serial arsonist was on the loose?

No, she couldn't think that way. That's why she was spending all her spare time with Robin and Val, trying to figure out what was happening. None of this was written in stone. She refused to accept that.

Monica looked at the third item on her list. "Jake, have you contacted the wineries about crush season promo?"

Jake sighed and jotted a note down on his legal pad. "I'll add it to the list."

"We gotta plan ahead," Monica said. "Always."

"Got it."

The three of them quickly ran through the rest of the schedule for the day before they went their separate ways, Monica to her office to call the tree company about clearing the back of Russell House, Kara to the front desk, and Jake to the boathouse.

Eve brought her a coffee midmorning. "I didn't see you this morning."

"I was behind on my schedule, but I'm feeling more caught up now." Monica reached for the caffe latte. "Bless you."

"No problem. It'll be quiet at my stand until the families start taking off and getting drinks for the road."

"Good." She tasted the delicious caffeinated goodness. "So you have time to gossip."

Eve sat in the chair and settled in with a smile. "Oooh, what are we gossiping about?"

"I happened to notice that my son and my manager were quite... cozy this morning."

Eve looked like a deer in the headlights. "Uh..."

"Jake already talked to me," she quickly added. "Neither of their jobs is at risk here. Unless it ends badly and Jake acts like a jerk. I told him he's more expendable than Kara is."

Eve snorted. "Harsh."

"Accurate." She sipped more coffee. "Besides, I will always be hardest on my own children."

"Good to know. Also, Kara works her butt off and she doesn't have much of a safety net, so I'm glad you're looking out for her."

"Oh?" Monica hadn't known that. Kara was pretty tight-lipped about her past.

"I don't know specifics—she's not a talker about personal stuff—but I don't think she has much family. Or if she does, she'd not on good terms with them."

"Oh, that's rotten. I'm sorry to hear that." Monica's mom heart wanted to immediately scoop Kara up and adopt her, but possible romance with Jake made the idea of it a bit awkward.

"She's very independent." Eve kept her voice low. "Very organized. But I kind of have the feeling it's because she's always had to be, you know? I just get that feeling from her."

"Good to know. So we keep an eye on her. She's got an apartment in town, right?"

"She rents a room at Bailey's."

Bailey's Boarding House was a popular spot for seasonal workers and long-term stays. It made sense for a single woman who spent most of her time at work. "You see her with any friends?"

Eve nodded. "A few. She's not a loner." She smiled. "And then... I've noticed a distinct uptick in late nights recently too."

Monica smiled. "Well, hopefully Jake has his head on straight for this one. She's a really nice girl."

"She is." Eve wiggled her eyebrows. "And how about you? Juggling the attentions of two silver foxes, Monica? I think I want to be you when I grow up."

Monica nearly choked on her coffee. "What?"

"Val told me you went out with West. Who is hot, I want to say, but also maybe not the most serious type?" Eve lowered her voice. "But I mean, if you want it, get it, girl. The man is old enough to be my father, but I can recognize the appeal."

"Oh." Monica put her hands over her eyes. "I don't know what to do about West."

"It's only been four years." Eve bit her lip. "Did you forget what goes where?"

Monica threw a balled-up napkin at Eve. "Brat! You're worse than Val."

Eve burst out laughing. "I learned from the master. And I tease because I love. But I'd be remiss in not mentioning you also have the very smoldering—pun intended—attention of our local fire chief. Who can't take his eyes off your legs every time you walk away."

Monica shook her head. "Do you see everything around here?"

Eve shrugged and spread her arms out. "No one notices the coffee chick even though I have blue hair. I'm the perfect spy."

"I'll say."

THE FIRE WASN'T an inferno that night—it swept from her feet like a carpet spread before her, rolling through the underbrush toward a destination shrouded by fog.

Was it smoke?

The fire cut through a towering grove of sequoias, the primeval giants rising from the forest floor in an eerie circle, surrounding a mother tree hollowed by fire.

LAVENDER'S GREEN, *dilly dilly,*
    Lavender's blue
    You must love me, dilly dilly,
    'cause I love you.

MONICA HEARD the voice like a ghostly apparition coming through the mist. She walked through the sequoia grove and into the fog. "Hello?"

I HEARD ONE SAY, dilly dilly,
    since I came hither,
    That you and I, dilly dilly,
    must lie together.

"HELLO?" Monica walked through the flames barefoot, but the fire didn't burn her feet and her dress wasn't scorched. "Who are you?"

"You must love me, dilly dilly, 'cause I love you…"

She saw a hunting cabin through the smoke. It was already on fire, and Monica saw a face peering through the window.

No. It made no sense.

The familiar face disappeared and a pale, moonfaced girl took its place.

"Bethany?"

Bethany's eyes went wide and she put a finger to her lips. "Shhhhh."

Monica heard the warning like a whisper in her ear.

"Wake up." The whisper came again. "Before it's too late."

MONICA SAT up gasping and reached for the phone on her bedside table. She dialed Sully's number without even pausing to write the dream down.

"Monica?" He was already awake. "Another one?"

"Another hunting cabin. It was near a grove of sequoias and there was water nearby. I heard something like a waterfall."

"Describe the cabin."

"Old. Older than the others. Redwood logs were square cut. Stacked. No siding. One story. Stone chimney."

"Square-cut redwood logs?"

Monica closed her eyes and tried to remember every detail. "Moss on the roof. Moss on the sides of the trees…" What side…? "Everything is turned around in my head, but I think the water or stream or whatever it is was east of the cabin."

Sully muttered, "Damn. This sounds remote."

"The fire's in the underbrush," Monica said. "It wasn't in the trees. I don't think she's lit it yet."

"She?"

Monica was crying because nothing made sense. "I don't know, Sully! I didn't see anyone for sure. It was all mixed up and there was a ghost—"

"I gotta get my map, okay? Then I'll call this in, but I gotta have a better idea of where it is. Just hang in there and don't panic."

———

SULLY CALLED HER HOURS LATER. The fire had been set in an old hunting cabin, but it was off a fire road south of town, within walking distance of Chaco's bar, and there was minimal damage.

"I don't know what to tell you," Sully said. "I was trying to locate the cabin you were talking about and I wasn't having any luck, but I called Gabe to give him a heads-up about there maybe being another fire, and he said someone had already reported it."

"So it wasn't near a sequoia grove?"

"Nope."

None of it made sense.

"The good news," Sully continued, "is that they caught this one early, like the fire at the Alison cabin, so there's a lot of evidence. Hopefully Val will be able to get something off the site in a day or two."

"The fires are happening every three or four days," Monica said. "We don't have much time."

"I know." Sully's voice was grim. "So far the damage hasn't been much, but I feel like he or she is getting bolder. This one was nearly in town."

"Do serial arsonists want to get caught?"

"I don't know." Sully cleared his throat. "Last night you said 'she' hadn't set the fire yet. Did you see someone?"

Monica paused. She didn't want to point fingers at innocent people when the rest of the dream hadn't proven true. "There was a ghost in the dream," Monica said. "The little girl who talks to Robin so much. Obviously she can't be the one who set the fire. Robin's sure a ghost couldn't do this, but I said she because I saw her."

"Right." Sully sounded doubtful. "Are you sure there's not something else you're not telling me?"

Monica took a deep breath. "I wish visions were more concrete, like the energy Val feels off objects, but they just aren't. Visions are messy. They're open to interpretation, and sometimes things don't follow. Like this time. No redwood cabin. No stream. No sequoias."

"Some of that is symbolic, you mean?"

"Yeah. In all these dreams, I'm walking though the fire barefoot and it's not touching me. I don't know what that means yet, but I'm working on it."

"Right." He sighed. "It's the middle of the night. Try to get some sleep, okay?"

"I'll try. Good night, Sully."

CHAPTER 14

*M*onica treated herself to coffee and scones at Misfit the next morning. She called in to Kara, who sounded as chipper as ever. Everything was running smoothly at Russell House, so Monica decided to hang with Val for a little if her friend had time.

She was sitting in a corner, enjoying a hot latte and blueberry scone, when she saw him walk in.

Gabe spotted her at almost the same time she spotted him. He lifted his chin in greeting, let his eyes linger for a moment, then nodded at the register.

Monica waved and paid attention to her own coffee.

"Hey, Ms. Velasquez!" Logan walked right up to her table, looking like a transformed kid. "How are you? How's Jake?"

Monica smiled immediately. "Hey, Logan."

He sat at her table without asking. "Thanks again for letting me go out with him. Did he tell you I tried a kayak too?"

"He didn't."

"So the next day, I biked down to the lake to the boat rental place, right?"

"Oh, that's great."

"And I rented a kayak and there was this really nice girl there. She got me all set up, and then we actually talked for a while and she gave me some tips and we went kayaking the next day. It was great." He held out his arm. "I'm a little sunburned though."

"I can see that." And a little dazzled by whatever cutie he'd met at the lake. "That's awesome! Well, not the sunburn part."

He shrugged. "I'll be brown by tomorrow. It's cool." He looked over at his dad. "My dad had another call last night. He's pretty tired."

"I remember those nights. You're probably pretty tired too."

He shrugged. "It's different when I'm with him. Most of the time I don't think much about what he does. It's a lot."

"Yeah, it is."

Gabe wandered over and set a frosty drink in front of Logan. "Coffee frapp-a-milkshake thing for you." He turned to Monica. "Do you mind if we join you, since my son didn't ask?"

Monica smiled. He did seem a little grumpy, but he was still polite. "Not at all. Logan was telling me about his kayak trip the other day."

That seemed to cheer Gabe a little. "Yeah, it sounds like he had a great time."

"And it sounds like you guys were busy last night too."

He took the lid off his coffee and blew on the steaming cup. "I know it's probably kids, but—"

"Doesn't make it any less dangerous," Monica said quietly. "I know."

Logan spotted someone across the room and perked up. "Oh hey, Dad."

Gabe turned toward the group of kids who'd entered Misfit. One of them was a girl with short blond hair. She waved at Logan with a big smile.

"Yeah." Gabe jerked his head. "Don't leave without me."

"Cool." Logan flashed a smile at Monica. "See you, Ms. Velasquez."

"Bye." She waved as Logan fled the adults for the teenagers. "Your son has very nice manners."

"I have to give his mom credit for that. She did a good job."

"And he looks a lot happier."

Gabe raised an eyebrow. "The power of getting out of the damn house and meeting a cute girl, right?"

She smiled. "Most of the local kids are really nice. There're always a few troublemakers, but by and large, the kids in town are pretty harmless."

"I wish he'd met some kids earlier in the summer, but late is better than never."

"It's possible they've been standoffish because they thought he was an out-of-towner. Once they found out you live here, they might have warmed up. I remember it being the same when I was younger. You don't want to make friends with someone who's going to forget you exist as soon as they leave town for their real life."

"Yeah, that makes sense." Gabe craned his neck to check on Logan. "He's a good kid. I hope he makes some friends.

His mom says he's kind of a loner at his high school in Emeryville."

"That's too bad." She nodded to the table where Logan was sitting. "Maybe he'll find his people here. I always told my kids you don't need a lot of friends, just a couple of good ones."

Gabe smiled, and the laugh lines around his eyes deepened. "That's good advice."

"How about you?" Monica tried not to get distracted by his mouth, which she'd just noticed had a little bit of foam on it. "Do you have a few good friends?"

He took a deep breath and let it out slowly. "Because I'm with the state, I've moved around quite a bit, so that's hard. But I'd count Sully as a good friend. Part of the reason I wanted this position was because I know some of the guys in the company too."

"Good."

"They speak very highly of your late husband."

Monica smiled. "That's good to hear. Everyone loved Gilbert."

"Heart attack?" Gabe shook his head. "He was young."

The ache was always there, like a bruise that never went away. "Yeah. He was always healthy, so he'd never gotten his heart examined for anything. Just his regular physicals, right? Apparently it was a congenital defect and he could have died even younger. Totally unpredictable."

"That's horrible. I'm so sorry."

"It was horrible. But after we learned that—how he could have died anytime—I tried to think about all the years we had together, all the years the kids had their dad, as a gift, you know? We could have lost him so much earlier."

Gabe's eyes were kind. "Still hard."

She blinked back a couple of tears. "Still hard."

"It's been three years?"

She nodded. "Almost four."

"You, uh... I mean, have you—" He cleared his throat. "None of the guys knew if you'd seen anyone since your husband passed."

Monica frowned. "Seen anyone? Like a therapist?"

His cheeks took on a ruddy tinge. "You know what, it's none—"

"Oh, like *dating*." She said that louder than she'd intended and felt eyes turn toward them.

Nice, Monica.

Gabe swiped a hand over his face. "You know what, you were just talking about your late husband and that was rude for me to bring up and I'm tired. I'm sorry. I shouldn't have asked—"

"Just once." Monica powered through her embarrassment since Gabe seemed embarrassed too. "Recently. I don't mind you asking. I'll always be sad about Gil. I don't think that ever goes away, but I can't stop living my life. Gil would hate that. I'm still young too."

"You are." His eyes traveled over her, from her lips to her cleavage, down to her legs. "And you obviously have a very... busy life."

"So I went on this date a little while ago." She smiled. "First first date in thirty years. It was fun. A little awkward."

The corner of his mouth inched up. "I can imagine. So is it serious with the guy you went on the date with?"

She cocked her head. "I might go out with him again. Not sure. It's not an exclusive thing though. We just met."

Gabe nodded. "Gotcha."

Monica felt bold. He was clearly interested and wasn't being very subtle about it. Monica leaned her elbow on the table and angled herself toward him, playing with her hair a little. "Are you thinking about asking me out, Chief Peralta?"

His eyes went to the fingers playing in her hair. "I'm... an investigator." He cleared his throat and looked her straight in the eye. "So I'm investigating."

"Is that so?"

His eyes moved to her lips. "Yeah."

Okay, this was... fun. She felt bold. Sexy. She crossed her legs at the ankles and saw his eyes drop to her thighs. "You'll have to let me know the results of your investigation when you're finished."

He shifted in his chair. "I think this may be a pretty complicated case. I may have to question you more specifically about certain... assets. Aspects." He cleared his throat again. "Might need to schedule a one-on-one." His eyes met hers, and Monica felt like she would melt under his gaze. If looks could seduce...

What was she talking about? Looks could definitely seduce, and the one Gabe was giving her had Monica ready to throw in the towel. Or her panties. Whatever it took to surrender.

Her brain flashed to the dream she'd had about him.

Not a dream, a vision. Was she falling into something inevitable? Or was her vision giving her a warning?

"Well." Monica took a deep breath. "If you need to schedule that one-on-one..."

Gabe's eyebrows went up.

"Monica!" Val grabbed her before Monica could finish

her sentence. "Hey, it's Sexy Gabe. Hey, Sexy Gabe, I need the woman you're flirting with right now—sorry for the interruption, but I need her. Bye, see you later."

Monica was yanked out of her seat and barely had time to grab her coffee. "Okay... what?"

Gabe's mouth opened, but he didn't get a word out before Val whisked her away, behind the counter, down the hallway, and onto the screened porch at the back of Misfit Mountain.

"Okay." Monica was finally able to speak. "What the—?"

"I am sorry." Val put both her hands on Monica's cheeks. "I am so so so so sorry, because you guys looked like you were about to make out at the corner table, and he's hot and I want that for you, but I need you to see this and it cannot wait because I'm freaking out and you have to see this."

"What?"

Val pointed to something on the table. Monica turned to look and saw a bundle of what looked like black clothes.

"What is that?"

"Look closer. I found it in the dumpster just now when I was taking out a bag."

"It's *burned*." Monica picked up a pen that was sitting on the table and poked at the bundle. "Are these...?" A section of the cloth revealed itself in a fold, the wool plaid still familiar even though she'd only seen it once. "Is this the same kind of blanket we found at the Alison barn?"

"Uh-huh. In my dumpster."

Monica's eyes went wide. "You think this came from the most recent fire?"

"Yes, but how did it end up in *my dumpster*? Of all the dumpsters in town, why mine? Chaco's is closer, and I know Sergio doesn't lock his bins. Why did she dump them in my dumpster? Do you think the arsonist is one of my customers? Do you think she knows we're looking for her?"

"I don't know. Has anyone come in smelling like smoke and kerosene?"

"Be serious!"

"I am serious!" Monica was actually annoyed. "I don't know what to tell you. Did you try reading them?"

"Yes. All I got was the same sense of confusion, except maybe more desperate. She's really scared now. She's really confused."

Monica tried to put what Val was feeling from the blankets together with what they knew about their arsonist. "Do you think this is someone who's lighting fires and doesn't realize it until afterward? Like... do you think you could do that? Set a fire and not realize it?"

Val blinked. "Like the worst case of sleepwalking ever?"

"Maybe? I mean, remember when Robin's cousin was on those pain meds and he ended up out in his boat in the middle of the night?"

"Oh, I do remember that. Her cousin Brent. He had all his fishing gear too."

"Exactly. I don't know, is it possible?"

"But Brent goes fishing all the time," Val said. "Like it's an automatic routine for him. It doesn't seem like setting fires with kerosene of all things would be routine for anyone."

Monica mused, "I don't even know where you get kerosene."

"You can get it at the farm supply store or most hardware shops," Val said. "People still have kerosene heaters."

"Really?"

"Yeah, so that's not really a clue." Val poked at the

blanket again. "Neither is this. I saw a pile of this kind of blankets at the sporting goods store. You can get them anywhere."

"This pattern?"

"I didn't see this one, no."

"I've *seen* this pattern somewhere." Monica frowned. "I'm telling you it looks familiar. I wish I could remember where." Monica felt her phone buzzing in her pocket. "You need to call Sully and give this stuff to him. It's probably evidence." She looked at her phone. "It's Robin."

"Put her on speaker."

Monica touched the screen to answer. "Robin, you're on speaker. I'm at Val's. She found some burned blankets in her dumpster just now. They're the same type that we found at the Alison cabin in the loft."

"I found something too." Robin's voice was quiet. "Can you and Val come over? I've been going through the online archives from the Glimmer Lake library and ran into a dead end, so Mark helped me access some records from Sacramento." Robin drew in a breath and let it out slowly. "I think I know why Bethany is scared. I think I know how she died."

CHAPTER 15

*R*obin and Mark's beautiful home was set at the end of a wooded neighborhood that backed up to the national forest. A broad porch surrounded the stone-fronted wood home.

They were sitting out on the porch, drinking iced tea while squeezed behind Mark's laptop so they could see the screen.

"I found it in this little article that was written after the dam was built," Robin said. "There were quite a few families who were unhappy with the payment they received from the power company—families that left after the fire got almost nothing for their land—and there was a reporter at the Sacramento paper who interviewed a bunch of them."

"There's something about Bethany?" Val asked.

"I can't know for sure, but it make sense. Remember what Gail told Monica? The fire started at the Sanger home and killed the father and the two children?" She pointed at the screen. "Look at the third paragraph on this page."

The computer screen showed a scan of an old newspaper; while the picture was scratchy, it was still readable.

Lucille Sanger, sister of the late Corbin Sanger, told the newspaper that her brother's and nieces' deaths did not mean the family land had been abandoned. Corbin Sanger, along with his daughters Rosemarie and Bethany, died in the 1932 fire that devastated much of the Grimmer Valley. The surviving Sanger family is petitioning to be compensated for their share of the settlement...

"Bethany." Monica blinked. "Bethany died in the fire. For some reason, I always assumed she'd drowned."

"I did too," Robin said. "I have no idea why."

"Because the town was drowned?" Val shrugged. "I assumed she drowned too."

"She died ten years before the dam was even built," Robin said. "It was her home that was the epicenter of the fire."

Monica remembered Bethany's words by the lake only a few days before. "Bethany said: 'It wasn't her fault. She didn't mean for it to happen.' Was she talking about her sister? Did her sister start the fire?"

Val said, "Didn't Gail say that it was probably a cooking fire? That would make sense."

"But why is Bethany still scared?" Robin said. "She died in a fire. There have been fires since. What's special about this fire?"

"There were wildfires last season," Monica said. "Not big ones, but there were a couple. I didn't have visions about any of them."

"Okay," Val said. "So there's something different about this fire, and someone knows about us or suspects we know something, because why else would they have dumped those burned blankets in my dumpster?"

"You *are* right on the main drag," Robin said. "Maybe that part is coincidence."

"I don't know, but something about it doesn't feel right." Val leaned away and kicked her feet up. "We're looking for an arsonist who doesn't seem to know she's starting fires. How do you forget starting a fire? Or is this person being framed? Is the real arsonist stalking this person I keep reading off the blankets? Is he following her and lighting fires, trying to kill her?"

"Is there a woman drifting through town? Have you guys seen anyone who looks unfamiliar and isn't on vacation?"

"It's practically impossible to tell this time of year."

Monica felt tired. "None of this is making any sense, and I feel like things are getting worse. Val, did you give the blankets to Sully?"

"Yeah, I called him. Told him they were on the back porch." She picked at her jeans. "Do you guys all feel it? Everyone in town is on edge."

"I know." Monica shook her head. "The guests at the lodge are the only ones having fun. Kara and Eve are putting on a friendly face, but I can see they're stressed out. Even Jake seems to be stressed. And when is he stressed out?"

Robin rubbed her bottom lip. "The kids were supposed to come home for a couple of weeks right before school started. Mark and I told them to go visit his parents. We made an excuse, but I think they know something's up here."

"I told Jackson to keep a go bag in his truck," Val said. "He thinks I'm being dramatic."

"Teenagers always think their moms are being dramatic," Monica muttered.

Robin closed the laptop. "What do we do?"

Monica said, "I guess I better start taking more naps. I'm starting to distrust my visions though. This last dream ended up being nothing like what actually happened. So why am I dreaming about that redwood cabin?"

"Do you think you've ever been there before?" Every kid in Glimmer Lake spent hours during the summer roaming around the woods, poking into old cabins and using them for forts. Most of the cabins were abandoned, but a few were still used by the forest service or campers.

"I don't think so. It looked really old. I'd remember one that old."

Val reached for her phone. "Sully's calling me."

Monica felt her phone buzz too. She took it out. "It's Russell House. I have to get back to work." She touched the phone and answered it. "Hey Kara, I'm sorry. I'm heading back right now."

"Good." Kara sounded nervous. "Um, that's great. Because... that fire inspector is here again."

"Gabe?"

"Yeah. He's been poking around, and he doesn't look happy."

MONICA PULLED up to the front of Russell House and saw Gabe's red-and-white truck parked right at the front door. She drove around and parked by the kitchen. By the time she got out of her car, Kara was practically running to her.

"I didn't know what to do." Words tumbled out of her mouth. "He asked to talk to Jake. Then they went to the boathouse and I heard arguing and then he stormed back to the house and demanded to see purchase records for the rec budget and I don't know where those are so—"

"Chill." Monica put a hand on Kara's shoulder. "Where is he now?"

"He's in your office." Kara looked guilty. "I didn't know what else to do. He just kind of... barged in. I haven't seen Jake."

Monica felt her stomach drop. What was Gabe looking for?

"He's there right now?"

"Should I call the sheriff? I mean... he kind of works with the sheriff, right?"

"I'll call Sully." She got her phone and called Val. "Hey, hon."

"Hey. Is Gabe there?"

Monica walked through the kitchen and through the dining room, waving and smiling at guests as they enjoyed an afternoon drink by the giant portrait windows. "Yeah. Do you have any idea what's going on?" She kept her voice low.

"Sully showed Gabe those blankets I found, and his kid was with him. His kid said something about the blankets being the same as the ones at Russell House, and Gabe just took off. Sully's been trying to call him, and he's not answering his phone."

"The same ones as..." *Oh shit.* "That's where I've seen the pattern." Monica blinked. "Oh my God."

She reached her office; the door was already cracked

open, and she saw Gabe Peralta standing at the table, looking through files. "Val, I gotta go."

"Okay, Sully is on his way out there."

"Thanks." She put her phone away and pushed down the sharp bite of anger. "Chief Peralta, can I help you? Would you like to explain why you're in my office, going through files that are not yours?"

Gabe looked up. He was leaning both hands on the table and his shoulders were tense. "Would you like to explain why we've found blankets that came from your boathouse at three arson scenes so far?"

"You have me at a disadvantage. I don't know what blankets you're talking about."

He reached down and pulled a plastic bag out of a box by his feet. In the plastic bag were the remains of the blanket Monica had seen that morning at Val's. On the table was one of the brown, cream, and blue plaid blankets that remained unburned.

The same blankets they'd seen at the Alison cabin.

The same blankets they'd ordered for Russell House. That was why they looked familiar. They were the same blankets Jake kept in the boathouse for guests to use in the evenings on the boat or when people wanted a picnic or when they just needed a cushion. They didn't use them in the house—that's why she hadn't recognized them immediately.

"So a mass-produced blanket we happen to order to use in our boathouse has also been found at an arson scene? You can get those blankets at any sporting goods store. They're very common."

"This color?" Color rode high on his arched cheekbones. "What are you hiding, Ms. Velasquez?"

"I'm not hiding anything." *Lie.* Where was Sully? This was bad.

"I asked your son for an inventory of these blankets, and he couldn't seem to come up with one."

"Good Lord, this is Jake. He thinks a yellow legal pad is a filing system."

Gabe's granite expression didn't move.

Monica huffed. "We order gobs of those blankets because they're guaranteed to get lost. People drop them in the lake when they're fishing. They get left in the woods or accidentally packed in bags and taken home. Any number of people have access to those blankets, Gabe."

"So you're saying that these aren't blankets from Russell House?" Gabe pointed to the plastic bag.

"They could be. They could not be. What I'm trying to tell you is that they go missing a lot, and that doesn't mean anything nefarious. Do you know how many new towels we order every season?"

"I also thought maybe I was overreacting," Gabe said quietly. "I thought all the same things you just mentioned. They're common. They can get lost. They might have been stolen—God knows your security system at the boathouse is nonexistent—but then the routine phone logs I asked for last week came in."

Monica felt the blood drain from her face. "Phone logs?"

"Sully got anonymous tips about two fires. He said they were anonymous, so it made sense to check the incoming calls to his house and his mobile phone. The calls were dialed into his government-issue phone."

Oh shit, oh shit, oh shit.

A pulse pounded in Gabe's temple. "So please—*please, Monica*—tell me why you called Sully in the middle of the night to report two wildfires that were already burning. Tell me you saw smoke or smelled something with an insanely accurate sense of smell or *anything* that will make sense."

Anything that will make sense? Monica let out a rueful laugh.

"You think this is funny?" Gabe was both furious and upset. "This doesn't look good."

"You were sitting across from me." She pointed to the chair at the end of the table. "Right there. We were together when you got that call on the second fire."

He shook his head. "That fire was started hours before it was reported. And that doesn't explain the other two. The two that no one else saw."

Monica nodded. "Right. No one but the arsonist."

"Give me a fucking explanation, Monica!" He slapped his hand on the table.

Monica stalked over and shut her office door firmly. "Do not threaten me, Gabriel Peralta." She walked back and got in his face. "I don't pull this out very often, but do you know who the hell I am? I am the widow of a career firefighter who watched her husband rush off to countless emergencies over twenty years and didn't say *shit* in complaint." She pointed to his truck out the window. "My husband gave the fire service the better part of his life, and I was the model department wife, and now you come to my business and accuse *me* of being an arsonist?"

He didn't move an inch. "Tell me something that will make it make sense, Monica."

Her eyes never wavered from his. "You won't believe me."

"Try me."

What the hell? Why not? What was there to lose? Gabe's respect? He already thought she was an arsonist.

"I saw them in a dream," Monica said quietly. "The fires. I had a vision about them. It happens sometimes."

Whatever explanation Gabe had been expecting, it was not that. He blinked. Opened his mouth. Closed it.

"Sully knows I have visions," she continued. "I've helped him on cases in the past, so I called him. I knew if I called 911 that no one would believe me."

"You are telling me that the explanation for why you called Sully in the middle of the night is because... you're psychic?"

"Yes."

Gabe blinked again. "Are you joking?"

"Why would I joke about this? You basically accused me of arson because I knew when two of the fires happened before anyone else. You think I'd joke about something like that?"

He took a step back. "You're... ridiculous."

His disdain burned, and Monica felt her self-control snap. "You think I'm ridiculous? What's ridiculous is you storming in here without any kind of warrant and looking through my files. My husband was a decorated firefighter. You think I don't know people? You are accusing Gil Velasquez's widow of *arson*." She pointed her finger in his face. "I tried to be nice. I told you information that I trust very few people with, and you are blowing me off. *Get out.*

And don't even think about touching any of my papers or setting foot in Russell House again."

He picked up the box with the burned blankets. "I'm reporting this. I'm reporting you."

"Good. Do it. Sully Wescott knows exactly where I live." Monica crossed her arms and pointed her chin at the door. "Out."

He was still pissed. "You know what? I was looking for some reason—*any reason*—to defend you. But this bullshit—"

"Get the fuck out of my office." She walked over and put her hand on the doorknob. "Know what else I had a vision about?"

Gabe narrowed his eyes. "What?"

"The two of us having sex. Good thing I know the future is changeable, because that is never going to happen." She opened the door wide. *"Ever."*

CHAPTER 16

*V*al's eyes were the size of saucers. "He thinks you started the fires?"

"You had a sex vision about him?" Robin reached for the wine bottle Monica had set on the dining room table. "And you *told him*? I don't know which one is more shocking."

"He didn't believe the psychic thing," Monica said. "This is exactly why I didn't call it in to 911. I knew I'd be a suspect, even with an alibi."

"But do you have an alibi?" Robin asked. "You were home alone."

"I have that alarm I set at night," Monica said. "Remember that ridiculous security system Gil insisted on? That sensor that attaches to my keys?"

"Oh right. I forgot about that."

"That key fob thing keeps track of when I enter the house and when I leave. Or at least it shows them my keys enter and exit. And does anyone actually think I'm walking to these places in the middle of the woods?"

"What would your motivation be anyway?" Val said. "Did he say that?"

Robin got up and refilled the bowl of pistachios they'd torn through. "To be fair, with serial arson, the fire is the point. There doesn't really need to be another motive."

"Can we talk about the fact that he was right on one thing?" Monica asked. "As pissed as I am at Gabe, I do think those blankets are coming from Russell House. I didn't say this to him, but we had to order that pattern. They were the same brand as you can get at the sporting goods store, but we had to order that particular pattern. And Jake has had to reorder quite a few. I was looking at the order history online, and we're missing significantly more this summer than last."

Robin asked, "Do you think someone stole some?"

"It's completely possible. The boathouse has a dead bolt, but if you know how to pick locks, it wouldn't be hard to get in there. It's not connected to the house security system—we just have a sticker on the window to make it look like it is."

"Shit." Val took a deep breath. "You need to tell Sully all this stuff."

"I did. He got to Russell House right after Gabe left."

Robin narrowed her eyes. "Did Gabe really say you were being ridiculous?"

"Yeah." It still burned. "He used that exact word."

Val raised her hand. "To be fair, I think I used the word ridiculous when I was in denial about our powers."

"Please do not tell me you're defending him," Monica said. "That man is an ass."

"I'm just saying that Sully is going to talk to him. All the psychic stuff can be a little hard to take when you first hear it —you can't deny that."

"Okay fine," Robin said. "But he's still an asshole for calling Monica ridiculous."

"He is without a doubt an asshole and will have to grovel before she forgives him and makes her sex vision come true. Can we talk about the sex vision again?"

"Valerie!" Monica nearly threw a wineglass at her. "As if I'd ever—"

"Groveling! Groveling, remember? He has to grovel. Then you can have the sexy sex with him."

"What about West?"

Val shrugged. "What about West? You went out with him once. You don't have to ask his permission for anything. He probably banged a random last weekend at that bike rally in Bridger."

He might have. West had invited Monica to join him at the rally, but when she said no—they'd had too many guests at Russell House for her to leave all day—she hadn't heard another word from him all weekend.

West was fun, but he didn't get her blood in a simmer like Gabe did. Had. Past tense. Because whatever might have been happening there was called off for sure after his attitude that afternoon.

"Gabe isn't happening," Monica said. "I hope Sully sets him straight about me, but I'm done with that man. I have other things to worry about. Like how my blankets are ending up at fire scenes."

"It has to be theft," Robin said. "I mean, you only have Jake, Kara, and Eve working there full time. And Jake's the only one who regularly goes to the boathouse."

"The idea that Jake would be an arsonist..." Monica shook her head. "That's what is ridiculous."

"Ridiculous?" Val said. "Try absurd. It has to be theft."

"Still," Robin said, "we've got to start putting things together. We have more information now. We know the fires have something to do with the past. We know the blankets are from Russell House. Do you guys think it's possible my grandfather's ghost is back?"

"No." Monica was sure of that. "His presence was centered on Russell House, but we've had no reports about any strange reactions from guests. I was in the attic the other day to put Fourth of July decorations away and there was nothing."

Val nudged her. "You did a smoke cleanse anyway, right?"

"Oh yeah. I used that cedar Robin dried."

Their first adventure with nascent psychic powers was banishing Robin's horrible grandfather from Russell House. The man had been abusive in life *and* in death. A little smoke cleanse to rid the area of negative energy was never a bad idea.

"Robin, have you tried calling Bethany again?" Monica was worried about the little girl. She'd died eighty years ago, but Monica was still worried. Did it make sense? No.

Val was staring out the window and into the forest. "Has anyone else wondered about the places this person is setting fires?"

Robin said, "Didn't Sully say that targets with a serial arsonist are usually random because it's all about the thrill of the fire?"

Monica sat up straight. "But these aren't random. Not really. He or she has only attacked one kind of target. Different places, but one kind of target."

"You're right," Val said. "It's all old cabins."

"Not just old cabins." Monica racked her brain. "If I remember correctly, all three of the places they hit, the Alison cabin, the Lewis place by the creek, and the most recent one—"

"It belonged to the Roberts family. No one in the family is left in town, but I think it's still in their name."

"Yeah." Monica nodded. "That's what I thought. Another family from Grimmer."

Val looked at Robin, then back to Monica. "Okay. All old cabins."

"All relics," Monica said. "All seasonal cabins left over from when Grimmer existed and people came up here for hunting or for the cooler weather."

Robin said, "You think the arsonist is only targeting old cabins that belonged to families from Grimmer?"

"Yeah." The pieces felt right. "I think that's exactly what they're doing. The fire took out a lot of Grimmer."

Val said, "The dam destroyed the rest."

Robin said, "But the cabins were still there. It's like... someone is burning the last pieces of Grimmer that remain."

"It's not *like* they're doing it," Monica said. "I think that's exactly what they're doing."

SULLY SAT NEXT to Val on Monica's couch. "I tried to set Gabe straight, but I can't lie. He's a skeptic. I don't think he believes you had anything to do with the fire though. He may think you're covering for someone."

"Who?"

Sully raised an eyebrow. "Your son does work at Russell House."

Val said, "See, that's where you guys don't realize what kind of mom Monica is."

"Yeah," Robin said. "If one of Monica's kids had done this and she knew about it, she'd be the one calling the cops."

"And I wouldn't bail them out either." Monica sat with her arms crossed. "The world isn't going to give my boys a break, so I can't either." She paused. "Maybe on their birthday."

"Fair enough," Sully said. "I'm just telling you what direction Gabe is looking in."

"Well, he's not going to find anything. Jake didn't do it."

"I'm going to question Jake anyway," Sully said. "Just so you know. That will let him get his alibis on the record. And I can't be seen playing favorites just 'cause I know the family."

"Arson." Robin muttered the word. "Arson is about anger. About making internal destruction external, right? Who in Glimmer Lake is angry at Grimmer?"

Monica spread her hands. "Who even thinks about Grimmer anymore? The last people who ever lived there have mostly passed away. I don't think an eighty-year-old arsonist is very likely."

Val said, "The old residents have passed, but their families are still out there." She turned to Robin. "Did you recognize any of the other names in that newspaper article? The one about the dissatisfied families?"

"You think an old resident of Grimmer—or a descendant of one—who didn't like their financial settlement is going after the last bits of Grimmer this many years later?" Sully frowned. "It's a stretch."

Robin said, "I'm worried about the ghosts."

"By definition, aren't ghosts pretty safe?" Sully asked. "They're already dead. What's the worst that could happen to them?"

"They're quiet." Robin continued, ignoring Sully. "There's something going on."

"So we keep trying to contact Bethany," Monica said. "Maybe once you tell her you know how she died—that no one blames her or her sister for the fire—she'll talk to you again."

"I'll try."

"We need to try to find the woman," Sully said. "The one Val keeps seeing waking up at the cabins. If we find her, we can tie these crimes together."

"But Sully, I don't think she's setting the fires. If she is, she's not conscious of it. Everything I'm getting from her is confusion, fear, panic—"

"Either way," Sully said, "victim or perpetrator, if she's at the scene, she's in danger. It's also possible this is someone who's just trying to get by sleeping in these abandoned cabins and she's being targeted. If that's the case, she's in danger and this arsonist is after her."

"So Robin is going to try to contact Bethany again," Monica said. "I'll go to the library and see if Gail has any old maps. Let's try to find out which cabins around here existed before the dam was built."

Sully said, "Good idea. I'll talk to the county surveyor and see what records he has too."

"Thanks. Val, are you going to try another read on the physical evidence they've saved from the scenes?"

Val and Sully exchanged a look. "I can."

He said, "It can't hurt. Head over to the fire house tomorrow and I'll work it out with Gabe."

"You can tell him about me," Val said. "If you want. It's a little easier to 'prove'" —she used air quotes— "my gifts. Maybe we can convince him."

"Just don't do it on my account," Monica said. "I don't care what that man thinks of me. I just don't want him going after my employees."

Sully shifted. "I can't lie, I was pretty skeptical about psychics at first. Cops and investigators have to deal with frauds all the time. Sometimes people are kidding themselves. Sometimes they just want to be close to the drama. I understand why he's skeptical because I was the same way until I met someone who was the real deal."

"In LA?"

He nodded. "It was on a murder case, and it was someone kind of like Val. She wasn't object specific, but she could read a scene, pick up pieces of what had happened. Emotions. Spoken words. Stuff like that."

"But no one who had visions?"

"No. Until I learned about you ladies, I wouldn't have believed anyone about visions."

"Why are visions so unbelievable?" Monica stood and started clearing the table. "No one questions ghosts. Or freaky energy readings. Even the psychic-friendly scientist friend of Mark's questioned whether visions were possible."

"It seems more mystical maybe?" Robin stood and went to the kitchen to help. "Don't take it personally, Monica. You've done more to help this investigation than any of us. We can only help after a tragedy has happened. You might have a chance to prevent it from occurring at all."

"But only if people believe me." And only if she could interpret this new kind of visions she was having. They were more than the snapshots of the future she'd gotten in the past. She had to interpret symbols and vague clues. "I just don't know if the information I'm getting is going to be able to stop whatever is coming."

Because it was coming. Something dark and angry was approaching Glimmer Lake. She felt it; the ghosts felt it.

Monica had to figure out the clues, or the whole town could be destined for tragedy.

CHAPTER 17

*J*ake poked his head out from under the sink. "Yeah, you're going to need a new garbage disposal."

Monica groaned. "Seriously? Of all the things happening right now, I don't need another one. You can't fix it?"

He smiled a little. "Mom, this thing is a relic. It's probably older than me. Just get a new one. They're not that expensive, and I can put it in for you."

Monica sighed. "Fine. I think it's the original one to the house, so you're probably right." The house had been relatively new when she and Gilbert had bought it when Jake was five, but "relatively new" in Glimmer Lake just meant it had been built in the previous ten years. "Do they have them at the hardware store, or will I need to go into Bridger?"

He crawled out from the cabinet. "Tell you what. I'll run by and see what they have. If they have the right one, I'll grab it. If they don't, I'll call Caleb and see if he can bring one up from Bridger this weekend. Does that work?"

She pinched his chin. "You are an excellent child and I'm glad I fed you."

Jake chuckled. "Me too. Even if there was too much spinach."

"It's good for you."

He groaned. "It's not. It's so gross. And you know what?"

She lifted a hand. "I don't want to—"

"I never eat spinach now. I eat no leafy greens at all. And I'm perfectly healthy."

She pinched his waist. "That is only because your mother fed you spinach every week when you were growing!"

Jake laughed and ducked away from her pinching fingers. "Sam and Sylvia agree with me. Caleb only eats it because he's a mama's boy."

A mama's boy who was built like a tank. "Did you get them presents?"

"They said they didn't want them."

It was the twins' birthday that weekend, and all her boys were coming into town for the day for a barbecue on Saturday. Sylvia would be video-chatting in for the dinner, probably complaining about not having any decent tri-tip in Berkeley.

"I don't care that they say they don't want presents, it's their birthday. They secretly want presents."

"Fine." He frowned. "I'll get them both a bottle of scotch."

"That's not a present."

"Sure it is." He started putting the tools back in Gil's old toolbox, which he kept in the laundry room. "Are you going to do something about this fire inspector?"

Kara had heard some of Gabe and Monica's argument in

her office. Not the vision part, thank God, but she could hear that Gabe was suspicious.

"What do you think I should do? If anyone questions me, I'll show them the security-system logs. I can't do anything else."

"Can't you call Dad's captain or something?"

"Sweetie, I think that's an overreaction." Despite what she'd said to Gabe the last time they talked, Monica had no intention of pulling a "do you know who I am?" She was fairly sure that Gabe investigating her would go absolutely zero places. She wasn't that exciting.

"I don't think it's an overreaction." Jake looked a little pissed. "This wouldn't even be a question if Dad were still alive. I mean, what does this guy think? That a middle-aged mom of four is going to randomly start fires all over town?"

"I don't know whether to be happy you are so sure of my innocence or pissed that you think I'm incapable of breaking the law."

He narrowed his eyes. "Don't joke about this."

Monica laughed. "Sweetie, why not? You think they're going to what? Railroad me? Who would arrest me? Sully? He knows I'm not an arsonist." She walked over, hugged him, and patted his back. "I'm going to ignore this. The man has nothing. I told him that those blankets are widely available and go missing all the time."

Jake hugged her back hard. "Just be careful."

"I will be. You be careful too. I'm more concerned that someone has been breaking into the boathouse. We need to do something about the security system down there."

Jake let her go and stepped back. "The only people who

have keys are me and Kara. I haven't noticed anything... out of place, I guess?"

"Be honest—that place is not organized. Would you even notice if someone stole something smaller than a boat?"

"Fair point."

"Speaking of Kara." Monica picked up the carafe and poured herself more coffee. "What's going on there?"

"Are you asking as my employer or as my mother?" Jake tried to hide his smile, but Monica caught it.

"As your mother of course."

"Then none of your business." He grinned and ducked away from the dish towel she threw at him.

"Fine! Then I'm asking as your employer."

"Nope. Doesn't work that way."

She picked up her phone and started to text someone. "Okay."

Jake's eyes went wide. "What are you doing?"

"None of your business." She was texting Eve about making her an iced coffee so it was ready when she got back to Russell House.

"Who are you texting?" Jake reached for her phone, but she kept it out of his reach.

"See you back at work," Monica said, walking toward her purse by the front door. "Take some of the leftovers if you want." She'd made chile verde that morning as a thank-you for Jake checking her garbage disposal on his lunch break. It was his favorite.

"Mom, you better not be asking Kara about us."

She would literally never do that, but she kind of enjoyed tormenting her oldest with the thought.

"Mom?"

"Lock up and don't be too long. Don't forget you have a fishing trip at five."

"Mom!"

THE AFTERNOON at Russell House had been routine. It was a Thursday, so guests checked in for long weekends and no one checked out. The hotel would be busy through the end of the month, but once Labor Day weekend was over, things were looking dead.

Monica was brainstorming promotion ideas at the kitchen table and picking at leftovers while she drank a cold beer. She heard the doorbell ring and looked at her phone, but no one had texted they were coming over. She switched over to the app that controlled her house system and checked the front door camera.

Sully and Gabe.

Was that heartburn? Monica snapped her notebook closed and stood, walking to the door and opening it just as Gabe had his hand raised to knock.

"Yes?" She crossed her arms over her chest.

She'd forgotten she was wearing an old V-neck shirt with the neck all stretched out until Gabe's eyes fell to her cleavage and got stuck.

"Can I help you?" She didn't move. Let him look. Let him wonder. He wouldn't be seeing any of it.

She might have hiked her boobs up. Just a little.

"Hey, Monica." Sully sounded bored. "You know this is routine, right?"

"Sure." She moved to open the door all the way and let them in. "You want a beer?"

"Still on duty."

"Right."

Gabe still hadn't managed to speak, but he entered her home and scanned it with narrowed eyes. She saw his eyes catch on the wall of family pictures in the entryway.

Gilbert and Monica on their twentieth anniversary. The kids' high school graduation pictures. Sylvia's college graduation. Kids riding dirt bikes and building tree houses. There was a little of everything on that wall, twenty-five years of life with a man she adored, raising four excellent kids.

She looked at Gabe and remembered the look of disdain when she told him about her visions. *Guess you only get lucky once.*

"Why don't we sit at the kitchen table." She pulled out her chair and sat down, reached for her beer, took a drink. Then she folded her hands and waited.

Monica would be damned if she offered them any information. She wasn't going to make it easy on them.

Gabe cleared his throat. "Thank you, Mrs. Velasquez. We had a few questions related to the three recent fires in the area."

"Should I have a lawyer present?"

Whatever Gabe had been about to say, he swallowed it. "Wha—? I don't... I don't think—"

Sully cleared his throat. "You were home the night of the first and the third fire, right?"

"Yes. I called you right after I woke up from the visions to warn you. I was home in bed."

Sully barreled through, ignoring Gabe's infuriated expression. "And the second fire? Where were you then?"

"I was actually with Chief Peralta all that morning. We were going over some changes we're making to the exterior of Russell House to create more defensible space before fire season."

Sully's eyebrows went up. "Oh yeah? What are you doing?"

"We're going to clear some trees along the back; then I'm gonna have Sam and Caleb build a gazebo and kind of a seating area around that area the porch overlooks. Add in some woodland-garden kind of plantings. Some flower beds. Very rustic. Kind of a craftsman look to fit the style of the house."

"That's a great idea. Good for parties and stuff, right?"

"That's what I'm thinking."

"Nice."

Gabe was glaring at both of them. "Can we get back to the fires please?"

"Sure." Sully turned back to Monica. "Is there anyone who can verify your movements during those times?"

"You mean other than Chief Peralta?"

"Was he in bed with you when you called me? Or just the one time at Russell House?"

"For fuck's sake, Sully!" Gabe looked ready to explode. "Can you take this a little bit seriously?"

"I told you I believe her, Gabe. You're the one who wanted to do this."

"Just because your girlfriend thinks she's psychic—"

"My girlfriend doesn't 'think she's psychic'; she's a veri-fied psychometric whose abilities were triggered by the same accident that triggered Monica's. And since I've seen the value of listening to Monica in the past—like the two fires she fucking predicted *this month*—I'm not so narrow-minded that I write her off."

"You expect me to believe she can see the future?" Gabe turned to Monica. "Okay, predict something. Predict something I can actually verify."

"Someone is going to burn down the entire town if we don't stop them," Monica said quietly. "Verify that."

Gabe shut his mouth.

"I've seen the same vision three times now. Every time I close my eyes these days, I remember it. The entire town of Glimmer Lake burning up. It has something to do with a redwood cabin. That was the dream I had before the third fire. I dreamed about a different cabin than the one that was burned. There's something different about it. It's old, and it's by a waterfall or a creek. It's made of square-cut redwood logs. The roof is covered in moss and falling down in parts. The fire will start in the underbrush, like the others, but this one will reach up to the top of the canopy. It's remote. Way off all the fire roads. By the time you get to it, it'll be too big to stop."

Gabe's face was pale, and Sully's was grim.

"Have you seen anything new?" Sully asked.

"Not since the last one I told you about. Has Robin found any cabins like that? Does the city have records? There's a small sequoia grove nearby."

"So far she hasn't found any record of a cabin like you're describing. Once she's narrowed down the cabins that were built before the 1940s, she'll look at the county records. Those probably go back further, but it's still a crapshoot.

Unless a surveyor went out there, there'll be no way of knowing who owned what land. People didn't exactly ask for permits back in the forties."

Gabe looked at Sully. "Why the forties?"

"Because that's when Grimmer was flooded," Monica said. "All the cabins that have burned—the Alison cabin, the Lewis cabin, and the most recent one—they were all built by families from Grimmer."

"Grimmer is the town that was here before the dam?"

"It wasn't here," Sully said. "It was in the bottom of Grimmer Canyon, which is now the bottom of Glimmer Lake. The cabins people built around here were all hunting cabins or seasonal summer houses for when it got hot in the valley."

"And you think the arsonist is targeting these old cabins?"

"They're remote," Monica said. "They're abandoned for the most part. Robin was going to try to find a list of cabins built during that time. She can talk to ghosts."

Gabe rolled his eyes. "So there's three of you."

"Yep." She opened her computer and turned it around so Sully could see the screen. "Here's the security log for the house. The tracker is attached to my car keys, so you can see anytime I leave the house or come back with my keys, because the system automatically disarms when I approach."

"Okay, so this tells us when you come and go." He scanned it and looked at Gabe. "Oh look, she was home all night the two nights in question."

"Unless you think I'm leaving my minivan here and riding my broomstick into the night to set fires at abandoned cabins around Glimmer Lake."

"Fine." Gabe stood and stuffed his phone in his pocket.

"This is useless. Email Sully a copy of that report and let's go."

"Okay." Monica rose and showed Gabe and Sully to the door. "So nice seeing you again, Chief Peralta."

Gabe said nothing.

Sully patted her shoulder. It was the closest he really came to hugging. "See ya tomorrow. I'll tell Val to call if she picks up anything new tomorrow on the evidence."

"Sounds good. I'll let you know if I see anything weird tonight."

"Thanks."

Gabe stood by Sully's truck, fuming.

Monica really wished he wasn't so handsome. It was just annoying at this point. When Sully turned his back, she crossed her arms under her boobs again, wiggled her fingers at Gabe, and mouthed *Bye*.

His jaw twitched. "You should trim your trees."

"Is that some kind of weird fire-inspector innuendo? I haven't heard that one before."

His expression never wavered when he pointed to the cedars that hung over her porch. "One hundred feet. You should cut them back."

"Sure, I'll get right on that at..." She looked at her phone. "Eight o'clock at night."

Monica turned her back and walked back into the house, making sure to put just a little extra swagger in her step. She could practically feel Gabe's eyes burning her backside.

Good.

Maybe she'd found her new middle-age hobby: annoying Gabe Peralta.

Who knows? Could be fun.

CHAPTER 18

*A*fter a night of fitful sleep, Monica went in to Russell House with a massive headache. She was annoyed by the late-night interview. Annoyed that despite his rudeness, she'd had *another* sex vision about Chief McDoubty-Pants that left her aroused and angry at the same time, and annoyed that someone was trying to set fire to her very nice hometown.

And doubly annoyed that Gabe was right, and she really did need to cut her cedar trees back. She was dialing the tree company when she pulled into her parking spot.

"Yeah. It's Pete."

Monica was relieved to hear a familiar voice. "Hey, Pete. It's Monica Velasquez."

"Monica! How you doing?" He cleared his throat. "Let me guess, you want some trees cut back."

She laughed a little. "Me and everyone else in town, right?"

"I tell ya, I called folks from Bridger City to come take some of these calls. I can't keep up. Everyone's finally cutting back those trees they've been meaning to take care of for five years now."

"Guilty as charged. I think the last time we got them cut back around the house was when Gil was alive."

"Sure." Pete was about seventy years old and he had known Gil. Everyone had known Gil. "Whatya need, hon?"

"I do need some trims around my house, but I'm actually calling about the hotel, so it's a bigger job. How soon can you fit me in?"

"For a big job, I'll make time." Clearing big trees paid a lot better than trimming back branches. "How many we talking about?"

She tried not to cringe when she said it. "About twenty."

Pete whistled. "You cutting around back?"

"Yeah. So it's dense and a lot more than what we needed when we built the ropes course."

He gave her some nonspecific muttering and a whistle. "I'm gonna need to look at my calendar and talk to the kid before I can give you a date. Probably not before end of the month at the earliest."

"The kid" was Pete's son Steve, and he'd graduated two years ahead of Monica. "As soon as you can get it in, I would really appreciate it." She had an idea. "And as a bonus for fitting us in, I'll give you and Dorothy and Steve and Taylor a couple of rooms at the hotel next month. You can take a weekend and let someone else do the cooking and cleaning."

"Is that so?" Pete sounded impressed. "Well, I might be able to squeeze you in the end of next week if something opens up."

Score. "That would be awesome."

She saw Eve approaching the car with a steaming cup of coffee. "Just give me a call and let me know. Thanks, Pete."

"You bet."

She opened her car door and was met with the scent of sweet, sweet caffeine. "Eve, you're a goddess. How did you know?"

"I saw you out the window still in the car, and Val mentioned this morning that Sully and Gabe had been over to the house last night." She presented the cup to Monica. "Your hazelnut latte, my friend."

Was it too dramatic to weep with joy? Did she care? She took the coffee. "You are my favorite person today. Well, you're up there with Pete the tree guy, but only if he fits us in next week; otherwise, you're definitely my favorite."

Eve nodded. "I'll take it. The tree service for my condo association told us that they can't come until next month. People are taking matters into their own hands."

"Oh, that's not good." She grabbed her purse and exited the relative safety of the minivan.

"Loooootta weekend warriors with chain saws out there. I hope the ER in Bridger is prepared to sew on some fingers this month."

She locked her car and walked toward the kitchen. "Anything else happening right now?"

"Not much. Jake and Kara are down in the boathouse."

Monica wiggled her eyebrows. "For business reasons, I'm assuming."

"Ha!" Eve grinned. "Jake said something about ordering a new security system for the boathouse, and Kara said she'd need to take a look at it, and I haven't seen them in about half an hour."

Should she be annoyed? Monica sipped her coffee and felt the irritation drift away. "It's fine. If they're gone another fifteen minutes, I'll call him."

"I have to say you're really understanding about all this." Eve looked impressed. "They are your employees."

"I know that, but he's my kid and I like her a lot. Have you noticed anything falling behind at the main house?"

Eve shook her head. "Not even a little. If anything, Kara has been working more lately, not less. She seems kind of stressed, to be honest. The only time she looks relaxed is when Jake is around."

"As long as he doesn't screw this up, I'm not going to make a big deal about it." She shrugged. "They're young and it's Glimmer Lake. Where else are they going to meet people other than work?"

"Good point."

She sat in her office, drinking her coffee and checking emails.

Still no new reservations for September.

An email from their insurance company, talking about fire safety and precautions.

An email from the winery who was very enthusiastic about creating some special events for Russell House. That was good news.

Someone tapped on her door. "Come in."

Kara popped her head in the office. "You have a minute?"

"Do you?"

The young woman's laugh was high and tight. Monica looked up. Eve was right. She looked stressed. "Hey, sweetie, come have a seat." It was impossible for Monica not to feel maternal. Kara was the same age as her own daughter. "You okay?"

"Yeah!" She quickly schooled her expression. "I'm great. I just wanted to suggest something for the security at the boathouse."

Monica sat back and really looked at her. There were faint lines under her eyes. Her jaw was tensed, and her nails were bitten down to the quick. "Are you sure you're okay?"

Kara sighed. "I'm just... Insomnia has always been a problem for me. My whole life. I've been having a really bad spell over the past month, probably just worried about work and the busier schedule with end-of-summer rush." She held up a hand. "I promise it has not affected my work."

"I know it hasn't; I just don't want you to burn out."

"I won't. I promise. I think after this month is over, I'm going to ask for a week off or so if that's okay. Maybe visit some friends at the coast. Just get a change in scenery, you know?"

The tension around her eyes was so obvious now that she was looking, Monica wanted to rub the girl's temples and force Kara to take a nap on the couch.

"If you feel like it needs to be this month, you better tell me." Monica had no idea how she would juggle the extra duties, but she'd find a way. She didn't want a sweet girl who was her best employee to burn out her second year on the job.

"I promise I will. But for now I wanted to recommend this security system for the boathouse. I saw it at the electronics store in Bridger, and I think it's perfect for older structures." Kara held out her tablet. "It's connected entirely by Bluetooth, so you don't have to run any new wiring."

"No new wiring? Tell me more."

Monica reclined on a large granite rock jutting up from the lakeside. It was more comfortable than it looked. Then again, she'd been scrambling on granite rocks her whole life, and she had a lot of padding in back to make her comfortable.

Yes, her ass was comfortable. It was just her knees that would make her pay later.

"Anything?"

Robin sat across from her on the beach in a folding chair, her eyes halfway closed and her hand moving over the page. "It's not like making a phone call, Monica."

She knew that. She did know that. But it was nearly sunset, and it was getting cold. She'd put all her electronics away—Robin had said something about electronics irritating ghosts—and she was trying not to think about all the junk emails in her inbox that she needed to delete.

She was over three thousand now. It was getting ridiculous. She had no time to go through every junk email that was sent her way. Was there a way to just delete everything prior to a certain day?

That was probably a bad idea.

Was it?

If she hadn't opened it or missed it in six months, did she really need to keep it?

The idea of deleting every unread email in her inbox gave Monica a dangerous thrill. She should do it. She should just go for it and throw caution to the wind. What did she have to—

"She's here." Robin's voice was soft.

Monica sat up slowly. "Is she alone?"

Robin had been trying to call Bethany, but the little girl hadn't been cooperating.

"Bethany?" Robin's voice was soft, soothing. It was the voice of a mother. "Hello, sweetheart. I think we know why you're scared, and we want to help."

Robin was quiet for a long moment.

"Robin?"

"She says we can't help. She says that it's all going to happen again because she's angry and Bethany doesn't know why. She never tells Bethany anything."

Robin and Monica exchanged a look. Being the parents of multiple children, they recognized the tone.

"Are you talking about your big sister?" Robin said. "Bethany, are you talking about Rosemarie?"

"We know about the fire," Monica said softly. "We know about the fire that took you and your sister and your daddy, Bethany. I am so sorry. I know you were probably scared."

Robin murmured, "She's listening to you, keep going."

"We know you were probably so scared, Bethany, and we don't want you to have to remember that. But we also don't want other little girls in Glimmer Lake to be scared. I have dreams." Monica took a deep breath. "I have horrible dreams about what is going to happen. We just want to keep everyone safe."

Robin had tears in her eyes. "She says no one kept Rosemarie safe, but Rosemarie kept her safe. She didn't mean for the fire to happen the way it did."

Monica's heart broke. "Was your father hurtful to your sister, Bethany?"

Robin whispered, "All she's saying is 'He drank a lot.'"

This was awful. This was so much worse than anything

they'd discovered before. The idea of someone hurting a child —even one dead for eighty years—made Monica's stomach churn.

Robin said, "She says Rosemarie was quiet for a long time. She thought she'd left, but then she came back and she won't tell Bethany what's wrong."

"When did she come back?" Monica was curious. What had been the catalyst for all this? When had things changed?

"She can't be sure. Time isn't the same. It was when the snow was on the ground."

So at least five months. Or five months and a year. Ghosts were notoriously bad at judging time.

"Okay, so Rosemarie is back. But Rosemarie isn't starting the fires. Does Bethany know who is?"

Robin shook her head. "I honestly don't think she does."

Monica had an idea. "Does she know about the cabin?" She turned to face the tree line Robin had been talking toward. "Do you know about the old redwood cabin by the waterfall, Bethany? With moss on the roof. The cabin with square logs and two windows on either side of a green door."

A shiver passed through Monica, a coursing cold streak that ran up her spine and settled on her neck, pressing against her and making her head pound. What was that? She let out a small gasp, and the cold entered her throat.

"Monica?"

"Something is wrong. Is anyone else here?"

Robin looked at her with wide eyes. "I think so. I feel something, but I can't see anything." Her head swung around to the edge of the trees. "Bethany?"

Monica felt the cold stiffen her neck before it fled as quickly as it had come. "It's gone."

"And so is Bethany," Robin said. "Damn, that was weird."

"Very weird."

Robin stood and stretched, flexing her knees gently. She'd been sitting for a long time. "That was the most information we've gotten from her though."

"Yeah." Monica stood and shook the shivers from her shoulders. "Funny thing though, I'm pretty sure I just met Rosemarie. And Bethany is right. She is pissed."

CHAPTER 19

*V*al pressed her fingers to her lips, absorbing the information Monica and Robin had related. "Corbin Sanger was abusing his daughter?"

Robin nodded. "We're pretty sure. We don't know how—"

"We don't need to," Val said. "We know it made her angry enough to burn down their family home."

They were sitting in Monica's living room, and she had the gas fire turned on. The summer night had a hard chill, and Monica was praying that meant an early fall was coming, along with possible rain.

"Arson can be a result of trauma," Monica said softly. "We read that."

"But a ghost isn't burning these buildings," Val said. "We also know that."

"But maybe someone else is in the same situation," Robin said. "Maybe there's something that Rosemarie saw or something she knows about what's happening in Glimmer Lake right now."

They were a close-knit community, and Monica hated the thought that any child in Glimmer Lake might be the victim of abuse and no one knew. Gil had been a first responder, which meant he'd had to go to more than one scene of domestic violence. They left him in an incredibly dark mood. The thought of child abuse of any kind was so outside Monica's experience she had trouble wrapping her mind around it.

Even her own parents, who hadn't been emotionally supportive, wouldn't have dreamed of laying a hand on her or her sister.

"People can hide things," Val said. "If there's a local kid in trouble and Rosemarie's ghost discovered it—"

"But what does that have to do with the redwood cabin?" Monica asked. "She came at me—and that felt very targeted. Very deliberate. She came at me when I mentioned the cabin."

"Maybe the abuse happened there?" Robin said.

"Or maybe that was her safe place," Val said. "Maybe that was where she ran away to and she doesn't want anyone finding it."

"Could that be what changed?" Robin asked. "Could that be the catalyst? Someone finding her cabin?"

Monica jotted something down in her notebook. "We need to find out if anyone is building anything new right now and if that building might threaten this place. I feel like—for good or for bad—the cabin I'm dreaming about is the key."

"But how could the person starting the fires know anything about all that? Do you think they're a medium like Robin?" Val asked. "Are they communicating with Rosemarie?"

"I've never seen Rosemarie," Robin said. "At least I don't

think I have. Other than Bethany, most of the ghosts in town are more recent. I haven't seen another girl or a young woman dressed the same style as her."

Monica said, "The feeling I got from Rosemarie tonight— if that was her that touched me—was angry and cold. Could a spirit be too scattered to talk? Too angry?"

Robin nodded slowly. "I don't know any other mediums, but I've found some message boards online that have helped me figure stuff out. From what I've read, not all spirits have a good sense of their own identity. Only those who do take form into what we see as ghosts. So it's possible she's not... formed the way Bethany is."

"But I still felt her," Monica said. "So what if she's communicating with the arsonist another way? A way that person might not even know?"

Val's eyes went wide. "Are you saying you think Rosemarie's spirit is... What? Possessing someone?"

Monica sorted through what they knew about the fires. About the blankets from the boathouse. The age of the cabins. "Val, the blankets you felt from the sites that burned, didn't you say that whoever was touching them was confused? Disoriented?"

"Yes." Robin sat up straight. "That's it. I think that's it."

Val cocked her head. "Seriously? Someone is possessed? Isn't that, like, movie stuff?"

"Isn't being psychic 'movie stuff'?" Monica said. "Think about it, Val. It's the only thing that makes sense. Whoever is starting these fires is being influenced by Rosemarie. She may not even be aware that she's doing it. That's why she's so confused."

Val crossed her arms. "Okay, say you're both right.

Someone in town is being... possessed by Rosemarie's spirit and starting fires, trying to destroy the last of Glimmer Lake. What the hell do we tell Sully? How does that help him find out who's actually doing this?"

"And why?" Robin said. "Why now? Why these places? The families who owned these cabins weren't the ones who hurt her."

"No," Monica said. "But maybe they knew. Maybe the whole town knew and they didn't do anything." She stared into the flickering blue and gold flames jumping in the fireplace. "Maybe that's why she wants to burn it all."

THAT NIGHT MONICA's dream was even more vivid. It was clearer, more sensory. She could feel the heat of the fire on her skin. Smell the smoke. She walked down the center of an ever-burning Main Street and turned left at the Ponderosa Lodge Hotel, which was also in flames as happy families pulled up to the check-in.

Tucked behind the lodge on a quiet street was the Glimmer Lake library, which was one of the oldest structures in town. Amazingly, though everything around the library was enveloped in flames, the library itself was a small oasis of calm.

She stepped on the porch, and immediately everything fell away. Monica walked through the doors and saw a very different library than the one she remembered.

It wasn't a library at all. It was a house, a small square structure that smelled like woodsmoke and wet leather. In the corner, with her back to the room, was a slim, willow-built girl with light brown hair braided down to her waist.

"Lavender's green, dilly dilly…"

The song was barely over a whisper. The girl tended to a pot on the stove, but unlike the pervasive smell of woodsmoke, she couldn't smell what was cooking.

Lavender's green, dilly dilly,
Lavender's blue
You must love me, dilly dilly,
'cause I love you.

The song resonated through the air like a string plucked in an empty room. It was a soft, clear sound poured directly into her ear. Monica walked like a ghost through the simple home.

She focused on the bending figure. The girl leaned down mechanically and fed the fire, opening the black grate, reaching for a quartered log, then feeding it to the hungry flames.

The girl's hand hovered over the glowing panel, and her voice hitched on the second verse of the song.

In a second, Monica knew exactly what she was thinking.

It would be so easy.

So easy.

It's just me and him.

So easy…

"Rose!"

When the blow came to the side of the girl's head, Monica felt it in her temple, a blinding, shocking blast of pain wrapped in a meaty fist.

"Whadid I tell you yesterday?" he slurred.

Monica watched her carefully set the fire poker down.

"It's past time I did more," the girl said.

"Tha's right."

While the man railed at Rosemarie, the girl turned and looked in the corner where Monica waited and observed. She slowly raised her eyes to Monica's, and Monica could see the tears of rage and anger gathering in the corners.

Her face was never clear. Monica saw eyes and shadows, but somehow the girl's face remained obscured.

"Do you see?" The voice came directly to Monica's ear.

She was frozen, staring at the girl who reached for the jar of clear fluid sitting on a table near a lamp.

"It all needs to burn." The voice came her ear again. "Burn burn burn until he's gone. Lavender's green; it grows again. Lavender's blue, blue, blue like me."

The girl's fingers curled around the mouth of the jar, and she kept her eyes on Monica as she picked it up.

"You must love me." Without another warning, she hurled the clear jar toward the fire, where it exploded in a ball of yellow flame. In the space of a second the entire house was engulfed in flames. Monica felt the heat on her skin and tasted the smoke on her tongue. Her eyes stung and something outside was screaming.

Screaming.

She sat up in bed and smelled the scent before she even opened her eyes.

Fire.

The fire alarm was the screaming she'd heard in her vision. The smoke was real. The flames were real.

Fire!

Monica swung her legs over the side of the bed and felt for a pair of shoes. Any shoes.

Her brain went into the automatic rehearsal of a hundred family fire drills. Cover your arms and legs. Cover your feet. She poured the glass of water by the bed over a headband and fitted it over her mouth, then grabbed her phone and stuffed it in her pocket before she ran for the door.

She felt the doorknob and it was cool. She carefully pulled the door open and immediately saw smoke filling the hall. She couldn't see flames in the house, but she heard something fall on the roof.

The trees.

The kids!

Monica threw open the door to Jake's room, but it wasn't right. All the furniture was gone. Where was his bed? She rubbed the sleep from her eyes, the piercing scream of the fire alarm making her temple pulse.

Shit! No kids. The kids were grown. She was in the house by herself. Her go bag was already in the car. She didn't see any flames inside the house; but she heard things falling on the roof.

Monica ran to the kitchen. The smoke was thicker, and she saw a red glow through the window over the sink. The outside of the house was burning, not the inside. She had to get out as quickly as possible and call the fire department.

Out first.

Go go go.

She grabbed her purse, her keys, and her computer. She ran for the garage door and felt the doorknob before she opened it.

Cool.

She threw open the door and smacked the button on the

wall to open both doors. The minute she did, flames flew up and smoke rushed into the garage.

Fire was everywhere. It surrounded the base of the house, reaching up and grabbing for anything edible. The smoke burned her eyes, but she could see the other side of the house through the black smoke filling the garage. There were flames there too.

She looked at her trusty minivan, filled with her most precious pictures and mementos from her kids' childhoods. She looked at the flames falling from the open garage doors.

"We can make it." She flung open the door and started the minivan, making sure the windows were firmly closed before she put the car in reverse and hit the gas.

Monica was always a careful backer. She inched her way out of parking spots so carefully it made her children groan.

She didn't inch that night. The pedal hit the floor as she backed out of the burning garage with tires screeching, up the driveway, bouncing into the quiet cul-de-sac where her house was situated. As soon as she was clear of the house, she reached for her phone.

"Nine one one. What's your emergency?"

"My house is on fire." She stated her address. "My house... It's all burning."

"Ma'am, are you outside the house? Is anyone inside? Have you evacuated your family and pets? Please wait for the firefighters to arrive. Someone already called and there are engines on the way. Ma'am, can you respond please? Do you need medical attention? Ma'am?"

Parked in the safety of the street with her car running, Monica couldn't bring herself to answer the poor operator. She was looking down on the cozy house where she and

Gilbert had raised four kids. The trees were burning, but that couldn't explain the unbroken line of fire running around the base of the house.

There was nothing natural about this blaze. It looked like someone had poured a can of gasoline around the perimeter of her house and dropped a match. Every inch was burning from the outside in.

Someone pounded on her window. "Monica!"

She jumped and put a hand over her heart. It was her neighbor Steve Hanson.

He pounded on her window. "Are you okay? I called 911! We could hear the alarms from inside our house."

She rolled down the window and shut off the car. "Yeah. I'm okay."

"Jake at his place? Just you, right?"

Monica nodded. "I better call him." Oh God. Her house. She started to cry. Sylvia had never cleaned out her room. All her stuff was still there. Sam and Caleb still had some things in the attic.

She sniffed and felt the tears come faster.

"Is there anything I can do?" Steve opened the door and helped Monica out. "Jessica's grabbing blankets." He looked over his shoulder. "Do you want a blanket? Or a sweatshirt?"

Steve left her with Jessica and ran down to the side of his house. He turned his hose on full blast and aimed it at the side of her house.

It was a little like pissing in the wind, but she understood the impulse.

More neighbors came. More hoses pointed at her house, wetting down the bushes and flowerbeds. Monica stood at the edge of her driveway, wrapped in Jessica and Steve's blanket, her sockless feet in the work loafers that had been sitting by the bed.

She stood at the end of her driveway and watched her house burn.

Then she turned her face to the woods and searched.

Are you there, Rosemarie?

Someone was there. She saw a movement behind the shed where the tree line started. She took a few steps closer, and for a second the fire lit up a face she recognized as clearly as one of her own children.

Monica blinked.

When she opened her eyes, there was nothing but darkness and she could hear sirens in the distance.

"Monica?"

She walked down her driveway as the engines approached. She could hear them through the narrow Glimmer Lake streets as she walked closer to the trees.

"Monica, what are you doing?" She felt hands on her shoulders, trying to bring her back, but she ignored them.

Someone was there in the trees. She'd seen them.

Someone impossible.

Someone who looked as horrified and confused as Monica felt.

Rosemarie, what have you done?

CHAPTER 20

*M*onica sat on the edge of Mark and Robin's couch while Mark made coffee in the kitchen and Robin sat next to her, looking as incredulous as Monica felt.

"No." Robin shook her head. "How? Why? Are you positive?"

Monica blew her nose. She'd taken a shower, but her sinuses were still angry with her, and her tissue looked like she'd been snorting charcoal. "You think I'm seeing things?"

"You were in shock."

"You think I want to even consider this?" Monica cleared her throat. "You think I want to even consider Kara is the one starting these fires?"

The face in the forest had been clear as day. Her own manager. Her son's new girlfriend. The sweetest, hardest-working young woman Monica knew.

"I feel like I'm accusing one of my own kids," Monica whispered. "But I saw her. She ran into the trees. Why would she do that?"

"Did she look...?" Robin shrugged. "I don't know. What did she look like?"

"She looked confused and upset. I only saw her for a second, but I think she was crying."

Robin sat back on her couch and covered her face with both hands. "Rosemarie has possessed Kara and is making her start fires?"

"It sounds insane!" Monica hissed. "I know. I know it sounds insane. I was expecting... I don't know what I was expecting, but not this."

"It sounds crazy." Robin shook her head. "I don't understand. You see her every day. Has there been any indication—?"

"Trust me, I have been racking my brain. The only thing I can think of is she said the other day that she'd been having trouble with insomnia. That she's always had it and it was bad right now. But other than that, she's been completely normal. Absolutely no indication that she was hiding anything." *Not that she spoke about her personal life.* "Not even a hint that she had any idea what was going on when people asked about the fires." *Maybe because she was as confused as the rest of them.*

"This does explain the blankets from the boathouse though. She's down there all the time for work."

"With Jake." She groaned again. "What am I going to tell Jake? What am I going to tell Sully?"

Robin rocked back and forth. "Do we have to tell Sully?"

"We have to."

"But Kara—"

"Is in danger." Monica stopped her. "She's in danger from this as much as anyone else. She clearly doesn't know what's going on. She could light herself on fire completely by accident. She probably feels like she's going insane, Robin. We have to find her."

"But they'll arrest her," Robin said. "And it's not her fault."

"I don't know what we're going to do, but we have to tell Sully. We need his help to find her before she hurts anyone else or herself."

Mark brought two mugs of coffee into the living room. "I've got a cream and sugar and a cream only."

Mark handed the sweetened one to Monica before he sat in the chair next to Robin's side of the couch and gave her the coffee with cream. "You think you saw Kara? That makes no sense."

"It does if Rosemarie is somehow taking advantage of Kara's insomnia," Robin said. "Maybe she's the cause of it. Maybe she can influence Kara more easily when she's low on sleep."

"Sleep deprivation can seriously mess with your mind," Mark said. "There are all sorts of studies about it. It's one of the fastest ways to break someone down."

"So if we put together what Bethany said about Rosemarie becoming more active 'when the snow was on the ground,' that fits with Kara. She arrived just before Christmas of last year."

"There was snow on the ground," Mark said. "What's so special about Kara?" He glanced at Monica. "You checked her references, right?"

"Yeah, of course. I called all of them. She had three different employers listed. She's been working in hotels since she was seventeen. No problems. No record. Nothing."

"This isn't about Kara," Robin said. "This is about Rose-marie and what happened to her."

"But you have to wonder why she targeted Kara," Mark said. "Is there something special about her?"

There were a million things special about her, and none of them lined up with Kara being a serial arsonist. She was friendly and loved socializing. She was cautious and responsible. She was careful with things and with people.

"What am I going to tell Jake?" Monica whispered. "I think he may love this girl."

Robin put a hand over hers. "I don't know, but we'll figure this out."

Monica ached. She heard a car pull into the drive and had the sneaking suspicion she recognized her son's Jeep engine.

Mark went to the door and let Jake in. He walked directly to his mom and pulled her up and into a hug. "Mami, it's gonna be okay." He held her tightly and rocked back and forth. "I just came from the house and they got most of the fire out before it even reached the inside."

Monica held her giant little boy and started to sniffle.

"Don't cry." Jake squeezed her tighter. "The garage isn't in good shape, and Sam and Caleb's room got a little singed 'cause it's on the corner, but there's more water damage than smoke damage. I promise. Dad's ugly old chair even survived." He squeezed her again. "So stop crying, okay? It's going to be fine."

Monica *couldn't* stop crying. None of this was fine. None of it was going to be fine. She was about to crush her son's heart, and she couldn't even tell him why. It wouldn't make sense to her levelheaded kid, and he'd only think she was losing it.

"Jake, I have to tell you something." She sniffed and pulled back. "I saw someone in the forest. I know there was accelerant used—"

"Gabe Peralta definitely thinks so. The way the perimeter of the house burned—"

She put a finger over his mouth. "Baby, I know. I already know who burned the house."

Jake frowned. "Did you call Sully?"

Mark stood and put a hand on Jake's shoulder. "It's going to seem confusing, but you need to listen."

Jake was looking between Monica and Mark. "What's going on?"

"Jake, I saw..." She cleared her throat. "She was behind the shed, right near the edge of the forest. She just disappeared into the trees, but I saw her."

"Mom, who?" He put his hands on Monica's shoulders. "You're freaking me out. Just tell me so we can call Sully."

"Baby, it was Kara." Her voice barely rose over a whisper. "It was Kara in the forest."

Jake blinked. "Kara what?"

"Kara is the one who burned the house." Monica swallowed the lump in her throat. "I'm pretty sure she's the one who's been setting the other fires too."

Jake laughed. "Mom. Be serious."

Robin put her hand on Jake's shoulder. "She is, Jakey. Trust me, we don't understand it either, but we're sure there's an explanation. This isn't who she is."

"I know!" He shrugged off both Mark and Robin's hands,

stepping away from Monica. "You guys are nuts if you think Kara — She didn't grow up here. She doesn't know where all the abandoned cabins even are, Mom. She's not the one burning them. And she..." Jake stuttered, and Monica could see the first threads of doubt working into his mind. "Just because the blankets they found were from the boathouse, it doesn't mean she did this."

"Has she been upset lately?" Robin asked. "Confused? Called you any mornings when she was lost or confused? Maybe she woke up someplace she didn't know?"

"What?" He glared. "She wouldn't do that. She's staying at Bailey's. She doesn't go out partying; she works, like, all the time. You know that."

"And we don't think she's consciously doing these things," Monica said. "We don't think that. But we think something is happening to her and she's in danger too."

"Are you... Are you insane? What is wrong with you?" Jake's eyes were wide and disbelieving. "You're going to tell Sully and Gabe this crazy theory, aren't you?"

"Baby, we have to."

"No!" He erupted. "She didn't do this! She couldn't. She's too..." His voice caught. "She's the best person I know. She couldn't do this. She couldn't."

Oh God, it hurt so much. There was nothing more awful than seeing your child in pain, and Jake's heart was breaking right in front of her. "Honey, where would she go? We have to find her. We have to make sure she's safe."

"So you can put her in jail?" He stepped back. "Fuck no!"

Mark started toward him. "Jake—"

"No!" Jake raised a hand at Mark, halting the man who'd been like an uncle to him. "You all think she did this, and she didn't. I'm not telling you anything." He turned and walked to the door, turning around before he opened it. "She didn't do this, and I don't know why you're blaming this on her. Kara didn't do anything to you. She told me..." He looked away. "She told me she felt like she found a family here. After a really long time being alone, she found a family. And now you're all turning on her. I don't even know who you are right now, Mom. Or you either, Auntie Robin. She's an innocent person, and you're accusing her of trying to kill you." Jake opened the door and slammed it behind him.

Monica collapsed on the couch. Robin sat next to her and put her arms around Monica's shoulders while Mark sat on her other side. She didn't even try to stop the tears from raining down her face.

"So that went well." Monica wiped her face and covered her eyes with both hands. "He's never going to forgive me, and I completely understand why. None of this makes any sense."

Robin hugged her hard. "You told me the other day that you felt like Kara was one of your own kids."

"Yeah."

"Then you do what any good mom does. You do what is right for them. Even if it hurts. Even if they get mad. Even if it's painful."

Monica met Mark's eyes over Robin's shoulder. "Can you call Sully and Val? Ask them to come to the house. And bring Gabe Peralta with them."

Sully and Val listened to Monica with open mouths and shocked expressions.

"Kara?" Val shook her head. "Not Kara."

"Think about it," Robin said. "The blankets from Russell House. The confusion you kept getting off them every time you read them. The timing that Bethany mentioned. Kara moved to Glimmer Lake just before Christmas."

Gabe leaned back in an easy chair with his arms crossed over his chest. "So this young woman works for you, has no grudges against you—completely good terms there."

Monica nodded.

"But she's had insomnia and been a little scattered. Then you saw her on the edge of your property tonight after you'd inhaled a lot of smoke and you were woken in the middle of the night."

Monica sighed. "You don't think she did it."

"I don't think there's any evidence she did. I don't think she has any motive for it—unless you two are amazing liars—but you're very quick to think this woman burned your house."

"We don't want to, but then why did she run away?"

"What if she witnessed something frightening? What if she was confused too? Maybe that's why she ran." He leaned forward. "Listen, I'm trying to be respectful of all the woo-woo stuff because I know this man isn't a fool." He pointed to Sully. "But I'm still an investigator. I'm going to look for Ms. Sinclair and ask her why she was there tonight, but if she has a good explanation, I'm *not* going to assume she did it because it fits into some narrative you three have dreamed up." He looked at Val, Robin, then finally at Monica. "You're exhausted and traumatized. All these feelings are normal, and you need to get some sleep, not keep brainstorming about all these psychic visions you claim to have."

"We *claim* to have?" Val muttered. "Hey Gabe, you think this shit is fun? You think we want this? You think Monica has a rip-roaring time having nightmares about the town burning down? You think some of these spirits don't scare the shit out of Robin? You think I enjoy picking up stray memories from every Tom, Dick, and Asshole in the mountains? We're not making this shit up, and we don't revel in it. We're not attention seekers, and if you can't tell we're worried as hell for this girl, you're a shitty investigator."

Sully growled, "Val—"

"No! I know he's your friend, but he ought to be observing a little more if you ask me." She pointed to Monica and Robin and glared at Gabe. "You think they're telling you this stuff for shits and giggles? You think they want to get Kara in trouble for some random reason? Look at them!"

Gabe's face was as expressive as a brick wall, but Monica knew he was listening to every word.

"Robin and Monica are worried sick," Mark added quietly. "We're all worried sick. She's not just a random employee, Chief Peralta. Kara and Monica's son are dating pretty seriously. She's like part of the family now."

Val said, "This girl is being harassed and controlled by a malignant spirit that is fucking with her life, targeting her, and doesn't care if she gets caught in the cross fire of her little revenge scheme. You think we're out of our minds and she's probably just a witness? Fine. But find her." Val turned to Sully. "Both of you. Find her before someone gets hurt."

$\mathcal{M}$onica managed to pull herself together with a solid coat of makeup, heavy caffeination, and some of the clothes she'd packed in her car. She hadn't been back to the house, but Mark was going that afternoon to meet the insurance adjustor while Monica was at work.

She pulled up to Russell House, surprised to see Grace's car in the driveway. She walked through the kitchen and grabbed coffee and a hug from Eve before she landed at the front desk where Grace was helping a family with young children check out.

"...and since you paid online, it looks like that's all I need from you." Grace spoke softly. "Thank you so much for your patience."

"Of course." The woman checking out handed her toddler to his father and reached for the receipt Grace handed her in an envelope. "I'm so sorry Kara's not here this morning. She and Jake made this vacation amazing."

"Yeah." The husband had one kid over his shoulder and kept the other from bolting with a finger hooked in the child's collar. "The fishing trip was everything we wanted for the boys' first catch. This is a really special place."

"We'll definitely be back."

Grace smiled graciously. "I am so happy to hear that. I'll pass the message along to Kara when she's feeling better."

"Thanks!"

"Bye. We'll see you again next summer."

One of the little ones said, "Tell Mister Jake thank you for the boat ride."

Monica walked behind the counter and sidled over to Grace, bringing up the morning schedule on the computer.

"Thank you," she said. "I didn't know they'd be checking out so early."

"Long drive to Ventura. They said they wanted to beat traffic." Grace took a deep breath and put an arm around Monica's shoulders. "How are you?"

"I'm okay." She blinked hard and tried not to give in to her emotions. "The roof is pretty damaged, but there's more water damage than fire damage inside from what Jake told Mark last night."

"You tell me and Philip if you need anything. Anything, Monica. I mean it." She patted the counter. "I'll be here the rest of the week. I don't know how to work all the computer things, but Eve helped me out a little, and I can smile and run a credit card when I need to."

"Grace, you don't have to—"

"Nonsense." She cut Monica off with a flick of her diamond-clad wrist. "Am I a partner or not? Now, what do we know about Kara? What is going on with that girl? Robin said she was at the fire? Surely there's some kind of mistake."

Grace had no idea that her daughter and her daughter's

two best friends had developed sudden psychic abilities, and Robin had no intention of filling her in.

Monica picked her words carefully. "We don't know what's going on with Kara. We think there must be some rational explanation, we just don't know what yet. The police are looking for her because Robin and I are worried she might be in some kind of trouble."

"If she's mixed up in any of these arson cases, I'd say she has a lot of trouble." Grace shook her head. "It just doesn't make any sense."

"I know. It makes no sense." She patted Grace's shoulder. "I'm sure Sully will figure it out though. We just need to find her and make sure she's safe."

As if on cue, Jake walked in from the kitchen area, making a beeline for the front desk. He kept his face stoic as he addressed Monica. "I'll be taking off this afternoon to go to the sheriff's office and answer some questions. Kara's missing, and I'm filing a report."

"Good." Monica could tell her soft words surprised him. "Do you need any help with the schedule this afternoon?"

Jake blinked hard. "No. I'm clear all afternoon, and I don't have anything on the schedule until a fishing trip early tomorrow morning with the Randall party."

"Okay. Let me know if you need anything. Or if Sully's found her."

Jake hesitated for a long time. "You told him. Last night you told him you think—"

"I told him."

"And?" His jaw clenched.

"Sully and Gabe both agree that this seems out of character and there's obviously stuff we don't know, but we need to find her and make sure she's safe."

"I tried calling her phone."

"And?"

He swallowed hard. "It went straight to voice mail. She hasn't logged anything online since yesterday morning."

Monica nodded. "Okay. Have you gone by Bailey's?"

"No."

"Why don't I run by and talk to Hettie? She knows Kara was working for me."

Jake lifted his chin in a quick jerk. "Fine." He walked back the way he came without a backward glance.

"He's angry," Grace said. "He's worried about her."

"He's angry that I think Kara was involved with starting the fires even though I don't think she's to blame for it."

"What a strange situation." Grace shook her head. "Maybe she was taking one of those medications that makes you do strange things when you sleep! Who knows? You remember Brent, don't you?"

Monica nodded. "Fishing in his sleep. Pretty hard to forget."

"I'm sure it's something like that," Grace said. "That poor girl. She's probably taking some pill that's making her sleep-walk and do dangerous things."

Monica began to see the beginnings of a narrative that could convince Glimmer Lake residents that Kara wasn't a horrible arsonist without trying to sell the town on the idea of ghostly possession.

"You know..." Monica spoke slowly. "I think she maybe was taking something. She said insomnia was a longtime problem."

"Then I'm sure that's what's going on. I bet if you changed those pills, she'd be fine."

"Right."

Right.

It didn't really matter if it was true or not. Monica could see that Grace had already worked it out in her mind and found it plausible. If Grace could find "sleep arson" believable, the rest of Glimmer Lake probably could too. What other reason could there be for a nice young lady like Kara Sinclair to start the fires?

"You know what? I'm going to make some calls," Monica said. "Maybe I can find someone who knows Kara's family. They need to know what's going on."

"I'll cover the desk." Grace put both hands on the shiny reception desk. "And I'll answer any calls."

"Right." Monica glanced at Eve, who was making reassuring hand motions and pointing her fingers to her eyes and back to Grace.

I'll keep an eye on things.

Monica gave her a surreptitious thumbs-up and went to her office to find Kara's employee file. She flipped it open and turned to the résumé in back.

She checked all the references Kara had listed and found nothing suspicious. Everyone she'd worked for—including the inn in Sacramento where she was from—had given Kara stellar performance ratings.

Sacramento...

She tapped the number to Pioneer Heart Bed and Breakfast. Maybe they knew some of Kara's family. She'd worked there when she was underage. Wouldn't she have needed a work permit signed by her parents?

Monica dialed the number and waited two rings for someone to pick up.

"Pioneer Heart B and B," an older voice said. "How can I help you today?"

"Hi! I'm calling to check a reference." She glanced at the paper. "Is Yvonne Willis still working there?"

"Nope. She retired. But I'm the owner, Doris Flemming. I'm filling in for my manager. If you need a reference check, I know just about everyone."

"I'm calling about a Kara Sinclair."

"Kara..." Papers shuffled in the background. "I don't think we've had anyone... Oh! You mean Caroline, I think."

"Do I?" What was this? Caroline? "The employee I'm asking about is named Kara. You may be thinking about someone else."

"Nope. 'Cause her mama's family name is Sinclair. That's why she went with Kara Sinclair. But it was all legal-like. She did the name change when she turned eighteen, I just didn't remember at first. Nothing criminal. No worries about that. Just looking for a break from her dad. Can't blame her; he was pretty useless."

"Right." So Kara Sinclair had once been someone else. "So Caroline—Kara to me—she's working here right now, at Russell House in Glimmer Lake."

"She's a gem of a girl," Doris said. "Hard worker."

"We love her here, but she's missing."

"What?"

"The sheriff, everyone's looking for her. But I was wondering if you had any family names or numbers you could give me. Her emergency contact number just goes to voice mail" —Monica had tried that last night— "and we want to make sure her family knows what's going on."

"Oh, that poor girl." Doris heaved a sigh. "Well, I don't have good news on that front. Her mama passed a few years ago. Some kind of cancer, sad to say. And her father's family... Well, I wouldn't call them. I don't think she'd want you to call any of the Sangers."

"Okay, but do you know *anyone*— Wait!" The name finally registered. "Did you say Sanger?"

"Yep. That's her daddy's name. She was born Caroline Sanger. Changed it to Kara Sinclair as soon as she could. She didn't want to have anything to do with that clan."

Caroline Sanger.

"Corbin Sanger, along with his daughters Rosemarie and Bethany, died in the 1932 fire that devastated much of the Grimmer Valley. The surviving Sanger family is petitioning to be compensated for their share of the settlement..."

"Thank you so much, Doris." Monica couldn't get off the phone fast enough. "Thank you for the help."

"Can you call me back when they find her?" Doris asked. "Sweet thing. I always hoped she did well in her life. Lord knows she worked hard enough."

"I will." Monica hung up and immediately called Robin.

"Hello?"

"Quick, add in Val so I don't have to tell this twice. I'm still processing, and I always hang up on you when I try to group call."

"Right." Robin grew quiet and Monica heard beeping.

Kara was a Sanger. A Sanger. Like the Sanger family from Grimmer, who settled in Sacramento. What were the chances of that being a random connection?

"Hello?"

"Val? Monica called me and I called you. You're both on speaker here."

Monica said, "Val, I have some info about Kara. Can you sneak out and come check her office? I think I know how she ended up in Glimmer Lake."

VAL RAN her ungloved hands over the small desk where Kara's laptop lay closed and plugged in. Everything on the desk, from paperclips to Post-its, was ruthlessly organized.

"So Kara is related to Bethany?" Val asked.

"If I'm right, she'd be a distant cousin or something. Her great-grandmother might have been the one we read about in the paper, who was trying to get money from the power company for their family's ranch."

"How common a name is Sanger?"

"It's not common, but there are quite a few listed in Sacramento. Think about it though. Kara ends up here, of all places, on what is left of her ancestral home, and right around that time, Bethany says Rosemarie 'wakes up.' You think that's a coincidence?"

"You think the blood connection is why Rosemarie can influence her?"

"Maybe." Monica stopped in front of the calendar board Kara had posted on the back of her door. "This girl is a treasure." The color-coding system was enough to make Monica weep. "It sounds like she wasn't close with the Sangers. She got rid of their name and took her mother's. Changed her name. Got out of town."

"They must have been a peach of a family," Val muttered. "Sounds like she had a good mom though."

"That definitely explains why she avoided talking about her family." That should have been a red flag. Monica just wanted to hug Kara harder.

"I'm not getting anything here." Val waved her hands around the room. "Nothing malicious. Nothing even hinting at the fires or any of the confusion or panic I got at the arson sites. She was happy here." Val looked up. "She loves working here. She loves Jake. There's nothing here but happiness and a few minor gripes about normal stuff. Guests being demanding, that kind of thing." Val frowned. "She was tired though. She wasn't sleeping much."

Monica's heart broke all over again. "She's out there somewhere. She's got to be so confused and frightened. And she's got a ghost relative who won't leave her alone. We have to find her."

"Come on." Val nudged Monica's shoulder while she slid on her gloves. "Take an hour and let's run by Bailey's. Hettie might have more info."

But when they drove into Bailey's, Monica's heart fell. There were two patrol cars parked in the lot, along with the distinctive red-and-white truck owned by Gabe Peralta.

CHAPTER 22

"*I*'m telling you." Hettie Bailey was standing behind her reception desk with her arms crossed over her chest. "That girl hasn't got a criminal bone in her body. And she hasn't been here in weeks. I think she's living with her boyfriend now."

Gabe glanced over his shoulder as Monica and Val entered the office, his eyes widening a fraction when they landed on Monica before he turned back to Hettie. "Ma'am, all I'm asking is for access to the room where she stayed."

"And I'm telling you I got a nice young man who's working the line for the power company in that room now, and I don't think you have the right to go through all his things while he's gone. Just wait a damn minute for him to call me back." Hettie was small but stubborn, and her expression was mutinous.

"Hey Hettie." Val waved.

"Hey there, Val. Hello, Monica. These fellas been pestering you too?"

"We're trying to find Kara." Val nudged Gabe to the side.

"I know the department's been looking for her to question her about the fires, but you know Kara's been seeing Monica's boy Jake, right?"

"Oh, she talked about him like he hung the moon." Hettie's eyes crinkled. "That sweet girl. Jake fixed the door-knob on the storage room when someone broke in last month." She frowned. "You saying she hasn't been staying with him?"

Monica shook her head. "Nope. He's worried too."

Gabe seized on what Hettie had said. "Tell us about the break-in. Was it reported?"

Hettie waved a hand. "Oh, I think I mentioned it to one of Sully's boys when I saw him at the coffee shop, but there was nothing but a couple of things gone. He told me to go file a report, but I got busy and never went in. Jake fixed the door and that was the end of it. Kerosene ain't that expensive."

"Kerosene?" Gabe narrowed his eyes. "The thieves took kerosene?"

"Sure. Lots of people still got kerosene heaters and lamps. To tell the truth, I figured if they needed the kerosene that bad, they could have it. You never know when people are down on their luck. I've been there."

"You're a sweetheart, Hettie," Monica said. "But I think Chief Peralta is worried because the kerosene might have been used to set a fire."

"That right?" She shrugged. "Lot of other things start fires too. I wouldn't put too much by it."

"Who noticed the break-in?" Gabe asked.

Hettie's jaw tightened. "Might have been Kara."

Oh shit.

Gabe leaned on the counter. "Mrs. Bailey, we really need to see that room."

"I AM ONLY LETTING you in here," Gabe muttered, "because Sully vouched for you. If you touch anything—"

"I have to touch things." Val laid her hand flat on the base of the lamp. "That's kind of how it works. Good Lord, there are so many different people in this room. The new guy likes company."

Monica winced. "Sorry, Val."

"I've seen worse." She kept running her hands over surfaces. "There's not a lot of Kara in this room."

"What's that supposed to mean?" Gabe asked.

"It means she didn't have very much emotion invested here," Monica said. "Val got a lot of her thoughts and feelings at her office at Russell House because she spent so much time there."

"And she loved it." Val walked down the small hallway to the bathroom. "Nothing about the fires though."

Gabe said, "I wasn't asking."

"Not out loud." Val stuck her head out of the bathroom. "Just like I know you want to apologize to Monica but you're not saying it. Stop being so emotionally constipated, Gabe."

His jaw clenched. Then he looked at Monica and his expression softened. "I'm sorry about your house."

Monica didn't know what to make of that. Being sorry someone's house burned down seemed like the bare minimum of human decency. Gabe didn't get brownie points for human decency.

"Thanks."

"The guys said it was all pretty fixable though. Mostly smoke damage?"

"I haven't been back." She sat in the rickety chair by the small table. "Robin's husband is meeting the insurance guy for me."

She should get back to Russell House. If Val hadn't been her ride, she would have left Bailey's half an hour ago. Now she was stuck in a small hotel room with Gabe Peralta, trying to ignore the tension between them.

And she was still picturing him naked. Dammit.

He went through the pile of magazines by the TV. "You know, it's not that I don't believe that this... kind of thing is possible."

Monica raised an eyebrow. "You just think it's possible for other people. Not housewives in Glimmer Lake."

His cheekbones were a little red when he turned to her. "You make it sound like I'm patronizing you."

"Aren't you?"

"No." He put his hands on his hips and turned to face her. "Maybe. It's hard to wrap my brain around the idea that someone I know, someone I'm..."

Monica cocked her head. "Someone you what?"

He looked into Monica's eyes and didn't look away. "Someone I'm very attracted to might have supernatural abilities. It's not a comfortable feeling."

"I can't do what Val does. I can't read anyone's thoughts." *And I'm just going to ignore the fact that you said that because I don't know how to respond to it.*

Also, you need to grovel.

The silence stretched between them.

Val poked her head out of the bathroom again. "It's true. Monica just has dreams. And sometimes they're not even very helpful."

"Also true." Monica didn't look away from Gabe. "Sometimes they're just really annoying. Like I can see that I'm going to drop one of my favorite dishes, but that doesn't seem to keep me from dropping it. The dish still gets broken even when I try to prevent it."

"So what does that mean for the town?"

Monica's voice went soft. "I don't know. That's probably why I'm afraid to fall asleep."

SHE WALKED through the burning forest, trying to focus on the details. She shoved back the instinctive panic and opened her senses.

The fire was hot, but it couldn't burn her.

The air smelled of smoke, but she was still breathing.

She walked barefoot across a soft bed of pine needles, her legs brushing against the green ferns that ran along the creek. She could hear water running and the distant crash of a waterfall threading through the crack and pop of the fire over her head.

Lavender's green, dilly dilly,
Lavender's blue
You must love me, dilly dilly,
'cause I love you.

The forest opened up and she saw the cabin in front of her, leaning haphazardly against a stand of granite rocks.

Monica stopped in her tracks.

I know this place.

She knew the cabin and the rocks. She knew the trail to get there.

I heard one say, dilly dilly,
since I came hither,
That you and I, dilly dilly,
must lie together.

The voice singing the old words was different than what she'd heard before. Monica stepped to the window of the leaning cabin and peered inside.

Kara was on the floor of the cabin, wrapped in blue plaid blankets from Russell House. Her knees were drawn up to her chest, and she was rocking back and forth. Ugly black and red burns marked her ankles, and her feet were bloody.

"Kara."

She looked up and saw Monica. Her face was covered in ash, and two lines of tears tracked down her cheeks. Her eyes were wide and frightened. She opened her mouth and started to sing the old nursery rhyme again, tears streaming down her face.

The fire around them started closing in.

MONICA WOKE with the smell of kerosene in her nose, confused until she remembered where she was.

Robin's guest room.

Mark and Robin's house.

Her house had been on fire. They put it out. There was water everywhere.

Water? Not water.

Fire.

The image of Kara's face flashed in Monica's thoughts, and the dream flooded her mind. She reached for the phone on the bedside table and searched for Gabe Peralta's number.

"Hello?" It might have been the middle of the night, but Gabe sounded alert.

Monica didn't wait to introduce herself or explain. "Kara Sinclair is in an old cabin off Cartwheel Road, south of Ranch Creek. Go east of the highway on Ranch Creek Road, turn right on Cartwheel. About two miles in there's a fire road. Turn left and follow the creek back to the old abandoned cabin. I don't think it's on fire, but it may be soon if you don't get to her. She's burned and she needs medical attention."

"I'll call Sully right now." Gabe hung up.

Monica dropped her phone and covered her eyes, fighting back tears. Kara had been so confused. So frightened. She was hurt and Monica had sent the fire department to her, knowing that they would probably have to arrest her as soon as they rescued her from whatever was tormenting her mind.

"Monica?" Robin tapped on her door. "Is everything okay?"

She rose and walked to the door, opening it and throwing her arms around Robin. "No. I saw Kara. Nothing is okay."

THEY WAITED for a knock at the door. They'd heard the sirens roaring down the highway south of town. Mark made coffee as Monica and Robin sat on the couch, waiting for news from Sully.

Monica heard a truck putter down the road and stop in front of the house. The knock came just as the sun was breaking over the horizon and the sky had turned from black to greyish blue.

Robin rose to answer the door.

"Is Monica awake?" Gabe's voice was rough.

"Yeah." Robin opened the door wider, and Gabe walked into the entryway.

He toed off his shoes in the entryway and walked without hesitation to Monica, kneeling in front of her where she sat on the couch.

"You knew exactly where she was." He stared straight into her eyes. "You knew about the burns."

"I saw her. Is she going to be all right?"

"I can't answer that." He braced his arms on the edge of the couch. "She's receiving medical attention right now. She had third-degree burns on her lower legs and they were infected. There was kerosene at the cabin, but no sign that she'd started a fire."

"Did she confess?"

Gabe nodded slowly. "You knew exactly where she was."

"I know. What did she say?"

"She wasn't making much sense."

Robin came and sat next to Monica, taking her hand and squeezing it. "Is she going to be okay?"

"Medically, I don't know how bad the burns are." Gabe couldn't stop staring at her. "I've seen people recover one hundred percent from worse, so it probably depends on the infection. I'm obviously not a doctor. She's heading to the hospital in Bridger right now. The EMTs have her."

Monica asked, "Did Sully arrest her?"

"Not yet. He's still trying to question her, but she's really confused." Gabe looked into Monica's eyes. "I need to know what's going on here."

"We told you," Robin said.

"Monica Velasquez, I am so..." Gabe cleared his throat. "I am so sorry that I didn't believe you. I don't know how any of this works, but that girl didn't have a phone on her. Didn't have anything but the keys to an old truck we found behind the cabin and the clothes on her back. And she was exactly where you said she'd be."

"I saw her." She patted his hand. "Don't worry—you'll get used to it."

He shook his head slowly. "I don't think I'll ever get used to you."

Was that a compliment? "Kara is not responsible for these fires. Robin thinks she's been possessed—"

"Not possessed," Robin said. "Not exactly. It's not like an *Exorcist* kind of thing. But today Monica called up to Kara's first job in Sacramento and found out that Kara is a blood relative of two sisters who were killed in a fire a long time ago in Grimmer. We think the ghost of one of those girls is trying to finish off the last of Grimmer. Burn any trace of the old town, like these cabins."

Gabe's eyes cut to Robin. "How does Monica's house fit with that? It can't be more than thirty or forty years old."

"Robin talked to one of the ghosts," Monica said. "The little sister. I was there, and I asked about the redwood cabin I keep seeing in my dreams. When I did that, something... brushed me." She shivered involuntarily. "She recognized me. I think burning my house was a warning."

"Don't interfere or you'll pay," Gabe muttered. "But it's Kara who is physically setting the fires."

"She's had trouble sleeping," Robin said. "If she's tired and her defenses are down... Val said that she only sensed confusion and fear when she searched what was left at the sites. Kara didn't know what she was doing."

Gabe wiped a hand over his face, looking exhausted. "How the hell am I going to write any of this into an investigation report?"

Mark walked over and handed Gabe a large cup of coffee. "I don't have any psychic powers or visions, but think I may have an answer for that."

"The bigger problem," Robin said, "is that now that Kara is out of Grimmer and safe in Bridger, who is Rosemarie going to target next?"

"Rosemarie?" Gabe asked.

"The ghost of the older sister," Robin said. "We think she started the fire in the 1930s that eventually led to the town being covered by the lake."

Monica put both hands around her coffee, trying to warm the chill in her chest. "You think she'll still try to burn Glimmer Lake?"

"I think Kara coming back to town woke her up," Robin said. "Kara is gone, but Rosemarie is still awake."

"And there are pieces of Grimmer still standing," Gabe said. "Robin is right. Kara is safe now, but there's no guarantee this ghost is finished."

CHAPTER 23

*M*onica walked through the trees, following the familiar thunk of an ax landing in the old pine stump behind the house. She brushed thick branches to the side and emerged on the far side of the clearing behind the house.

Gilbert heaved the ax over his shoulder, straining the cotton T-shirt he wore in the bright afternoon sun.

"We have enough." Monica pointed to the large pile of split wood stacked in the notch of twin cedars behind the back porch.

Gil turned to her, squinting into the sun. "I know, but what else are we going to do with all this dead wood?"

Monica looked around and saw the logs scattered through the clearing. "What happened?"

Gilbert shrugged. "Just time. Everything dies eventually."

A manzanita bush lay on its side, the twisted red branches like skeletons against the underbrush. "But it was all alive."

"And now it's dead." He lifted the ax and placed another

log on the old stump. "Don't get upset, babe. That's the way it goes."

Twin cedars lay across the firepit, toppling the carefully placed stones that ringed the circle. Monica walked through their backyard in confusion. "But our house..."

"Look." He pointed to the fresh green saplings waving in the breeze. "New ones are already growing."

Monica felt like crying. "But I want to keep the old trees. They were beautiful, and they shaded the house."

He walked over and put his arm around her shoulders. "These will grow too. They're different, but they'll grow. They'll shade the house."

The dead trees around her seemed to multiply before her eyes. "I don't want to lose them all!"

"You won't." Gil pointed toward a stand of young pines that were already reaching the top of the house. "Look at that. See?"

"Gilbert, I don't want to lose all these trees." A knot of dread tightened in her chest. "They've been around the house since before it was built. These are important trees. The house won't be the same if they're not here."

A crash over her shoulder made Monica turn. Gilbert was already there, walking toward a fallen sugar pine with a chain saw in his right hand. "Babe, forests die. If you don't cut the dead parts away, the new things won't have a chance to grow."

"Why are you doing this?" She stomped her foot, crushing a new pine beneath her boot. "I don't want all this."

Gilbert turned and his smile was soft. "I know you don't think you do. But I promise you're going to love it, babe."

She felt the wind brush against the tears on her cheeks.

"No. I want things back the way they were. I want what I had. I want our old trees."

He pointed to the pile of firewood. "They're all still there. They're going to keep you warm while the other trees grow. Trust me. You're going to be fine."

"But the house—"

"The house is strong." Gilbert walked across the clearing, bent down, and kissed her forehead. "This house? This is what you and I built, babe. It's real strong. Nothing is gonna make this house fall, okay? Trust me, the new trees are going to be beautiful. They're gonna grow so fast you won't even feel like you missed anything." He pointed to the woodpile. "And if you do, just remember they're still all there."

Monica sat on the wood-chopping stump and stared at a small evergreen pushing up from the forest floor. "It's not the same. Nothing will be the same."

"But that's okay." He walked toward the fallen sugar pine, throwing her a grin over his shoulder. "Just because it's different doesn't mean it won't be great."

MONICA WAS STILL THINKING about the dream while she and Robin drove to visit Kara in Bridger City. So far the girl was responding well to the burn treatments, and the doctors were talking about different courses of therapy to best repair the damage.

Robin was chattering about something to do with antique rugs, and Monica was not paying attention.

"...so I told her a dealer can print up any kind of certificate that he or she wants, but that doesn't mean—"

"Have you ever seen Gilbert's ghost?"

Robin stopped talking completely.

Monica forced her eyes to remain on the road.

"Why are you asking that?" Robin asked.

"I had a dream about him."

"Oh."

"Yeah." Monica changed lanes to avoid a merging big rig. "It didn't feel like a vision. But it didn't feel like a dream either."

"Have you ever dreamed about him before?"

"Of course." Monica thought of the countless dreams she'd had of her late husband. She'd dreamed about him being back, about the kids being young again, even about their fights. "But this was different. I can't explain how, it just was."

"But you don't think it was a ghost?"

"Do you ever see ghosts in dreams?"

"No. They look corporeal to me."

"Yeah. So this wasn't like that. So I don't think it was Gilbert's ghost."

Robin let out a long breath. "Good."

"Why good?"

"Wouldn't that be... upsetting?"

Monica shrugged. "I don't know. Maybe it would be flattering."

"No." Robin shook her head. "Most ghosts aren't happy spirits. I mean, they're not all violent like Rosemarie, but they have something unfinished here or they don't feel like they can move on for some other reason."

"And you don't think Gil had that?"

"I don't want to think he did," Robin said. "I know his life was shorter than we expected—"

"Like, half as long." Gilbert had died when he was only forty-four. "He was barely in middle age."

Robin's voice was soft. "I know, Monica."

She felt her throat tighten, but she was determined not to cry. She'd cried plenty, and she was done with that. "So maybe he'd think there was something left here to do. Maybe he'd want to see his kids."

Robin was silent for a long time. When she finally spoke, her voice was slow and thoughtful. "I think Gil knew the kids were in a good place. Even Jake."

Monica snorted. "Jake was a ski bum."

"But he was happy. He's always been a good guy. Even if he wasn't the most ambitious, he's always been a good person who cares about people. Sam and Caleb had their own plans. Sylvia was ready to conquer the world."

"And he missed it," Monica said quietly. "He did all the hard stuff and missed the reward."

"What are you talking about? *You* were the reward." Robin angled her shoulders toward her. "You and Jake and Sylvia and Caleb and Sam. You *were* the reward. What did he miss out on? His life was full and joyful and happy, Monica."

She blinked the tears away. "But he should have had longer."

"I know. And it sucks that he didn't. It sucks for both of you."

Monica sniffed and reached for a tissue in the center console. "Do you think it would be disrespectful to Gilbert if I went out with Gabe Peralta?" She snorted. "God, can you imagine? Their names both start with G. I'd end up calling Gabe the wrong name constantly. The kids are bad enough."

"Why would you ask if it was disrespectful? It's been four years. You went out with West."

Monica shrugged. "West was... fun." In fact, West had been calling her again, and while Monica didn't mind the ego boost, she wasn't exactly in a party-time mood.

"He wasn't serious."

"No."

Robin paused. "But Gabe Peralta might be."

Monica shrugged again, but she didn't say anything.

"Yeah," Robin said quietly. "That makes sense."

"I just... I felt ready to *date*. I know I'm young. If I'm anything like my grandmother, I'm going to live until I'm ninety-seven. I'm not even halfway there."

"And your grandma outlived three husbands," Robin said. "Each one a few years younger than the last. Grandma Trujillo was an icon."

Monica frowned. "She really was. So I'm not even halfway done with life. I don't want to be alone all that time. But I don't want to fall into some relationship that's destined to—"

"Whoa!" Robin leaned forward and caught her eye. "Brakes please. Not literally, we're still on the highway, but you know what I mean. Brakes on this destiny crap."

Monica rolled her eyes. "It's kind of hard not to believe in destiny when I literally see the future, Robin."

"You dreamed about sex with the man! Maybe all you are destined to do is have a really hot affair! Maybe that's all it's going to be and you're supposed to just live a life of sexy adventures because you've been responsible for literally the entire rest of your life."

Okay, that didn't seem all that bad. Sexy adventures.

Oh shit. She didn't know how to have sexy adventures.

"But what if I like him? What if I don't want to just have a sexy affair?" She felt her cheeks getting hot just thinking about it. "I don't think I'm even capable of having a fling. That's probably why I haven't called West back." She glanced at Robin. "I'm not Val. I'm not daring and cool."

"You are so cool."

"I drive a minivan. And I like it. When this one dies, I'm probably going to go out and get the exact same model. 'Cause I am not cool."

Robin patted the dashboard of the car. "The minivan is the utility belt of vehicles, and you know who wears a utility belt?"

Monica frowned. "Electricians?"

"Batman."

Monica snorted. "You're crazy."

"I'm right."

She took the turnoff for the hospital and followed the signs for short-term parking. "I don't know what to do about Gabe Peralta. I'm attracted to him. He's very open about being attracted to me. I don't know what to do with him."

"I recommend kissing him," Robin said. "Start there and see what happens."

"Okay." Why the hell not? "Once we figure out what's happening with Kara, stop the town from burning down, and get rid of a vengeful ghost, I'll kiss Gabe Peralta."

Robin pointed her phone at Monica. "Say that again. I'm going to record it."

"Do you want me to leave you in Bridger without a ride? Because I will."

"I CAN'T REALLY EXPLAIN IT." Kara glanced at the door that Jake had just exited. "I feel like my brain is playing tricks on me. I've taken antianxiety medication for years, Monica. I've told you—"

"This is not about your anxiety, honey." Monica took the hand that didn't have tubes running out of it. "Do not feel like this is your fault or that this has anything to do with your mental health, okay?"

Robin sat next to Kara, her purse stuffed next to her on the seat and a drawing pad open on her lap. "So we're going to tell you some stuff that might make us seem a little weird. But we have a feeling that you might be a little relieved too."

Kara's face was even paler than when they'd first come in. "There's something weird about Glimmer Lake, isn't there? This all started when I moved here."

"Can I ask why you moved here?" Monica asked. "It might help explain a few things."

Kara shrugged a little. "I guess it was partly to do with my dad. I didn't know him much—his whole family is kind of a mess—but I knew they were from around here, and I was curious. I love hospitality work and I love the mountains, so when I saw the opening at Russell House, it kind of felt like..."

"Destiny?" Monica asked.

The corner of Kara's mouth turned up. "Yeah."

Robin nodded. "Okay. So you moved here, and when did you notice that things started getting..."

"Weird." Monica finished the thought. No need to scare the girl right away.

"Okay." Kara took a slow breath and let it out. "Pretty quickly. My insomnia got a lot worse, and that's part of why I take anxiety medication, so I talked to my doctor in Sacramento—I haven't found anyone here yet—and he told me that it wasn't uncommon when you have a big move, so we adjusted my meds, and that seemed to work for a while."

"Okay."

"But then... I think it was the beginning of summer, when things started to get really busy." Kara's voice fell back. "I had these crazy dreams. I'd been hiking with a friend I met at Bailey's and we were following all these old trails. We'd found this beautiful trail that led along the creek. There was this cabin there. I took so many pictures because it was really beautiful. Abandoned, but just covered in moss and ferns. So gorgeous."

"You have pictures?"

She nodded. "When Jake gets back, he can show you. I sent some of them to him."

"Cool," Robin said. "What happened after you found the cabin?"

"I can't say for sure, but... it almost felt like someone was following me. Does that sound crazy? Like that feeling you get that someone is watching you sometimes, you know?" She shook her head. "And I know I was probably imagining things, but then the other stuff started happening."

"What other stuff?" Monica pulled up a chair and sat next to Kara.

"I had these really vivid dreams that felt like they were from the old West. I was living in a cabin and cooking at an old woodstove. I was boiling water for laundry and hanging it to dry. I was baking bread in a stone oven. Like all this pioneer stuff, you know? And I don't know how to do any of that."

"But in the dream, you did."

"Totally." Kara's fingers twisted in the sheets. "And then it started getting stranger. I'd wake up in places I didn't remember going to. My truck would be outside, but I had no memory of driving. And then the fires started." Her eyes filled with tears and she bit her lip so hard it looked like it was on the edge of bleeding.

Monica stroked her arm. "Kara, be calm. No one blames you for any of this."

"There was a man in my dreams. An older man with a long white beard and a terrible temper. I can't remember him ever hitting me in the dreams, but like... I knew he would. In the dream, I knew he would beat me if everything wasn't done exactly right."

Robin asked, "Do you think you could describe him?"

Kara shrugged. "I mean, does it matter? He was part of a dream."

"We think it does matter," Monica said. "We think what you've been dreaming about haven't just been dreams. They're memories."

Kara frowned. "Whose memories? Not mine."

Robin and Monica exchanged a look.

Monica said, "Her name was Rosemarie Sanger. She was killed in a fire in the 1930s that burned much of the town of

Grimmer, and it's part of the reason they flooded it to create Glimmer Lake."

Kara's mouth dropped open, but she didn't say a word.

Robin added, "We don't know for sure, but we believe Rosemarie started the fire, possibly to try to kill her father. Unfortunately, it also ended up killing her little sister, Bethany. It's Bethany's ghost that I can see and talk to."

"And I have been having visions," Monica said. "Premonitions about a fire destroying Glimmer Lake. Visions of a cabin in the woods that's covered in moss and near a waterfall or a stream."

Kara narrowed her eyes, but she still didn't speak.

"Bethany," Robin continued, "is worried about Rosemarie, who's very angry and very protective. Something happened to wake her up. Ghosts can't start fires. They're not strong enough. But they can influence people."

"You think..." Kara blinked hard. "You think a ghost—"

"We think Rosemarie used you to continue her mission," Monica said. "None of this is your fault."

Kara stared at the empty wall across from her bed. "What's her mission?"

"To destroy Grimmer," Robin said. "To destroy every part of it that's left."

CHAPTER 24

"Well, she took that better than I expected," Robin said. "And she gave us pictures."

Monica shut the door of the minivan. "I just wish her memory of the location was a little better, but at least she gave us Carlisle Creek. That's a starting point." She started backing the car out of the parking space. "You think she'll tell Jake?"

"Would you?"

Monica shrugged. "I have no idea. Do you think she believed us?"

"Oh yeah." Robin nodded. "Come on, if you were in her situation—having dreams that you couldn't explain, waking up in strange places, starting *fires* for reasons you didn't understand—wouldn't you believe something supernatural was causing it?"

"I just hope she can work through the guilt." Monica turned and headed out of the lot. "I could see it all over her face, and none of this is her fault. The poor girl had no idea what she was doing."

"Mark has already talked to a lawyer about it, and he's been looking up cases of weird behavior caused by medication." Robin was texting as they drove toward the highway. "He's hoping if he can give Sully and Gabe any reason not to charge her, she might be able to get probation or counseling or something instead of jail."

"I wish she hadn't confessed," Monica muttered. "It's kind of hard to get past that."

"But that just goes to her being confused and frightened. I don't think it's a bad thing."

Monica wasn't going to debate that. She was far more suspicious of law enforcement than Robin was. "The main thing for her is that she knows, no matter what, we do not think she's responsible for all this. She needs to know we are in her corner."

Robin smiled at Monica. "You know who I'm impressed with?"

"Jake?"

Robin nodded.

Monica's heart felt so full. "He's sticking with her. Did you see him? He's like a dragon guarding that girl."

"He gets it from his dad. Velasquez men protect the people they love."

She nodded and tried to blink away the tears before Robin saw them.

No luck. "Don't cry. It's a good thing."

"I just wish they didn't have all this hanging over them." Monica forced the words through the lump in her throat. "They should be young and enjoying a romance, not worried about ghosts and fires and jail time."

"We're going to figure this out. We have a lead on the

cabin now, and I'm going to look in the archives for pictures of Corbin Sanger."

"Why?"

Robin frowned and leaned back in her seat. "I have a theory about that cabin in the woods, and I have a feeling I know why Rosemarie woke up after all these years."

MONICA DROPPED Robin off at Russell House to relieve Grace from front-desk duty. They'd both been chipping in hours while Monica dealt with the fallout from her house fire. She called the adjustor on the way to her property and got an update on the claim. By the time she arrived at the house, she was feeling a little calmer.

Which was why she was able to smile when she saw Gabe Peralta and his son Logan tossing burned shingles and other detritus in a dumpster in front of the house. Logan paused and stood up straight, waving at her with heavy brown work gloves on his hands.

She parked at the base of the sloped driveway and rolled down the window. "Hi."

"Hey, Ms. Velasquez!" Logan kept waving.

Gabe leaned against the porch posts with his arms crossed over his chest, his biceps straining against the blue uniform shirt he wore. He was wearing dark sunglasses, and the silver sprinkled in his hair winked at her in the midday sun.

Damn it, why was he so attractive? Just really ridiculously hot.

She got out of the car and walked toward them. "What

are you doing here? I think my insurance is going to send people over to do all that."

Gabe shrugged and tugged off the work gloves he was wearing. "I had to come by and get a few more details for my report. Logan was with me, so I told him it would be nice to at least clean up the driveway, you know?"

The driveway of the house was filled with torn-up wood, shingles, and wet insulation from where the firefighters had ripped open the attic to attack the flames.

"Thank you both so much." She pointed at the minivan. "Logan, there's a little cooler in the center console of my van with some sodas in it. You can grab one if you want."

"Oh cool." His face lit up. "I didn't know minivans had stuff like that."

She remembered what Robin had said that morning. "They're the utility belt of vehicles."

Logan snickered. "Like Batman."

"Exactly."

Gabe cocked his head at her, the corner of his lips turned up. "You have a way with teenage boys."

"I had three of them." She walked to him and looked up. "Trust me, it gets better."

The half smile turned into a full one. "I'll have to take your word for it." He looked over his shoulder at the house. "Have you been inside yet?"

She took a long breath. "No. Jake did a walk-through right after the fire was put out, but he's been focused on Kara. Sam and Caleb wanted to come up, but I told them to wait until the insurance was done because they'll want to start fixing stuff right away. That's just their personality. And Sylvia's all the way in Berkeley."

Had it only been two days? How had it only been two days?

Gabe propped one foot on the first step of the porch. "Want some company?"

Did she want the company of a man she'd had sex visions about while she went through the wreck of her life? Debatable. Did she want a trained firefighter to walk her through a house with fire damage?

That was an easier answer. "Sure."

Gabe held his hand out for the keys and then opened the door, blocking Monica from walking in right away. "From what I can see, it's very repairable. But the drywall and floors..."

Monica walked into the entryway and froze.

Disaster.

Oh.

My.

God.

Disaster.

She wasn't going to cry. She told herself she wasn't going to cry. It was just stuff. Nothing was irreplaceable.

But she did. She couldn't help it.

"Shit." She took a shaky breath, and the tears started falling. "Dammit." She wiped her eyes and hardly even noticed when Gabe's arm came around her shoulders.

It wasn't just the destruction, it was the work. All the work it would take to put her life back together. To replace everything. To supervise the reconstruction. She was barely getting out from under the avalanche of work that Russell House had been, and now all this...

"I give up." She sniffed. "They should have just let it burn down. I'll get a room at Bailey's."

"Okay." Gabe's voice was steady. "You're not going to live in a room at a boarding house. I want you to focus on the big stuff." He handed her a clean cotton handkerchief from his front pocket. "Is the house still standing?"

Monica nodded.

"And you have good insurance."

"Yeah. Yeah, we do." She took another shaky breath. The living room was a disaster. Everything was waterlogged and already smelling musty. The stone fireplace was the only thing that had escaped the water damage. Ink ran down the walls from their family pictures. Gilbert's old recliner was sagging to one side. Her immaculately kept couch was soaked. All the windows were blown out, and their hardwood floors were warped and cracking.

They walked toward the kitchen.

"Appliances are all still good," Gabe said. "No damage to any of your dishes or anything like that. Anything that was waterproof is still fine."

"Mm-hmm." All Monica could do was shake her head. The smell of smoke was everywhere, mingling with the smell of damp and mildew.

"The drywall is all going to have to go," Gabe said. "So you'll get all new walls. Fresh paint everywhere. New ceilings. You like that popcorn texture shit on the ceiling?"

"No." She sniffed. "Gil and I hated it, but it wasn't a high priority, you know?"

"Well, you won't have that anymore. You'll be able to get everything exactly the way you want it. Redecorate the rooms. Freshen everything up." He kept talking to her as they walked down the hall and pushed open the doors to all the bedrooms. "You can make everything exactly the way you want it. You have a home office? Exercise room?"

She stared at Sam and Caleb's room that still had car posters and school pictures on the walls. They were curling off now, wilting in the damp, smoky air. "I was using the boys' desk in here for a home office."

"See? You'll be able to completely redo that now." Gabe walked her through the remains of her home and forced Monica to see the possibilities and not just the destruction.

"You're good at this." She wiped her eyes with the handkerchief. "You must do this professionally or something."

He chuckled, and the sound shook something loose in Monica's chest. She looked up at him and Gabe looked down, meeting her eyes.

His arm was around her shoulders. Her eyes were wet with tears. Her gaze landed on the carved architecture of his mouth. His lower lip was fuller than his upper. They looked soft but firm.

Capable lips. Lips that knew what they were doing.

"I really want to kiss you right now." Gabe's voice was rough. "But you're upset and I'm pretty sure I'd be taking advantage of that. Then there's that whole subject of a sex vision we haven't talked about."

Her libido was not in favor of his restraint. *Booooo! Kiss him, Monica!* "Did I say we were going to talk about it?"

"I'm an investigator, Mrs. Velasquez." His lower lip was flushed. Bitable. "I'm going to need to know every detail."

"For professional reasons?"

"For very unprofessional reasons." His eyes never left her mouth. "Val said something to me about groveling."

"Right. Because you doubted our formidable psychic powers. I think you can hold off on that for a while since we have a ghost arsonist we need to catch."

"It seems unbelievable, but that statement isn't even the strangest thing I've heard today."

She frowned, still staring at his mouth. "I'm almost afraid to ask."

"Something about political action via K-pop memes on TikTok. I have no idea what Logan was talking about." His arm around her shoulders tightened.

"Give up now and nod politely. He's going to speak an unknown language for about five more years." Monica allowed herself to lean her breast into his chest. She wasn't imagining things. He groaned.

Gabe smelled so *good*. It was like cedar and clean laundry and leather all put together and why did that smell so good? If she put her face in the crook of his neck, would that be bad? Probably unprofessional. But not illegal or anything. Too forward? Probably not very conducive to solving a decades-old mystery that could destroy the town.

Monica said, "So we have a ghost arsonist."

"And a mysterious cabin that has something to do with all this, but we don't know where it is."

"And my house is destroyed and my front-desk manager is in the hospital because of the ghost arsonist."

"Right." That seemed to snap him back to reality. He moved his arm from around her shoulders and cleared his throat. "How is she?"

"In a lot of pain but feeling safer now that she's not on her own trying to deal with all this."

There was that little smirk again.

"What?"

Gabe hooked his thumbs in his front pockets. "I'm just saying... sometimes it's good to remember you don't have to do everything yourself."

"Are you trying to point out I'm a workaholic?" She turned and walked back down the hallway. Did she put a little sway in her step? Of course not. She was just being very careful where she walked. And maybe that made her ass sway. A little.

"I know you're a workaholic, and I don't mind that. I'm just not too sure about you and your friends charging into the woods to tackle ghosts. What if the next person this ghost possesses is a big burly guy and not a girl who barely comes up to my shoulder?"

"We've dealt with ghosts before." She opened the front door, happy to have been distracted by Gabe and his smell and his lips. "We've dealt with murderers." She turned as he was locking the front door. "Trust me, we can handle whatever is at that cabin."

He faced her with a frown and dropped the key into her waiting palm. "You are not going out to that cabin alone."

"We haven't even found it yet. Don't get bossy; it's a sure-fire way to piss me off." Monica saw Logan wandering around the side yard, staring into the thick stand of trees that surrounded the property. "Just keep in touch with Sully. Val will tell him when we're ready to go into the woods."

Gabe nodded, then glanced at Logan. "Hey, bud, you ready to go?"

Logan turned; he looked distracted. "What?"

"You ready to go?"

"Oh." He started back toward the porch. "Sure thing,

Dad." He crumpled the Coke can in his fist. "Thanks for the Coke, Ms. Velasquez."

"You're very welcome." Monica waved as they walked up the driveway and to Gabe's truck. "Gabe, thanks for helping me go through the house."

"Sure thing." He opened Logan's door and waited for the young man to climb in before he shut it. "Don't go into the woods without me."

She waved at him. "We'll be fine."

"Don't—"

Logan rapped hard on the window and yelled, "Stop flirting with Jake's mom."

"You should bring him by Russell House tomorrow." Monica waved at Logan. "Jake is working on the boat. He could hang out again. I think they had fun the last time."

"And I told you I'd help you tag trees." He nodded. "So I'll see you then."

Monica watched them drive off down the cul-de-sac before she got in her own car and headed to the library. They had a ghost arsonist to find, and Robin was waiting.

CHAPTER 25

*M*onica found Robin at the library, going through boxes of old photos from Grimmer.

"Any luck?"

Robin kept her voice down. "Not so far. There was a lot documented around the time the dam was constructed, but before that?" She shook her head. "Really spotty."

"If you can't find anything here, our best bet is finding that cabin."

"Yeah." Robin propped her chin on her folded hands. "You know what I'm thinking?"

They'd been friends for almost forty years. Of course Monica knew what Robin was thinking. "You think Corbin Sanger is still at that cabin."

She nodded slowly. "We both know domineering men have a problem letting go. Even after they die."

Robin's grandfather had hung around the attic of Russell House for years before Monica, Robin, and Val had managed to banish him. Who was to say Corbin Sanger wasn't as stubborn?

224

"Yeah." Monica sat across from her. "It wouldn't be the first time we've had to get rid of one."

"Rosemarie might have gone off the rails in death, but I think she burned that house down—the first one—because she was trying to protect Bethany. I think she was trying to keep her father from going after her sister and things got out of control."

"And eighty years later, her distant cousin comes back to the mountains and stumbles onto the cabin Corbin is haunting."

"Corbin wakes up maybe?"

Monica drummed her fingers on a picture of three Depression-era girls standing in front of the Grimmer schoolhouse. "Corbin wakes up, forcing Rosemarie to wake too. She's angry and confused. She's lashing out, trying to finish her father off and using the one person she identifies with the most."

Robin nodded. "Rosemarie isn't the real problem. Rosemarie is trying to protect her cousin from Corbin."

She flipped through a stack of black-and-white pictures from Grimmer. Old men, many with beards. Dressed in overalls. Smoking pipes. Boots propped up on a split rail fence. "Corbin Sanger could be any of these guys."

"Yeah." Robin sighed and set down the stack of pictures. "I think Kara might be a better bet if we want to get an idea of what he looks like. Because unless I can draw him, there's no guarantee we'll be able to summon him. And if we can't summon him—"

"We can't banish him." Monica tapped her fingers on the table. "Why don't you head back to Bridger and talk to Kara? I'll keep at this for a while and try to find some old maps from around Carlisle Creek. There have to be maps somewhere in here." She glanced around the quiet reading room of the Glimmer Lake library. "I can tell Gail I'm looking for historical stuff for Russell House if she gets curious."

"Okay. Val's going to get off work soon. Should I call her?"

"Maybe see if she can go to Bridger with you. I'll be fine up here, and you might need someone to drive you home if you get tired."

Robin nodded. "How was the house?"

Monica fell forward and banged her head quietly against the lacquered wood top. "My life is a disaster."

"I'm so sorry." Robin ran a hand over Monica's hair. "You know you can stay with us as long as you want. Or take a room at Russell House if that's easier. Let someone else do the cleaning for a while. It's the slow season."

Monica lifted her head. "That might be the way to go. Jake's at Russell House. I can use his kitchen if I want to cook." She covered her face with both hands. "I just want my house to magically be back to what it was. Even the parts I didn't like. The idea of doing..." She waved her hands around. "...all this is exhausting. I don't have the energy or the time. I told Gabe I was going to abandon the whole thing and get a room at Bailey's."

Robin lifted an eyebrow. "Gabe was there?"

"Yeah." She sighed. "He and his son were cleaning all the burned shingles and insulation out of the driveway so I wouldn't have to walk through it."

"That was really nice."

Monica propped her chin in her palm. "He is nice, especially now that he's not as skeptical about the psychic thing. I can tell it's still a little weird to him, but he's dealing with it. And he walked through the house with me and gave me a handkerchief when I was snotty and crying."

"An honest-to-goodness handkerchief?"

Monica nodded.

"Lumberjack red?"

"Just plain white cotton."

"Classy."

"Yeah. His lips look like they kiss well." She tapped her fingernails against her own lips. "I wanted to kiss him."

"And you didn't because...?"

"Ghost arsonist. Innocent girl caught in the middle of messy family history. Emotional overload at my destroyed house."

Robin nodded. "Fair points. That said—"

"Yes, Robin. Once we catch the ghost arsonist and banish the bad ghost, I *will* make an effort to kiss Gabe Peralta and test the competent-lips thing."

Robin shrugged. "I'm just saying it's kind of for science."

Monica couldn't stop her laugh.

SHE DIDN'T FIND any pictures she could be sure were Corbin Sanger, but she did find an old map of Grimmer and a newer hiking guide that mentioned several trails near Carlisle Creek.

Three hours after she got to the library, she headed back to Robin and Mark's house with a bundle of papers under her arm and a stack of copied photographs. She had no idea if any of it was helpful, but at least the stack of papers made Monica feel like she'd accomplished something.

She walked in just as Mark was opening a bottle of wine. "How did you know?"

He smiled. "Robin called. She and Val are on their way home. Apparently the trip to Bridger was successful."

"So she got a picture of Corbin Sanger?"

Mark blinked. "Was that what she was trying for?"

"Yes?" Shit. Had Robin not told Mark about the new creepy ghost? "I mean, it's just a theory we had."

Mark looked a little pissed. "Do we need to banish another ghost?"

"Think about it this way—at least this one isn't in your wife's family home."

The knife Mark was using to slice cheese seemed to need a lot more concentration all of a sudden. "You know," he said, "it's not that she has this ability. It's part of who she is now. But she has the biggest heart and she thinks the best of everyone. I worry one of these days she's going to..." He set down the knife and took a deep breath. "It's hard caring about someone who always puts other people's needs first."

"You wish your wife were more selfish?"

"Maybe." He picked up the knife again and shook his head. "Maybe a little more self-preservation, you know? Last winter she almost got killed by an Olympic sharpshooter."

"So did you."

Mark took a long drink of red wine. "I was looking forward to an active retirement, but I'm not sure I was prepared for this."

Monica walked over, refilled his glass, and poured one for herself. "What do you think Gil would think about all this?"

He smiled. "I was just thinking about that the other day. He'd be so in. He'd think all this was awesome."

"Because he was an adrenaline junkie."

Mark shook his head. "That guy had no fear."

She sat at the counter and watched Mark slice cheese. "What do you think of Gabe Peralta?"

"Don't know him well enough." Mark shrugged. "Seems okay. Sully likes him."

"Yeah. And Sully doesn't like that many people."

"So... that's worth something." He glanced up. "You like him?"

"I'm attracted to him. I *think* I like him."

"Hmm."

"Do you think I'm being—?"

"You better not mention Gil." Mark spoke quietly, glancing up at Monica. "Just don't."

Mark and Gil had been friends, close friends, for over twenty years.

He took a deep breath and braced his hands on the counter. "Gil's gone. And I can't tell you whether he'd approve of you dating or not. No one thinks about that shit, you know? And honestly, it doesn't matter. It matters what you want."

"Would you want Robin...?"

"I guess, if I think about something happening to me, I'd want Robin to find someone again. Someone who made her happy and was good with the kids, you know? I wouldn't want her to be alone." He picked up a knife. "Not unless she wanted to be because I'm such a kick-ass husband that no one could compare."

"I mean, obviously it would be that." Monica raised her glass and Mark toasted her. "Thanks."

"For?"

"Wine. Dude wisdom."

He put a hand over his heart and gave her a small bow. "I do what I can."

"Now give me cheese."

He handed over the plate. "Yes, ma'am."

MONICA WAS READING in bed when her phone rang. She glanced at the old-fashioned clock on the wall. Who was calling her at ten o'clock?

There better not be anything else burning.

"Hello?"

"Hey." Someone cleared their throat. "This is Gabe."

"Oh. Sorry, I didn't recognize the number."

"I'm calling from the house. We still have a landline because... not important. Do you happen to know if Jake has Logan with him? I know he doesn't live with you anymore, but I can't get ahold of Jake, and the number—"

"Logan is with Jake? I thought they were working on the boat tomorrow."

"I thought so too, but Logan came in earlier tonight and said that Jake was back at Russell House and he needed a hand with something. I didn't think much of it—I was kind of happy, to be honest. At least he'd be getting out of the house, you know?"

"Okay."

"But it's almost ten and he's not home. And he's not

answering his phone. I don't know if the reception out at the boathouse is bad."

"It's not." Monica sat up. "Let me try calling Jake. Maybe he doesn't recognize your number either."

"Right. Call me back."

Monica hung up and immediately called Jake. The phone rang four times, then switched to voice mail.

Weird.

She got up and walked out to the hall. She tapped on Robin and Mark's door, waiting to see if they were still awake.

Robin came to the door, her reading glasses sliding down her nose. "What's up? You need something?"

"When you were at the hospital earlier, did Jake mention working on the boat tonight?"

Robin frowned. "I don't think so. He was staying till the end of visiting hours, then heading home. So like... eight o'clock? He might have just gotten home."

So Jake hadn't called Logan. So Logan was lying to his dad or Jake had changed his plans about staying with Kara.

"He's not answering his phone, but Gabe called and supposedly Logan went out to Russell House because Jake called him for something."

Robin pursed her lips. "Okay, your boys were good kids who told you everything. Mine was not. Is Gabe sure Logan isn't out with some other friends? He might have just told Gabe he was going to be with Jake because Gabe would be less likely to ask questions."

Mark opened the door wider. "What's up?"

Monica was already calling Gabe back. "Gabe can't find Logan."

"He's eighteen? Nineteen?"

"Sixteen."

"Oh." Mark's voice got serious. "And he was hanging out with Jake?"

"He's been teaching Logan about the boat engine."

Gabe picked up on the first ring. "Monica?"

"Jake's not answering for me either." She started back toward her room to put her shoes on. "Is there anyone else he might have gone out with?"

"I don't think so. And I used the Find My Phone feature on his mobile and it shows that he's at Russell House. But no one is answering."

"Did you call the front desk?" Andrew, the night manager, should have answered.

"I didn't. I didn't want to bother them."

"I'm getting shoes on. I'll drive out."

"I don't want to ruin your evening because my kid—"

"My kid isn't answering his phone either," Monica said. "And I can't play the Find My Phone card with him anymore. He's got his own plan." She waved at Mark and Robin as she walked toward the front door. "I'll meet you there. I'm sure we're being overly cautious, but let's make sure everything is okay."

"Okay." He sounded relieved. "I'll meet you there."

Not five minutes later, as she was pulling into the driveway to Russell House, her phone started buzzing. It was Andrew. Monica heard the sirens turning off the highway as the words spilled out of his mouth.

"Monica, he's going to be okay, but someone hit Jake."

"*What?*"

"I already called 911. There were all these lights on

down here, and one of the guests commented that the boathouse door was open, so I walked down to ask Jake to turn some of the lights off and that's when I found him and he's going to be okay. I know he's going to be okay."

Monica's foot hit the pedal. "Andrew, where are you?"

"I'm at the boathouse with Jake. He's kind of awake but also kind of falling asleep."

"Keep him awake. Is Logan there?"

"Logan? Chief Peralta's son?"

"Yes."

"No." There was a shuffling sound. "I wonder if that's whose phone this is. I thought it was weird Jake had two. He doesn't usually carry two."

"Logan's phone is there?" She hit the gravel and swerved a little before she raced across the arching driveway and parked as close to the boathouse as she could. She leaped out of the car and sprinted across the lawn.

"Jake!"

Andrew came to the door and held up a hand. "He's awake, but he's still groggy. He says Logan hit him!"

Her mind was racing. *What if the next person this ghost possesses is a big burly guy and not a girl who barely comes up to my shoulder?*

Gabe had been right. Rosemarie hadn't gone after another delicate woman. She'd gone after a kid. A big kid who probably had no idea what he was doing or why.

CHAPTER 26

*J*ake was sitting up and holding an ice pack to his head by the time Gabe arrived.

Gabe's eyes were wide and terrified. "Where's Logan?"

Jake shook his head a little. "Chief, I have no idea what is going on. I got back from Bridger and I saw his truck out front. I thought he was maybe wanting to hang out or wanting some advice. See, there was a girl—"

"Girl's not important right now, sweetie." Monica stroked a hand over Jake's cheek. "Logan was in the boathouse?"

Jake frowned. "Yeah. It was weird. He... What did he have?" Jake's eyes went wide. "It was a can of lighter fuel. The stuff we use for the firepit. And like a..." He frowned. "I think they were blankets. The blue ones like Kara..." Jake's face went pale. "Mr. Peralta, is Logan taking any medication right now?"

Gabe was too distracted to answer clearly. "He had lighter fuel? And blankets?"

Jake nodded. "And he was getting on one of the quads."

Jake pointed over his shoulder. "The green-and-orange one. So I came in the door and asked him, 'Hey dude, what's up?' All casual-like, right? No biggie. I thought maybe he wanted to hang out, but I was super tired from being at the hospital all day."

"Did he say anything?" Gabe took Logan's phone from Andrew's hand. "Did he say where he was going?"

"No."

There was shouting on the driveway and Andrew rose, handing a phone to Monica. "I think those are the EMTs."

"Drew, dude, I didn't need an ambulance."

The night manager's eyes went wide. "You're joking, right?"

"You were out cold. Do not complain about an ambulance," Monica said. "Think, Jake. Did he say anything? Give any hint where he was going?"

"I don't think..." He frowned, then winced. "Something about two wrongs." Jake closed his eyes. "'Sometimes you need two wrongs to make a right.'"

Monica looked at Gabe, whose jaw was clenched. "We're going to find him."

His dark eyes turned to hers, filled with bone-chilling panic. "How?"

"I have maps. We have pictures from Kara." She rose and took his hand. "Let's get back to Robin and Mark's house. We need to find that cabin."

"I'll call Sully."

"Wait." Jake lifted the ice pack from his head. "You guys are leaving?"

The EMTs came rushing into the boathouse and surrounded Jake.

"I'll call you when we know something," Monica shouted over the rising noise. "But right now we need to find Logan."

Both Monica and Gabe walked to Monica's minivan without a word. Gabe put the phone to his ear.

"Sully, I—" He bit back what he was going to say. "Not right now, man. Logan is gone. He hit Jake Velasquez over the head with something at Russell House, took some lighter fluid and a quad, and now he's gone." Gabe's voice caught. "I'm with Monica. We're going to Robin and Mark's house. We've got to find him."

Rosemarie, what are you doing now? Monica tapped Robin's number. "Robin?"

"What is going on? Is Jake okay? I heard more ambulances heading toward—"

"Rosemarie has Logan." Was it by her house? Had the ghost found Logan there? He'd been hanging out in the forest by Monica's house. "You need to call Bethany. We have to find out where that cabin is. I think that's where she's taking him. Tell Bethany we know about Corbin. Tell her we know he's still there."

"I'll call her." Robin's voice was soft. "Are you coming back here?"

"Yes. I have Gabe with me."

"I'll ask Mark to make coffee."

Gabe was biting his fist, his teeth digging into the flesh so hard Monica thought he might make himself bleed. She reached over and grabbed his hand, taking it in hers.

"We'll find him."

She could not even imagine the terror he was feeling. Her son probably had a concussion, but he was alive. He had all his senses. He had control of his own mind.

"You found Kara," Gabe said. "Can you find him?"

"I can't just turn it on or off like that." Monica turned left onto Mark and Robin's street. "I wish I could, but I can't."

"Can you try sleeping?"

"There is no possible way I'd be able to sleep right now. And if I force it, I'll get nothing. Our best bet is Robin talking to Bethany and maybe Val reading Logan's phone."

Gabe nodded, keeping the phone clutched in his hand. Then he thought better of it and dropped it in the center console. "Evidence."

"Yeah. Kind of." She squeezed his hand. "But remember, he hasn't done anything yet. He's in danger, but it took months for Rosemarie to control Kara enough that she lit a fire. We are going to find Logan before he lights a fire."

Gabe nodded, but he didn't say anything. He didn't say a single blessed thing until they reached Mark and Robin's house.

Monica came to a rolling stop and Gabe was out. He plucked the phone from the console and held it with two fingers while he charged toward Mark and Robin's front porch.

"Hold on, cowboy," Monica muttered, but she couldn't blame him. She parked the van at the bottom of the hill and climbed up the walk to the front door.

Mark was opening it, and Gabe was inside.

"Hey." Mark held out his arm and squeezed Monica with a one-armed hug. "You girls will find him. Sully is on his way with Val."

"Okay. I got some maps from the library today. Did Robin—?"

"Already found them. They're in the kitchen along with some survey maps I found online and printed out."

"Has Robin tried calling Bethany?"

He nodded toward the back porch. "Why don't you go out with her and I'll spread everything out on the dining room table?"

"Sounds good." Monica walked through the house and out the french doors to the back porch where Robin was sketching silently with her eyes closed.

Four fat white candles were burning at the corners of the table, and Monica saw sprigs of lavender sprinkled around.

"Lavender's blue, dilly dilly," Robin sang. "Lavender's green."

"When I am king, dilly dilly,
You shall be queen."

Robin sang the familiar lyrics that Monica also knew, not the more disturbing version she'd heard Rosemarie singing in her dreams.

"Who told you so, dilly dilly,
Who told you so?
'Twas my own heart, dilly dilly,
That told me so."

Monica felt something in the air shift, and the candle flames rose for a second before they settled down.

Robin raised her head, looked to the corner of the porch, and smiled. "Hi, Bethany."

Where is your batshit-angry sister, little girl?

"I know you like that song. Your sister sang it to you, didn't she? Rosemarie sang it to you."

It was always weird watching Robin have a conversation with a ghost.

She nodded. "The words I know are a little different."

Monica didn't want to wait, but she knew the child ghost was already shy.

"I think you know the reason I called you." Robin set her sketchpad to the side. "We found our friend, the one that Rosemarie had visited. She's okay, but now there's a boy missing. He would be around Rosemarie's age. He's sixteen and his father is very frightened. No one knows where he is, but we think Rosemarie might have told him to go somewhere."

Monica watched the corner, trying not to say a word. She reached out and took Robin's hand.

"I know it wasn't Rosemarie's fault, but we have to stop her from hurting anyone else. She wouldn't be happy if that happened, would she?"

"Their father," Monica whispered.

"Bethany, I think we know why Rosemarie is still angry." Robin took a deep breath. "Monica had a dream about the cabin. We know that was your father's cabin."

They didn't know that. It was a guess, but Monica was hoping Bethany would confirm it.

"The cabin by the waterfall," Monica said. "It's by a stream, and there are ferns all around it."

Robin was listening. "She said she asked the ranger to keep people away from the cabin last year." She frowned. "Sully? When did you ask Sully..." Robin gasped. "In the snow. You asked him to keep the snowmobiles away. No... you asked him to keep the loud machines away from the west side of the dam." Robin looked at Monica. "The cabin is on the west side of the dam."

"But Carlisle Creek..." Unless Kara was mistaken. Unless she'd mixed up the trail where she'd stumbled on Corbin

Sanger's cabin. "There are a couple of different waterfalls on the west side of the dam." Monica rose and went inside. "Gabe, we may be looking at the wrong side of the lake."

Sully, Val, Mark, and Gabe were gathered around the table.

Monica walked over and looked for a map of the lake. "We're looking in the wrong spot."

"What?" Val lifted a map. "Kara said Carlisle—"

"Sully, last winter Bethany asked you to keep the loud machines away from the snow park on the west side of the dam." Monica put her finger on the dam. "Where was she talking about?"

"There." Sully traced a finger up the lakeshore and inland. "There's a snow park right around here that has a bunch of snowmobile trails going up into the mountains."

"Do hikers use them in the summer?"

"I don't know why they wouldn't. They're wide enough trails for a quad."

Gabe stared at the map. "There's a fire road that goes up that direction. We have some work scheduled to start in the next month."

"What kind of work?" Mark asked.

"Tree removal." Gabe pursed his lips. "Forest service says there's a huge amount of bark beetle damage on that side of the river."

Monica was focused on the creeks. "There are two creeks that could have waterfalls on them running through that area. They might be dry this time of year, but they're marked." She pointed at the map. "I'm seeing Horseshoe Creek..." Her finger slid up to the next thin blue line. "...and Sand Creek."

"Sand Creek doesn't sound like it's likely to have much water."

"You never know." Mark grabbed a stack of papers. "Let me see if I can find anything in these survey reports."

Gabe frowned. "Where did you find those?"

"Online," Mark said, flipping through the pages. "The power company did a survey of the whole area in the 1940s when they were settling with the families from Grimmer." He scanned the page and his eyebrows rose. "This could be it." He tapped on the page and flipped it. "Redwood hunting cabin in good repair. Abandoned. No record of ownership. It's listed in the Horseshoe Creek area."

"How do we know it's the Sanger cabin?" Val asked.

"Remember that article Robin found?" Monica asked. "The Sangers who'd moved to Sacramento were pissed because the power company was trying to deny their claim. They weren't going to list the Sanger family on any property surveys."

Mark was still looking at the surveys. "There's a cabin along Sand Creek, but they don't list it as made of redwood, and they say the owners were the Haverfords."

"Horseshoe Creek," Sully said. "I'd be willing to bet it's there. That area has a lot more exposed rock, and the creek runs all year unless it's really dry."

"Then let's go." Gabe started toward the door. "How are we getting there?"

Sully said, "Gabe, it's the middle of the night."

"And my kid is out there, being controlled by a deranged ghost who likes to burn things." He opened the door. "Trucks and quads have headlights; I'm going."

Monica walked to the door. "I've seen the cabin; I'll recognize the area. I'll go with Gabe."

Robin walked inside from the back porch, her face pale and wan. "Someone give me some juice and a Tylenol. I'll go too."

"What did she tell you?" Val asked.

Mark rushed to the fridge while Monica started toward Robin.

"Monica," Gabe said. "We need to go."

"Put the brakes on." Robin looked like she was about to puke, but she nailed Gabe with a glare. "You need to understand what's out there." She took the glass of juice Mark gave her. "And we're going to need some salt. A lot of salt."

CHAPTER 27

*M*onica looped her arms around Gabe's waist as they bumped over the trail that ran along Horseshoe Creek.

"You three have done this before?"

"Once," she yelled. "I don't know how similar ghost banishings are though. We may have no idea what's going to happen."

"Comforting."

For a man whose sixteen-year-old was missing, Gabe was doing pretty well. Monica leaned against his back, wishing she knew enough to reassure him.

She couldn't. They were heading into a situation with two violent spirits, one of whom had hold of a sixteen-year-old boy carrying lighter fluid. It was nearly midnight, and they were riding three quads slowly along an unknown trail. Sully was in the front, leading the pack and kicking up dust that threatened to choke all of them despite their protective equipment.

The trail led up and into the forest, and the higher they

climbed, the more damp the air grew. Soon the dust had died down and Monica could smell the water in Horseshoe Creek.

"There must be a spring," Gabe said.

"Has to be." Snow wouldn't still be melting this far into the summer.

It was hard to tell how long they'd been riding. They had parked their trucks at the end of the fire road and unloaded the quad bikes from the trailers. Mark and Robin were behind them, Gabe and Monica in the middle, with Sully and Val leading the crew.

"This is bad." Gabe's voice was barely audible over the sound of the engine.

"What's bad? I mean... other than the obvious."

"The trees." Gabe pointed with his left hand. "Look how many dead trees there are."

Once Monica noticed, it was all she could see. Bark beetles had eaten through the pines, leaving dead evergreens standing in wide swaths over the hillside.

"If a fire starts back here—"

"There's enough fuel to sweep down this mountain, jump the river, and head straight into town."

Monica gripped his waist harder. They couldn't get to the cabin fast enough.

If they were on the right trail.

If the cabin existed.

If Logan was there.

"We're going to find him."

Gabe reached down and squeezed her hand, but he didn't say another word.

A sharp whistle cut through the air. Monica leaned to the

side and saw Sully pointing off to the right. There was light flickering through the woods.

"There." Gabe veered off the trail, nearly throwing Monica off the back of the quad. Her jaw was rattling from the rough forest floor as they crashed through the underbrush. They passed through a small grove of sequoia trees; even through the jostling, she recognized the terrain.

This was it. This was the cabin.

A full moon hung over a clearing in the woods, the dead trees surrounding the cabin seemingly at odds with the lush ferns and underbrush along the creek bank.

In the center of the clearing, Logan sat on a fallen log, staring at flames flickering in an old stone firepit. The remains of a wooden spit leaned haphazardly on either side of the pit and logs were ringed around, creating a seating area.

Logan didn't look up, not even when they shut off the quad bikes. He was staring intently into the fire.

"Logan!" Gabe ran toward his son but stopped when Logan looked up and put a finger over his mouth.

"Shhh." He glared at his father before he looked over his shoulder at the abandoned cabin. "Don't you know he's sleeping?"

Monica grabbed Gabe's hand and squeezed hard before he could say anything else.

Logan wasn't injured, but something was very not right.

Robin stepped forward and sat across from the boy. "Who's sleeping?"

The corner of Logan's mouth turned up, and he gave Robin a sideways glance.

"You know." His voice was singsong, higher than his normal tone.

"Rosemarie?" Robin asked. "Why don't you leave Logan alone? You can talk to me on your own."

Logan shook his head. "Nope. I can't do that. I'm not like Bethany." For a second, a frown wrinkled the boy's forehead. "Stop it. You're confusing him."

"I don't think I'm the one confusing him." Robin waved Monica over. "We're worried about him. Worried about you."

The laugh Logan let out was more than unsettling. It was eerie. "No. I don't believe that. You all knew. You all knew what he was like and you didn't do a thing." Logan looked up, and any amusement that was in his eyes had distilled into a cold, hard rage. "Not a damn thing."

Monica said, "You're talking about your father. About Corbin."

Logan looked Monica up and down, curling his lip. "I thought I got rid of you. You're just like all of them, believing the lies he told, ignoring all the signs." Logan looked back at Robin. "You're the only one in Grimmer who listens, and that's only because you know Bethany."

"You're confused," Robin said softly. "Grimmer is gone. It was flooded eighty years ago. The people here now? They don't know you. They didn't know Corbin. And if they'd known what he did to you—"

"Why can't you do anything right, girl?" Logan stood and yelled at them. He reached down and tossed another log on the fire, showering sparks into the air.

Monica hissed in a breath. She looked at Gabe, but he and Mark were already running back to the quad bikes to grab the extinguishers they'd packed.

Sully came to stand near the fire, his thumbs hooked in his front pockets. "Logan, you need to sit down."

There was another moment when Monica saw Logan behind Rosemarie's anger. The boy was frightened and confused. He recognized Sully, but he couldn't seem to connect. He shook his head and Rosemarie turned her eyes back to Robin.

"Why did you bring all these people?"

"We're trying to help," Sully said.

Rosemarie turned to look at him. "You the ranger?"

"I'm the sheriff."

"Bethany said the ranger was supposed to keep people away, but you didn't do that, did you?" Logan crossed his arms over his chest and pursed his lips. "You got the winter machines away, but did you stop the hikers? Did you stop the noisy machines you're all riding? No! You didn't." She leaned dangerously close to the fire. "You went and let a *Sanger* near this cabin! What did you think was going to happen?"

"What happened, Rosemarie?" Robin asked. "Did the girl make Corbin angry?"

"She woke him up." Rosemarie pointed over Logan's shoulder. "Do you know how long I've been keeping him asleep?"

Monica felt a prickle of cold roll down her back, and a wave of malevolent energy emanated from the redwood cabin.

"Thank you," Robin said quietly. "I know you were protecting everyone from him. But don't you want some help?"

Val came and sat next to Robin, a large bag of salt

plopped between her feet. "We can help you get rid of him, Rosemarie. You won't have to keep working so hard."

Something in the air was telling Monica that they needed to go. Now. They needed to walk down the hill and not turn back. They needed to—

"You guys feeling that?" Val asked quietly.

Sully spoke beside her. "Hell, I'm feeling that, and I'm not even psychic."

"He wants us to leave," Robin said. "He wants us to leave him alone and leave you alone. But we're not going to do that."

Monica saw it now, saw it so clearly that everything that had happened made sense. The other cabins. The fires. Kara's confusion and Rosemarie's rage. "This is the last place he knows, isn't it?"

Rosemarie swung her eyes to Monica. "I knew I needed to get rid of you."

"All the other places he knew in some way. The Alison cabin, the Lewis place, those were all places Corbin knew. He might go there. But now they're gone, so he's trapped here. You've finally got him."

Logan's head swung back and forth; Rosemarie was shaking it hard. "I can't be sure."

"So you're going to burn it," Monica whispered. "You don't want him to know, but you're going to burn this cabin down."

"Fuck," Gabe muttered behind Monica. "Logan, you can't—"

"Logan is taking a nap," Rosemarie hissed at Gabe. "Do not wake him up."

"No, he's not," Monica said. "I can see him. Logan's

awake and he's confused and he's scared, Rosemarie. If you burn this cabin, you're going to kill him and all of us."

"So leave." She sat down and reached into Logan's backpack, which was propped against the log where he was sitting. She pulled out the can of lighter fluid and opened it. "It's not as good as kerosene, but it'll work."

"Not without Logan," Gabe said. "Not without my son."

Rosemarie's eyes held no pity. "It's nice that you care about him." She shot a stream of lighter fluid into the fire and the flames shot up.

Robin let out an involuntary yelp. "Rosemarie, don't!"

"What is wrong with you?" Gabe was nearly shaking. "Your father was awful to you, so you want to take my son away from me?"

"Some things can't be helped." Rosemarie's expression through Logan's face was stoic. "Some wrongs need to be righted. Even if that means people get hurt."

"You're not making any sense," Robin said. "We can get rid of him. We can protect—"

"Like you kept the people away?" Rosemarie shook her head and started pouring lighter fuel all around the fire. "Why should I trust you?"

Monica watched in shock as Rosemarie stood in Logan's body and started pouring lighter fluid everywhere, dousing the pine needles around the stones and getting dangerously close to Logan's clothes.

"Oh, I do not think so." Monica stood and grabbed the fire extinguisher from Gabe. "Enough, young lady. This is ridiculous." She broke the seal on the can and shot a heavy stream of foam at the roaring campfire.

It might be a good size campfire, but it was still just a

campfire. It went out in seconds, leaving Rosemarie standing in Logan's body, gaping at her while Monica stood with one hand on her fist.

"Doesn't matter. I have a lighter." Logan reached in his pocket and drew out a Zippo while he held the lighter fluid in his other hand. "I can still—"

"Nope. I don't think so." Monica shot a stream of foam at the base of the boy's feet. His hands. His arms. Rosemarie was sputtering in rage, and Monica saw Logan's expressions start to break through.

"Dad?"

"Fight her, Logan!" Gabe grabbed another fire extinguisher and started laying down retardant on the pine needles around Logan. "Shake it off."

The boy's face twisted in pain, he collapsed to the ground and threw up. "Dad?"

Gabe ran to his son, tossing the extinguisher to Mark, who continued to spray around the extinguished campfire.

Monica handed her can to Sully; then she walked over and sat next to Robin, who already had her sketchpad out. "Did you see her?"

Robin had her eyes closed. "I think I saw enough. I'm trying to make the picture clearer."

Val was on her right and Monica sat on her left. Rosemarie's spirit might have left Logan, but it was still out there. It could still wreak havoc if they didn't trap her and whatever malevolent entity was in the old redwood cabin.

The sky was growing lighter. Sully, Mark, and Gabe were crouched around Logan protectively.

Monica stood and held her hand out to Robin. "Will you be able to summon her?"

Robin took a deep breath. "Only one way to find out. The real question is, will Corbin Sanger show his face? All I have is Kara's description."

Val said, "Now we find out just how good a sketch artist you really are."

"Let's hope it's better than what I'm expecting."

Monica felt dread settle in her gut. "We can do this. You got the stuff, Val?"

Val patted the backpack and held out the giant bag of salt. "Mark has more."

"I think we'll need it." Robin nodded at the cabin. "Let's put a circle around the whole thing."

"Are you sure?" Monica walked to the quads and grabbed a battery-operated lantern.

"Yeah." Robin looked to her husband. "We need a circle, Mark. As soon as we're all inside. Not a single break in the line."

Mark and Monica exchanged a look, and she read every word in his eyes.

You better protect her.

We will.

Robin strode to the cabin and stood a few feet from the door. "One nightmare down. One to go."

With Monica and Val standing behind her, Robin walked through the black doorway.

CHAPTER 28

*R*osemarie's whispering voice was already singing inside.

"Lavender's green, dilly dilly,
Lavender's blue
You must love me, dilly dilly,
'cause I love you..."

Monica held the lantern up, lifting it as high as she could in the center of the old cabin as her eyes swept the room. "There's nothing in here."

Val turned in place. "There's something in here."

"Well, I was talking about furniture, but I know what you mean." Monica scanned the floor. "But still, nothing much to trip over, so that's good." The only structure left in the cabin was the stacked stone chimney and hearth.

"I heard one say, dilly dilly,
since I came hither,
That you and I, dilly dilly,
must lie together."

"I am so sick of that song," Val muttered.

Monica found a hook in the ceiling and hung the lantern. The wooden walls were open to the weather outside, the chinking long rotted away. Two windows were boarded up and covered with what looked like plywood.

"Rosemarie?"

The singing had stopped, but someone was still humming in the background. Robin leaned against one wall, holding her sketchpad under the light. She picked up the song and started singing under her breath as she drew.

Monica walked over to Val, who took three smudging sticks and four white candles from the backpack she carried. "Are we sure the candles are a good idea with Rosemarie?"

"I think we're pretty safe." Val handed Monica the three bundles of dried herbs for burning. "She only went after young people. All three of us know who we are and know our own minds. I don't think she'd be able to influence any of us."

"Middle-aged moms are too damn stubborn to be possessed?"

Val gave her half a grin. "Too damn opinionated."

"We are that."

Monica peeked out the doorway. The guys were laying a thick border of salt around the whole cabin, trapping whatever energy Robin was calling within the barrier.

The energy of the cabin was depressing. Monica wanted to leave. She desperately wanted to leave, but she knew enough about ghostly oppression by now to know that it was the spirit pushing her toward the door. She turned and faced the old stone fireplace.

"Come on out, Corbin." She lit her cedar and stuffed the lighter in her pocket as Val placed four white candles at each corner of the cabin, far enough away from the walls that they'd be safe even if they tipped over.

A rippling black shadow grew in the corner to the right of the fireplace.

"I think I got him," Robin said quietly. "Come on out, Corbin Sanger."

The thing in the corner growled.

"We're not little girls," Val said. "We're not scared of you."

As Robin sketched furiously, the black shadow began to take shape.

"Holy shit." Val glanced at Robin. "Can you see this?"

"I see him." Robin's jaw was tight. "You're only seeing his shadow."

"He's big," Monica said.

"He likes that," Robin said. "You like people being afraid of you, don't you, Corbin?"

Monica might not have been able to see more than a shadow, but she could hear the ghost's voice.

"Know your place."

Robin didn't miss a beat. "You've been hanging around for a long time, Corbin. There's no place left for you to go, is there?"

The growling whisper came back. "This... my house."

"Wrong." Robin kept her eyes on the corner, but Monica could see her distracted by something across the room. "It's not your house. You're dead, Corbin."

Monica said, "I'd say sorry to break it to you, but you seem like a horrible person."

"You're dead," Val said. "Dead, dead, dead. Worm food.

Your daughter lit a fire and killed you. Which means you must have been a really big asshole."

"My... house." The growling voice drew out the *s* at the end of "house." It felt like a fingernail scraping down Monica's back.

"Smoke him," Robin said. "Keep him away from the fireplace."

The one point of entry they couldn't control was the chimney, ironically enough. Monica walked to the hearth and placed a small brass bowl in the center; then she placed smoldering cedar in the bowl. She carefully added the two other bundles of dried herbs to the cedar. Lavender for protection. Rosemary for cleansing. They had all been taken from the gardens at Russell House.

"There." Monica straightened and watched the smoke curl up the chimney and around the room, filling the space with its fragrance. "That should keep him contained."

"Rosemarie?" Robin called. "I see you over there. I understand you're frightened."

"Is this who you let into my house, girl?"

The shout was so loud and violent Monica took a step back. She and Val exchanged a look.

"Robin?" Mark was calling from outside.

Val stuck her head out the door. "We're fine."

"What the hell was that?"

"Corbin doesn't like company." Val handed Monica another bundle of cedar. "Rosemarie Sanger, time to come out."

"She won't." Robin was still sketching. "Not until he's gone."

The walls of the cabin began to shake, and Monica

looked up. The lantern was swinging wildly from the shaking. "Robin?"

"Almost done." She swept her fingers over the sketch and stood up straight. "Corbin Sanger, you're dead. It's time for you to go."

The cabin shook again, and the voice came even louder.

"Rose! Get these women out of my house."

The last faint sound of humming went silent, and a hollow energy filled the cabin.

Robin laid down a pencil sketch of a middle-aged man with an angry brow and the body of a grizzly bear. His head was bald, but a long, tangled beard fell down his chest.

"There you are, Corbin. Did you think you'd escape forever?" Robin sat down next to the sketch. "She tried to kill you with fire and ended up killing herself and the sister she was protecting."

Val handed Robin a bag of salt.

"Rosemarie isn't responsible for that fire or Bethany's death," Robin said softly. "You are."

"She's a crazy bitch," the shadow growled. "Just like her mama."

"No," Robin said firmly. "You are a bully and a monster." She started pouring a line of salt around Corbin's picture. "It's your fault, Corbin, you weak, sad man. You killed them, and it's time you faced your judgment."

Monica walked in a circle around the cabin, waving smoke into every corner except the one where the shadow lived. In that corner, nothing drifted. All the light seemed to vanish into the shadows.

"He's not moving," Monica said. "Do it."

Robin took a match from Val and struck it on one of

the stones in the fireplace. "Time to go, Corbin." She placed the match in the center of the sketch, and the roar that shook the house was enough to break open the panels covering the windows. One of the candles tipped over.

"I got it!" Val shouted. She dove for the candle and threw dirt on the flame that was already trying to creep up the wall. "I got it, keep going."

"You bitch!" The voice got louder and louder. Unintelligible yelling that made Monica's toes curl. It was animalistic, the sound of pure hatred.

Robin didn't flinch. She struck another match and placed it on another corner of the sketch. "Leave this place, Corbin Sanger. Go into whatever dimension will have you, but you cannot stay here."

Monica watched as the malevolent shadow in the corner shook, fracturing like glass before it seemed to fall like ash to the ground.

The shaking stopped, and the wave of cedar smoke that Monica directed into the corner filled the space and expanded. The smoke crept into the chinks between the logs and drifted into the pearled-grey morning sky.

But even as Corbin disappeared, Monica could still feel another presence in the room.

"You can come out, Rosemarie." Robin took a deep breath, and Monica could see the lines furrowed between her eyebrows. "It's safe. He's gone."

Someone pushed at her back. Monica looked over her shoulder and glared at the rippling shadow behind her. "Don't even think about it, kid. You're not out of the woods yet."

But she would be. Monica could already see Robin's hand moving over her sketchbook.

"It's time to go," Robin said. "Rosemarie, it's time."

Val and Monica circled the room, smudging smoke into every corner.

"No," Robin continued, "that's not your job. Corbin is banished. He's not going to be bothering Bethany." She set her pencil down. "It's time for you to go. Who knows? Bethany may follow you if you go willingly." Robin's expression changed. "You've been guarding her for eighty years. Longer than that even." She nodded. "Rest. It's time for you to rest."

Monica couldn't describe the feeling of lightness that filled the formerly oppressive cabin. It was as if a pressure valve released.

"Okay." Robin nodded. "I can do that." She put a picture of a beautiful young woman in the center of the salt circle. The paper lay on top of the ashes of Corbin Sanger. Very gently, Robin struck a match and lit the corner of Rosemarie's picture.

"Lavender's blue, dilly dilly," Robin sang. "Lavender's green."

Val and Monica joined her, singing the sweeter words of the old folk song.

"When I am king, dilly dilly,
You shall be queen."

The three women sang together as the sketch of Rosemarie Sanger curled and blackened in the safety of the salt circle.

"Who told you so, dilly dilly,
Who told you so?

'Twas my own heart, dilly dilly,
That told me so."

Monica watched the picture burn, and when the last pieces of Rosemarie's picture went black, a gust of wind like a heavy sigh swept through the room and carried cedar smoke up and out the chimney.

Robin curled into a ball and fell to the side. "Get Mark."

Val ran for Mark while Monica laid Robin's head in her lap. "You did so well." She put a hand over Robin's eyes, knowing that an excruciating headache was just around the corner. "You did so good, honey."

"She was so tired," Robin murmured. "She was in so much pain, and she was so tired."

"Rosemarie can rest now." Maybe someday Monica would have more sympathy for the girl who'd tried to kill a monster in life only to have to tame it in death, but for now she was just relieved.

She wanted a cold drink.

She wanted something for her headache.

She wanted to close her eyes, lay her head down, and fall into a dreamless sleep.

CHAPTER 29

"*M*onica?"

Her eyes flickered open, then closed again. Where was she? The chair she was sitting on was so hard. She wanted to put her feet up. She could already feel her ankles swelling, and her legs ached. Where was she?

Hospital. Right. Hospital.

"Mom?" There was a hand on her knee. "Mami, wake up."

"Maybe she doesn't want to wake up, Sam. She's probably fucking exhausted."

"Dude, don't use that kind of language. You know she hates that."

Another voice intruded on the twins. "Idiots, leave them alone. They were awake all night looking for Logan."

"We got coffee."

Monica was leaning on something soft and warm. It smelled like cedar, clean laundry, and leather.

Oh. Gabe. She had fallen asleep on Gabe's shoulder. That was nice.

"Just get out of here," Sylvia hissed at her brothers. "Go to Kara's room, okay? I'm sitting with Logan until Chief Peralta wakes up."

Heavy footsteps receded down the hall, leaving Monica and her shoulder pillow in silence.

"If you don't open your eyes," she whispered, "they'll eventually leave you alone."

"Your kids must think you're the heaviest sleeper on earth."

"Pretty much, yes."

"Are you?"

"God no. I'd wake up if one of them skipped a breath at two a.m."

Gabe's shoulder shook, and Monica cracked one eye open.

He was looking down at her with warm dark eyes and a soft smile. "Hey."

"Hey," Monica whispered. She didn't move her head. "Thanks for the shoulder."

"Thanks for banishing the ghost that was haunting my kid."

"It's not usually a service the hotel offers, but we try to go above and beyond for the fire department."

Gabe smiled again. "Why are we still whispering?"

"Because my children have ears like cats, and before they get back, I want to do something."

"What's that?"

Monica put her hand on his neck and drew his mouth down to hers.

Gabe's lips immediately moved over hers with *purpose*. He'd thought about kissing her, and it was evident. One hand cupped her cheek and the other tucked her hair behind her ear before it slid to the back of her neck. His lips were warm and firm; his tongue touched the corner of her lips without being pushy. His teeth caught her lower lip in a gentle bite before he drew back to take a breath.

"Yep," Monica said.

"Yep what?"

"I thought you were going to be a good kisser, and you are."

He raised an eyebrow. "Not too bad yourself."

"Thanks." She pressed her lips together for a second. "Darn it. I forgot about my breath. I am so sorry."

"Can I be honest? I didn't even notice and my breath is probably pretty bad too. We drank a lot of coffee last night."

"What time is it?"

Gabe's arm stretched across her shoulders and he looked at his watch. It was an old-fashioned watch with a regular display. Nothing smart or electronic or connected to anything. Just a watch.

"It's nearly two."

"In the afternoon?"

"Yes."

She wiped a hand over her eyes. "I wonder when the kids got here."

"I think it was a few hours ago. Pretty sure I heard Sylvia taking charge and ordering her brothers around while she got reports on Kara and Logan."

"She'll do that."

"Order everyone around?"

"Yes. She was always my second-in-command. When you have three boys, it's necessary."

"Chain of command. I can understand that." He reached out both his arms and stretched his shoulders. "I am going to be sorry that I slept that long in a hospital chair."

"I don't think we had an option." Monica flexed her ankles. "My hips are going to hate me later."

They both stood and stretched. Monica could hear the popping and crackling of both their joints.

"I would make a comment about the next time we sleep together being on a flat surface," Gabe said, "but that seems forward."

"More forward than telling you I had a sex vision about you?"

His chuckle was low and seductive. "About that vision—"

"Mom!" Caleb charged into the waiting room. "We got you coffee. I think it's still hot."

"Thank you, baby." She patted his cheek when he bent down to hug her. "Gabe, this is my youngest, Caleb."

"Youngest by four minutes."

"But I felt every four of those minutes," Monica said, "so they count."

Caleb turned and held his hand out to Gabe. "You're Logan's dad. He seems like a cool kid."

"Thanks." Gabe looked up, swamped by the linebacker-sized man who was her baby. "Is he awake?"

Sylvia charged into the waiting room, her hands on her hips. "I told you not to wake them up!"

"They were already awake."

"Did you get them their coffee then?"

"No, I was—"

"Get their coffee while it's still hot." Sylvia turned to

Gabe. "Sorry. Caleb got you coffee with milk. There's sugar on the side. We don't know how you take it."

"He doesn't take sugar," Monica said. "Thanks, honey."

Sylvia raised her eyebrow. "So you know how he takes his coffee?"

Monica glanced at Gabe, then back at her daughter. "We're not talking about this right now. I want to see Kara and Logan."

Sylvia shot Gabe a smile. "Later." She took Monica's arm and leaned down. "*Tan guapo*, Mami."

"You think he doesn't speak Spanish?" Monica shook her head.

"I'm a little rusty," Gabe said. "But I got that."

Sylvia cackled. "This is gonna be fun."

At the end of the day, Logan was treated for dehydration, a few cuts and bruises, but nothing more serious than that. He was confused by how he'd gotten up to the old cabin, but he didn't remember much.

There had been no fire, so there was nothing for Gabe to investigate. The two Peraltas went home that afternoon when Logan was released.

Kara's case was another story. Two of her burns would require skin grafts, and she was facing criminal arson charges.

Sully sat with Monica, Val, Mark, and Robin in the waiting room. "I'm doing what I can."

"Can Gabe alter his report to make it seem more...? I have no idea." Monica took a deep breath. "It's bad."

"I think her state of mind is the key," Mark said. "The lawyer seems to be pretty optimistic."

The lawyer Mark had contacted to represent Kara was already talking with the district attorney about her history of anxiety and the unexpected side effects of her medication. He was optimistic that since Kara had turned herself in and confessed and none of the fires had caused significant property damage or injuries to anyone other than herself, she had a good chance at probation and counseling instead of jail time.

"I know Gabe is going to do everything he can to help her out," Sully said. "As will I. Some of this is out of our hands, but we've both got a pretty good relationship with the DA. Kara is cooperative, and it's obvious she's telling the truth about not remembering the fires."

Robin said, "I just wish she'd come to us earlier."

"She had no idea what was going on," Val said. "I cannot imagine how freaked out she was."

"Well, Russell House is sticking by her," Monica said. "I already talked to Grace and Philip."

"Mom and Dad are fully in Kara's corner," Robin said. "They both love her."

"God knows she's missed," Monica said. "I'm moving Drew to the day shift, and he's not happy about it."

"It's all going to work out." Robin rubbed Monica's back. "We've caught the ghost arsonist and banished not one but two tormented ghosts, one of whom was a very bad dude."

Monica looked at Robin. "I told you I would."

"Would what?" Val asked.

"Kiss Gabe," Robin said. "So did you?"

Sully stood. "Okay, I don't need to be here for this."

Mark joined him. "Yeah, I'm gonna check on Kara."

The men both left and Robin and Val stared at Monica. "Well?"

Monica smiled. "I may need to repeat the experiment once I'm showered and have clean teeth. For science."

Val held her hand up and Robin gave her a high five. "It was good."

"It was definitely good."

Monica smiled. "You don't have to be so smug about it."

"We're your best friends," Robin said. "Of course we're smug about you bagging a hot fireman."

"I was married to a hot fireman for twenty-five years."

Val leaned forward. "And now you have another one. Icon."

Robin pretended to wipe a tear from her eye. "Grandma Trujillo would be so proud."

Monica snorted. "You two are ridiculous."

"That's why you love us."

Monica stared at her two best friends and realized that while she'd felt pretty lost after Gil had died, she'd never felt alone. And she never would. "I love you guys."

"Love you too," Robin said.

Val said, "It would be ridiculous *not* to love you. And I'm not ridiculous."

Sometimes Monica saw the future; sometimes she didn't. But with friends like she had, no matter what happened, she could handle it.

No matter what.

EPILOGUE

The house was ready. For the first time in six months, the house was actually ready. Monica wanted to giggle in relief and dance at the same time.

New furniture? Check.

Fresh paint? Check.

New floors? Check.

It had taken a long time, but her house finally felt like home. A new home. Familiar pictures hung on the walls and a few things had been saved from the home she'd shared with Gil, but most all of it was new.

Gabe swept in from the back porch, a plate of barbecue in his hand. "Here. Try this."

She bit into the tri-tip he held out for her to taste and bit the end of his finger playfully. "Delicious." She smiled.

"Hmm." The corner of his mouth turned up, and he leaned in to kiss her. The kiss started out playful and turned hot and heavy within seconds. "Very delicious." He moved a hand to her waist and slid his palm over the curve of her hip as he took her mouth again.

"Gabe."

"Mmm." He kissed from her lips across her jaw, teasing the sensitive spot behind her ear. "You're wearing that perfume I got you."

"The meat."

"The meat?"

"On the grill?"

"Oh." He drew back. "Right."

"We should call everyone and tell them not to come." Monica let out a breath and tried to calm the heat in her face. "It's Valentine's Day. Who has a housewarming party on Valentine's Day? They probably all want to stay home anyway."

Gabe kept the door cracked to the back porch. She could hear him laugh.

"Everyone wants to see the house."

"I guess we can accommodate them for one night."

"Are Jake and Kara coming?"

"Yes, but later. They're hosting the Valentine's dinner at Russell House, then coming over for drinks. Probably around ten or so."

"Logan gave me a curfew."

Monica laughed. "That kid cracks me up."

"Me too."

Logan had decided that he liked Glimmer Lake enough to try a year of school in the mountains. His mom had been reluctant at first, but when Logan talked about all his new friends and learning to ski, she got on board. Gabe was being a full-time parent and a fire chief for the first time ever.

It was a lot, but he and Logan seemed to be doing pretty well.

Monica was still working full time at Russell House, but since Kara's case had finally been settled and the house was finished, she felt like two mountains had been taken off her back.

Mandatory counseling and a year of probation had been the resolution to Kara's case, which put her back to work as soon as she'd healed from her skin grafts.

Even though she'd technically been on sick leave, since she was staying in the caretaker's quarters with Jake, Monica didn't feel like Kara had gotten much of a break.

"I think I'm going to send Kara and Jake on a vacation before the summer rush crashes into us." Monica set out wineglasses and a bucket of beer for Sully. "They need a break."

Gabe came into the kitchen bearing a foil-covered plate. "You're a nice boss." He kissed her cheek.

"I try."

"I'm going to send my guys up to Northern California for a three-week intensive training session before summer."

"Awww." She kissed his cheek back. "You're a nice chief."

"I know. They love me."

Monica heard something buzzing and scanned the room. "Is that you?"

Gabe held up his phone. "Nope. You."

"Nuts." Her gaze raced around the family room. "Where did I put it?"

"Did you leave it in the bedroom?"

"No, I hear it."

"Is it by the—?"

"Oh!" Monica opened the fridge. "Found it."

Gabe laughed, but it wasn't the first time she'd found her phone in the fridge.

She answered it before she looked at the number. "This is Monica."

"Mrs. Velasquez?" The voice on the phone sounded a little out of breath and more than a little panicked. "Is this Monica Velasquez?"

"Yes." She pulled the phone away, but the number didn't look familiar. "Are you okay?"

"I just... I'm not sure how to ask this. I don't even know if you remember me."

"Does this have something to do with Russell House? If there's a guest emergency, I'm not on site, so you'll have to call—"

"What's Russell House? I'm sorry." She took a deep breath. "I do apologize; I'm not making any sense. My name is Dr. Katherine Bassi, and I believe I spoke to you around seven months ago about—"

"Precognition." The name and voice settled into place. "Yes. Yes, I do remember you. Are you okay?"

"I'm fine. I'm... unsettled. But I'm fine."

"Okay."

Gabe was making questioning faces at her, but Monica could only shrug. She had no idea why Mark's old friend was calling her.

"I'm calling because something happened very recently, and I don't understand it, but I remembered our conversation months ago." She cleared her throat. "And I am so sorry if I seemed dismissive at the time. I admit, hearing about your... friend's experiences seemed so out of the realm of scientific possibility that I was probably patronizing. I apologiz that."

Monica felt a knot form in her stomach. "Dr. Bassi, what happened?"

"Are you the friend, Mrs. Velasquez?" Her voice was urgent. "I need to know if you were using a common distancing tactic to—"

"Yes," Monica told her without hesitation. "I'm the friend I was talking about. I experience precognition through dreams."

"Then I need your help." The woman's professional tenor had dropped away and her voice was barely over a whisper. "Someone tried to commit a violent crime yesterday. A shooting. It could have been very bad, but it wasn't. Because... I saw it happen before it happened. And I helped stop it."

"Okay." Monica let out a long breath just as the doorbell rang. Gabe went to answer the door as Monica continued talking. "Katherine, I'm going to get your number and call you back in about five minutes with some friends of mine. Everything is going to be okay, but I have a feeling you're going to want to talk to all of us."

"Thank you. I don't know what's happening, but... thanks."

"Trust me." Monica caught Robin and Val's worried expressions and waved them toward the back porch. "You are not alone."

your next Paranormal Women's Fiction

en you meet three new friends in the

Cove series by Elizabeth Hunter.

...n exclusive sneak preview of the first book,

Runaway Fate, coming Fall 2020.

for

FIRST LOOK: RUNAWAY FATE

If Katherine Bassi could have predicted a time and place for her life to change irrevocably, it would not have been at the Blue Wave Gym on State Street at four forty-five on Thursday afternoon.

Her yoga class started at five o'clock, so at four thirty, Katherine hopped on one of the few available treadmills to warm her muscles up. Properly warmed muscles were a prerequisite to get the most out of her twice weekly yoga class. The class was focused on flexibility and joint mainte-nance, two areas Katherine knew were vital for older women.

Dr. Katherine Bassi wouldn't have predicted that her life would change that Thursday. She wouldn't have predicted it would change at all, and she was perfectly happy with that.

She was a forty-seven year old physics professor at Central Coast State University. She'd been married for twenty years to a man she adored. She was the happy and indulgent aunt to four children her siblings and in-laws were raising and had no desire for kids of her own.

Her life didn't need to change. It was exactly what she wanted.

As she pushed the buttons to increase her workout pace, she glanced around the gym.

On her right was a young man wearing a college sweat-shirt, his head down as he listened to music and jogged at a steady pace.

In the row before her was a middle-aged blond woman in ruthlessly coordinated sportswear sweating her heart out on an elliptical machine.

The Blue Wave Gym gave a discount to student and faculty at Central Coast State, so the number of blue and green sweatshirts and t-shirts around the aerobic machine room was noticeable, but plenty of ordinary people from town were mixed in as well.

It was one of the reasons that Katherine enjoyed going to this gym. She was too often surrounded by academics since she and her husband Baxter were both professors, and it was nice to break out of her limited social circle.

"Hey!"

Katherine looked over her left shoulder.

"You dropped your towel." A freckled woman with a curly cap of short dark hair held a white towel out to her.

"Thanks." Katherine reached back and grabbed it, then folded it in thirds and placed it on the small bar below the control panel on the treadmill, all the while never slowing her pace. "Were you waiting for this machine?"

The woman shrugged. "I'm good. I've got time." Her eyes seemed focused farther down the row of machines.

Katherine glanced at the clock on the wall. "I'm just warming up before the five o'clock yoga class. I'll be done in a few minutes." It was four-forty, and she would need at least ten minutes to walk to the yoga classroom and set up. Katherine hated being late for anything, but especially classes. She slowed her treadmill to cool down.

"I can wait." The woman's eyes swept around the gym before coming back to rest on something or someone farther down the row. Her eyes narrowed, but she didn't move from her spot near the wall.

Katherine turned back to the closed captioned television that was broadcasting the local news. There was something about the classic car show on Beach Street that weekend. The weather forecast jumped onto the screen. Seventy-five and sunny on Friday. Seventy-three. Seventy-six. Yep, pretty much perfect all week.

When you lived on California's Central Coast, you didn't get to complain about the weather.

At four forty-four she stopped the treadmill and grabbed her towel. She dabbed her forehead and looked for the dark-haired woman, but she was already on a different machine.

Gym goers were shuffling locations as some left for the day and others switched workouts. Katherine saw the color-coordinated blond woman heading toward the hallway where the yoga classroom was located and wondered if she was a new attendee.

She walked toward the aisle, passing another young man running steadily on a treadmill. A blue and green hoodie covered his head, and something familiar about him made Katherine pause at the back of his machine.

It came in a flash.

Katherine saw the man stop and pull a black handgun from his sweatshirt. It was black and had an odd bar sticking out from the brown wooden handle. The world moved in slow motion as the young man raised the gun and started firing across the gym.

Once, twice, again and again. He didn't stop. The world around her was muffled, but she heard people screaming. Glass shattered. More screaming.

She blinked and the world around her came back into focus. No one was screaming. The gym was filled with the sounds of treadmills and pumping workout music. The clock on the wall read four forty-five.

She was standing at the base of the young man's treadmill when she saw it start to happen.

He unzipped his blue and green sweatshirt and reached inside.

It wasn't a dream.

"Gun!" Katherine screamed and dove for the man, knocking him off balance. He toppled back and fell on her. The treadmill track shot them off the rear of the machine and into the aisle.

"He has a gun!"

The world compressed around her. She was struggling with the man, but he was so much stronger. Where was the gun? She saw it in his hand, and she reached for it.

He elbowed Katherine in the temple and rolled away, trying to lift the firearm and take aim.

"No!" The blond woman stood over them, her face red and angry. She reached her hand out and the gun jumped into her palm.

Katherine blinked.

The young man elbowed her again, snapping her head to the side. She saw stars and rolled into the still-spinning treadmill as the man scrambled toward the blond woman who had his gun. He was on his knees when the compact, dark-haired woman leapt over two treadmills and jumped on the attacker, forcing him back to the ground with a thud and a solid punch to the jaw.

"Stay down!" She looked to be about a third of the size of the man with the gun, but the woman grabbed his shoulders, forced him to the floor, and yelled into his face. "Calm down! Stay down!"

As if by magic, the man's body went limp and he relaxed completely.

The blond woman was holding the gun on the man, but her hands weren't even shaking. She glanced at Katherine. "Ma'am, you doing all right?" She spoke with a pronounced southern accent. "He hit you pretty hard. Think you might be bleeding on your forehead a little."

The dark-haired woman glanced at the woman with the gun. "You a cop?"

"No." The blond woman laughed a little. "Just grew up with a lot of good ol' boys. You doin' okay?"

"I'm good." The dark-haired woman didn't move off the man. "Please tell me someone is calling the police."

Katherine rolled up to sitting and propped herself against the front of a stair-climbing machine. "I'm okay." She watched their attacker lying completely still under the small woman. "I think I'm okay."

Everyone in the gym had fled and most were milling around outside on State Street. Katherine could see them through the windows.

A man in a bright blue shirt ran over to them. "We called 911." His muscles bulged from beneath his shirt and the word "trainer" was emblazoned on the front. "What can I do? Do you want me to hold him, Toni? How can I help?"

The blond woman didn't move an inch and the dark haired woman the man called Toni didn't budge.

"I think we'll just stay right exactly where we are until the cops come." Toni kept her hands pushed into the man's shoulders, but the young man who'd wrestled so fiercely with Katherine had gone limp. He showed not a hint of resistance.

The trainer looked at the woman with the gun. "Uh... miss?"

"It's Megan, sweetie. Megan Carpenter. I'm good here," the blond woman said. "I'm new at the gym, but I'm real good with guns and I can wait with these nice ladies for the cops." She glanced down. "This is a real fancy extended magazine, young man. I don't think this model is legal in California."

The young trainer was running his hands through his brown curly hair. "Oh my God. Holy shit. Patrick and Jan are gonna kill me."

Katherine cleared her throat. "If you're talking about the owners, I doubt you're going to get in trouble. No one could have predicted this."

Except she had.

She had seen the man pull the gun from his sweatshirt. She'd seen him raise it and shoot people. She'd heard screams and glass shattering.

But it hadn't happened yet.

Katherine glanced at the clock. It was four forty-nine. In four minutes, everything about her life had changed.

She looked at the two women named Megan and Toni. All three of them were exchanging nervous glances and trying to pretend not to notice the others' scrutiny. Katherine had never seen either of the women before that day, but she could read the question on both their faces.

What on earth just happened?

Subscribe to my newsletter for more information about MOONSTONE COVE and my other works of fiction.

ACKNOWLEDGMENTS

I want to thank all the Fab13 authors who originally banded together to push and promote Paranormal Women's Fiction.

Thank you to:
KF Breene, Deanna Chase,
Jana DeLeon, Christine Gael,
Darynda Jones, Eve Langlais,
Shannon Mayer, Kristen Painter,
Robyn Peterman, Michelle Pillow,
Mandy M. Roth, Denise Grover Swank,

And me. I am not too shy to thank myself for taking this risk and doing something different.

Because while it may seem like an obvious success months now after the launch, when we first started talking about writing these books: by women, for women, focusing on challenges in the middle of life and writing stories that reflected the good, the bad, and the ugly chin hairs of paranormal, it felt really risky!

Would readers want main characters who didn't have perky boobs and baby faces? Would they hang with heroines who didn't have romance at the front of their minds?

With three books finished in this genre and another three book series planned, I am thrilled to say that YES. Readers were game for all that. They were game for wise-cracking women who didn't take life too seriously. They were game for heroines who didn't ask permission, but maybe needed to take the stairs a little slower. They were eager for friendship and loyalty, and if romance came along, that was fun too.

The success of this genre belongs to you. There are other authors now exploring this rich, funny, and refreshing part of women's lives. There are younger authors who are seeing that yes, women don't become irrelevant or stop wanting magic when the wrinkles show up.

In time, the magic just becomes more powerful.

I hope this genre continues to expand and encompass many more stories of friendship, fantasy, and family. I am so very grateful that I get to be a part of it.

Many thanks. To my assister Gen and my publicist Emily at Social Butterfly. Thank you for the work you do that allows me to write and focus on writing.

Jenn, I miss you. Enjoy your retirement, but you better still read my books.

I want to give special thanks to the marvelous Lisa Wilson, who not only keeps my back healthy, but also took the time to beta read this book and offer her fire-fighter wife wisdom. As the wife of one firefighter and the mom of another, I was so grateful for her insight and expertise.

Special thanks to the team at Damonza who continue to create the beautiful covers for all my books. I am so grateful to work with such professionals. I say, "Make it pretty!" And you do. Wizards, every one of you.

Always and forever thanks to my editing team, Amy Cissell, Anne Victory, and Linda at Victory Editing. I would not be the writer I am without the three of you cleaning up after me.

To my wonderful family and friends, thank you for everything you do to keep me sane and mostly socially well-adjusted, despite my hermit-like tendencies. Your job is not easy; I owe you all tamales.

And to my husband. Silver hair is sexy, especially on you. All my love forever, E.

ABOUT THE AUTHOR

ELIZABETH HUNTER is a *USA Today* and international best-selling author of romance, contemporary fantasy, and paranormal mystery. Based in Central California, she travels extensively to write fantasy fiction exploring world mythologies, history, and the universal bonds of love, friendship, and family. She has published over thirty works of fiction and sold over a million books worldwide. She is the author of the Glimmer Lake series, Love Stories on 7th and Main, the Elemental Legacy series, the Irin Chronicles, the Cambio Springs Mysteries, and other works of fiction.

ElizabethHunterWrites.com

A Fall of Water

The Stars Afire

The Irin Chronicles

The Scribe

The Singer

The Secret

The Staff and the Blade

The Silent

The Storm

The Seeker

Linx & Bogie Mysteries

A Ghost in the Glamour

A Bogie in the Boat

Contemporary Romance

The Genius and the Muse

7th and Main

INK

HOOKED

GRIT

Made in the USA
Middletown, DE
15 December 2021

55940166R00177